Praise for

# NEVADA BARR

**and the award-winning Anna Pigeon novels . . .**

"Nevada Barr is one of the best." —*The Boston Globe*

"A constant source of pleasure." —*San Francisco Chronicle*

"Nevada Barr writes with a cool, steady hand about the violence of nature and the cruelty of man."
—*The New York Times Book Review*

"A true original . . . like a combination of Henry David Thoreau, Mark Twain, Sherlock Holmes, and Maureen O'Hara, the engaging character of Anna Pigeon is the only reason most readers will need to return to this series again and again. But it doesn't hurt that Barr can write rhapsodic passages about America's beautiful parks and cobble up page-turning whodunits." —*The Denver Post*

"Nevada Barr can take the most improbable plot and turn it into a fascinating foray into the human psyche, then dress it up with eloquent description of the great outdoors she so obviously adores. . . . She's also one of the more eloquent mystery writers around, having the ability to make you feel the chill of the night, smell the smoke of a campfire, experience the isolation of the wilderness. She's worth reading just for that alone." —*Chicago Tribune*

"Barr combines primo mysteries with what always feels like a virtual reality tour of one of the parks. . . . There is beauty here. Still, Anna never loses her edginess in a world where your life depends on having a backup light for your backup light." —*Detroit Free Press*

Praise for

# HUNTING SEASON

"Genuinely thrilling." —*Los Angeles Times*

"Thoroughly enjoyable." —*The Seattle Times*

"Suspenseful, atmospheric, [and] pulse-pounding. . . . *Hunting Season* ranks right up there with the best in this excellent series." —*Chicago Tribune*

"An engrossing and deftly written thriller. . . . [Nevada Barr] provides us with a backstage view of our national park system that is both fictionally exciting and factually enlightening." —*The San Diego Union-Tribune*

"Will keep readers guessing until the last page." —*The Denver Post*

"Satisfying [and] shocking." —*Pittsburgh Post-Gazette*

"In *Hunting Season*, [Barr's] descriptions are so vivid a reader almost feels the leaves on the forest floor cracking beneath her feet and the misty fogs soaking into her pores." —*The Memphis Commercial Appeal*

"A good, exciting read. [Barr] has a deft touch with suspense." —*The Charleston Post and Courier* (SC)

"The edgy, fast-paced tale generates plenty of tension . . . and Barr does a good job of developing the character of Anna, adding romance to the mix, and giving the ranger plenty of opportunity to display her slightly dark, off-center wit." —*Booklist* (starred review)

"First-rate. . . . Barr outshines most other authors in the mystery genre." —*Publishers Weekly*

Praise for

# BLOOD LURE

"Well-baited suspense." —*People*

"Barr's red herrings and sly twists culminate in one huge payoff." —*Entertainment Weekly*

"A must-read for Barr fans and a great place to start for everyone else." —*Rocky Mountain News*

"Downright spine-tingling. . . . *Blood Lure* is an exciting read, and its wilderness setting puts it in a league of its own." —*Pittsburgh Post-Gazette*

"A captivating story distinguished by her keen appreciation of nature, both Mother and human." —*The San Diego Union-Tribune*

"One of Barr's best . . . a tightly plotted, satisfying read. The author's masterful descriptions of the natural world immeasurably enhance an exciting, suspenseful story." —*Publishers Weekly* (starred review)

"Barr's biggest triumph is in detailing Anna Pigeon's 'falling-out' with nature, and her inner journey back to a place of trust for the world she so reveres. . . . As in all of Barr's novels before this one, Anna is the heart and soul behind the story. And with *Blood Lure*, Barr will take a well-earned spot on bestseller lists across the country." —*The Denver Post*

"Anna is at her best in the great outdoors, and so is Barr, both in her passages detailing the wonders of the natural world and in tense, action-packed sequences. . . . Armchair campers will enjoy the vicarious thrills." —*Orlando Sentinel*

"Anna Pigeon . . . remains one of the most engaging characters in modern whodunits." —*Fort Worth Star-Telegram*

## Titles by Nevada Barr

### FICTION

*Boar Island*

*Destroyer Angel*

*The Rope*

*Burn*

*Borderline*

*Winter Study*

*Hard Truth*

*High Country*

*Flashback*

*Hunting Season*

*Blood Lure*

*Deep South*

*Liberty Falling*

*Blind Descent*

*Endangered Species*

*Firestorm*

*Ill Wind*

*A Superior Death*

*Track of the Cat*

*Bittersweet*

### NONFICTION

*Seeking Enlightenment . . . Hat by Hat*

# ANNA PIGEON: TRACK OF THE CAT

Previously published as *Track of the Cat*

NEVADA BARR

BERKLEY
New York

BERKLEY
An imprint of Penguin Random House LLC
1745 Broadway, New York, NY 10019
penguinrandomhouse.com

ISBN: 9798217193165

G. P. Putnam's Sons hardcover edition (*Track of the Cat*) / March 1993
Avon Books mass-market edition (*Track of the Cat*) / May 1994
Berkley mass-market edition (*Track of the Cat*) / June 2003
Berkley trade paperback edition (*Anna Pigeon: Track of the Cat* TV tie-in edition) / June 2026

Printed in the United States of America
1st Printing

The authorized representative in the EU for product safety and compliance is Penguin Random House Ireland, Morrison Chambers, 32 Nassau Street, Dublin D02 YH68, Ireland, https://eu-contact.penguin.ie.

*For my mother and sister*

# CHAPTER 1

There hadn't been a god for many years. Not the nightgown-clad patriarch of Sunday school coloring books; not the sensitive young man with the inevitable auburn ringlets Anna had stared through in the stained-glass windows at Mass; not the many-armed and many-faceted deities of the Bhagavad Gita that she'd worshipped alongside hashish and Dustin Hoffman in her college days. Even the short but gratifying parade of earth goddesses that had taken her to their ample bosoms in her early thirties had gone, though she remembered them with more kindness than the rest.

God was dead. Let Him rest in peace. Now, finally, the earth was hers with no taint of Heaven.

Anna sat down on a smooth boulder, the top hollowed into a natural seat. The red peeling arms of a Texas madrone held a veil of dusty shade over her eyes. This was the third day of this transect. By evening she would reach civilization: people. A contradiction in terms, she thought even as the words trickled through her mind. Electric lights, television, human companionship, held no allure. But she wanted a bath and she wanted a drink. Mostly she wanted a drink.

And maybe Rogelio. Rogelio had a smile that made matrons hide the hand with the wedding ring. A smile women would lie for and men would follow into battle. A smile, Anna thought with habitual cynicism, that the practiced hucksters in Juárez flashed at rich gringos down from Minnesota.

Maybe Rogelio. Maybe not. Rogelio took a lot of energy.

A spiny rock crevice lizard peered out at her with one obsidian eye, its gray-and-black mottled spines creating a near-perfect illusion of dead leaves and twigs fallen haphazardly into a crack in the stone.

"I see you," Anna said as she wriggled out of her pack. It weighed scarcely thirty pounds. She'd eaten and drunk it down from thirty-seven in the past two days. The poetry of it pleased her. It was part of the order of nature: the more one ate the easier life got. Diets struck Anna as one of the sourest notes of a spoiled country.

Letting the pack roll back, she carefully lowered it to the rock surface. She wasn't careful enough. There was an instant of rustling and the lizard vanished. "Don't leave town on my account," she addressed the seemingly empty crevice. "I'm just passing through."

Anna dug a plastic water jug from the side pocket of her backpack and unscrewed the cap. Yellow pulp bobbed to the top. Next time she would not put lemon slices in; the experiment had failed. After a few days the acid taste grew tiresome. Besides, it gave her a vague feeling of impropriety, as if she were drinking from her finger bowl.

Smiling inwardly at the thought, Anna drank. Finger bowls, Manhattan, were miles and years away from her now, Molly and AT&T her only remaining connections.

The water was body temperature. Just the way she liked it.

Ice water jarred her fillings, chilled her insides. "If it's cold, it'd better be beer," she would tell the waitress at Lucy's in Carlsbad. Sometimes she'd get warm water, sometimes a cold Tecate. It depended on who was on shift that day. Either way, Anna drank it. In the high desert of West Texas moisture was quickly sucked from the soft flesh of unprotected humans.

No spines, she thought idly. No waxy green skin. Nothing to keep us from drying up and blowing away. She took another pull at the water and amused herself with the image of tumbling ass over teakettle like a great green and gray stickerweed across the plains to the south.

Capping the water she looked down at the reason she had stopped: the neatly laid pile of scat between her feet. It was her best hope yet and she'd been scrambling over rocks and through cactus since dawn. Every spring and fall rangers in the Guadalupe Mountains followed paths through the high country chosen by wildlife biologists. These transects—carefully selected trails cutting across the park's wilderness—were searched for mountain lion sign. Any that was found was measured, photographed, and recorded so the Resource Management team could keep track of the cougars in the park: Where were they? Was the population healthy?

Squatting down, Anna examined her find. The scat was by no means fresh but it was full of hair and the ends twisted promisingly. Whatever had excreted it had been dining on small furry creatures. She took calipers out of the kit that contained all her transect tools: camera, five-by-seven cards with places for time, date, location, and weather conditions under which the sign was found, data sheet to record the size of the specimen, and type of film used for the photograph.

The center segment of this SUS—Standard Unit of Sign—was twenty-five millimeters in diameter, almost big enough for an adult cat. Still, it wasn't lion scat. This was Anna's second mountain lion transect in two weeks without so much as one lion sign: no tracks, no scrapes, no scat. Twenty of the beautiful cats had been radio-collared and, in less than three years, all but two had left the park or slipped their collars—disappeared from the radio scanner's range somehow.

Ranchers around the Guadalupes swore the park was a breeding ground for the "varmints" and that cattle were being slaughtered by the cats, but Anna had never so much as glimpsed a mountain lion in the two years she'd been a Law Enforcement ranger at Guadalupe. And she spent more than half her time wandering the high country, sitting under the ponderosa pines, walking the white limestone trails, lying under the limitless Texas sky. Never had she seen a cougar and, if wishing and waiting and watching could've made it so, prides of the great padding beasts would've crossed her path.

This, between her feet, was probably coyote scat.

Because she hated to go home empty-handed, Anna dutifully measured, recorded, and photographed the little heap of dung. She wished all wild creatures were as adaptable as the coyote. "Trickster" the Indians called him. Indeed he must be to thrive so close to man.

Piled next to the coyote's mark was the unmistakable reddish berry-filled scat of the ring-tailed cat. "MY ravine," it declared. "MY canyon. I was here second!"

Anna laughed. "Your canyon," she agreed aloud. "I'm for home."

Stretching tired muscles, she craned her neck in a backward arc. Overhead, just to the east, vultures turned tight circles, corkscrewing up from the creekbed between the narrow walls of Middle McKittrick Canyon where she hiked.

Eleven of the big birds spun in a lazy whirlwind of beaks and feathers. Whatever they hovered over was hidden from view by the steep cliffs of the Permian Reef. A scrap of rotting carrion the size of a goose egg drew vultures. But eleven? Eleven was too many.

"Damn," Anna whispered. A deer had probably broken a leg and coyotes had gotten it. Probably.

A twelfth winged form joined the hungry, waiting dance. "Damn."

Anna pulled up her pack and shrugged into it. "You can have your rock back," she addressed the apparently empty crevice, and started down the canyon.

While she'd been sitting, the glaring white of the stones that formed the floor of Middle McKittrick Canyon had been softened to pale gold. Shadows were growing long. Lizards crept to the top of the rocks to catch the last good sun of the day. A tarantula the size of a woman's hand, the most horrifying of gentle creatures, wandered slowly across Anna's path.

"As a Park Ranger I will protect and serve you." She talked to the creature from a safe three yards away. "But we'll never be friends. Is that going to be a problem?"

The tarantula stopped, its front pair of legs feeling the air. Then it turned and walked slowly toward her, each of its legs appearing to move independently of the other seven.

"Yes. I see that it is." Glad there were no visitors to witness her absurdity, Anna stepped aside and gave the magnificent bug a wider berth than science or good sense would've deemed necessary.

Half a mile farther down the canyon the walls began to narrow around boulders the size of Volkswagens. Anna scrambled and jumped from one to the next. Middle McKittrick was an excellent place to break an ankle or a neck; join the buzzards' buffet.

The sun slipped lower and the canyon filled with shadow. In the sudden cooling a breeze sprang up, carrying with it a new smell. Not the expected sickly-sweet odor of rotting flesh, but the fresh smell of water, unmistakable in the desert, always startling. One never grew accustomed to miracles. Energized, Anna walked on.

The walls became steeper, towering more than sixty feet above the creek. A rugged hillside of catclaw and agave showed dark above the pale cliffs. The boulders that littered upper McKittrick were no longer in evidence. In the canyon's heart, Anna walked on smooth limestone. Over the ages water had scoured a deep trough, then travertine, percolating out of the solution, lined it with a natural cement.

Not a good place to be caught during the Texas monsoons in July and August. Each time she walked this transect in search of cougar sign, Anna had that same thought. And each time she had the same perverse stab of excitement: hoping one day to see the power and the glory that could roll half a mountain aside as it thundered through.

The smell of water grew stronger and, mixed with the sighing and sawing of the wind, she could hear its delicate music. Potholes began pitting the streambed—signs of recent flooding. Recent in geological time. Far too long to wait for a drink. Some of the scoured pits were thirty feet across and twenty feet deep. A litter of leaves and bones lay at the bottom of the one Anna skirted. An animal—a fawn by the look of one of the intact leg bones—had fallen in and been unable to climb out again.

This was a section of the canyon that Anna hated to hike, though its austere beauty lured her back time and again. The high walls, with their steep sloping shoulders sliding down to slick-sided pits, put a clutch in her stomach. Farther down the white basins would be filled with crystal waters, darting yellow sunfish: life. But here the river had deserted the canyon for a world underground and left only these oddly sculpted death traps. Anna entertained no false hopes that her radio signal would reach up over the cliffs and mountains to summon help if she were to lose her footing.

She crawled the distance on hands and knees.

Even heralded by perfume and music, the water took her by surprise. Sudden in the bleak bone-white canyon came an emerald pool filled by a fall of purest water. The plop of fleeing frogs welcomed her and she stopped a moment just to marvel.

Aware of the ache across her shoulders, Anna loosed the straps and let her pack fall heavily to the limestone. At the abrupt sound there was an answering rattle; a rushing sound that brought her heart to her throat. With a crackling of black-feathered wings and a chatter of startled cries, a cloud of vultures fought up out of the saw grass that grew along the bench on the south side of the pool.

They didn't fly far, but settled in soot-colored heaps along the ledges, looking jealously back at their abandoned feast.

Anna looked to where they fixed their sulky eyes.

Saw grass, three-sided and sharp, grew nearly shoulder-high along the ledge beyond the pool. From a distance the dark green blades, edged with a paler shade, looked soft, lush, but Anna knew from experience anything edible in this stark land had ways of protecting itself. Each blade of saw grass was edged with fine teeth, like the serrated edge of a metal-cutting saw.

The sand-colored stone above it was dark with seeps of water weeping from the cliff's face. Ferns, an anomaly in the desert, hung in a green haze from the rocks, and violets the size of Anna's thumbnail sparked the stone with purple.

In the grasses then, protected by their razor-sides, was the carrion supper she had stumbled upon. Not anxious to wade through the defending vegetation, Anna reached to roll down her sleeves to protect the skin of her arms. Fingers touched only flesh and she remembered with irritation that, though, come sunset, West Texas still hovered in the cool grip of spring, the National Park Service had declared summer had arrived. Long-sleeved uniform shirts had been banned on May first.

Balancing easily on the sloping stone now that the drop was softened with a shimmer of water, Anna walked to the edge of the pool and entered the saw grass. She held her hands above her head like a teenager on a roller coaster.

The sharp grasses snagged at her trouser legs, plucked her shirt tight against her body. It matted underfoot and, in places, grew taller than the top of her head. Her boots sank to the laces in the mire. Water seeped in, soaked through her socks.

A high-pitched throaty sound grumbled from her perching audience. "I'm not going to eat your damned carrion," Anna reassured them with ill grace. "I just want to see if it's a lion kill." Even as she spoke she wondered if talking to turkey vultures was a worse sign, mentally speaking, than talking to one's self.

She must remember to ask Molly.

At the next step, stink, trapped by the grasses, rose in an almost palpable cloud. Death seemed to rot the very air.

In a sharp choking gasp, Anna sucked it into her lungs.

Crumpled amongst the thick stems was the green and gray of a National Park Service uniform. Sheila Drury, the Dog Canyon Ranger, lay half curled, knees drawn up. An iridescent green and black backpack, heavy with water and whatever was inside, twisted her almost belly-up. Buzzard buffet: they didn't even have to dig for the tastiest parts.

Anna knew Drury only to say hello to—the woman had been with the park just seven months. Now she lay at Anna's feet, her entrails, plucked loose by greedy talons, decorating her face, tangling in her brown hair. Mercifully the thick loose tresses covered the dead eyes, veiled the lower half of the face and neck.

One vulture, bolder than the rest, dropped down from the ledge on wide-spread wings, stirring up the putrid air. Unheralded, a Gary Larson cartoon flashed into Anna's brain. Vultures around a kill: "Ooooooweeeeee! This thing's been here a looooooooong time. Well, thank God for ketchup."

Gagging, Anna turned and stumbled toward the pool. Razor thin lines of red appeared on her face and arms where the saw grass cut. Oblivious to their sting, she fought free of the vegetation.

Her stomach was long emptied before the heaving stopped. She crawled to the water's edge, wiped her mouth with a handkerchief wet from the pool and, without hope, pulled her King radio from its leather holster on the hip belt of her pack.

"Three-eleven, three-one-five."

Three times she tried. Magic number, she thought, filling her mind with irrelevancies: the Holy Trinity, three wishes, three strikes and you're out.

"No contact. Three-fifteen clear."

The vultures had settled back to their interrupted supper. A squabble of black wings pulled Anna's reluctant attention to the saw grass. A shadow rose into the sky, something slippery and snake-like held fast in its talons. Another followed, snatching at the prize.

Not such a bad thing, Anna couldn't help thinking, to be so celebrated in passing. Half the naturalists in the park would be honored to play to such an appreciative audience. "Sorry, Sheila," she said aloud, knowing few shared her strange sensibilities. "I'll be quick as I can."

She belted the radio on and, looking only where she put her hands, began to climb. Daggers of agave, needle-sharp and thrusting knifelike up from the rocky soil, catclaw in a bushy haze of tangled branches and small hooked spines, and jagged-toothed sotol, the black sheep of the lily family, tore at her skin and clothing. These dragons of this tiny Eden were the reason it had yet to be trammeled by humanity in the form of coolers full of beer and sunbathers slathered with cocoa butter.

Forty or fifty yards above the canyon bottom, Anna found a secure niche between a rock and a stunted yucca clinging determinedly to the thin layer of soil. "Three-eleven, three-one-five," she repeated. This time there was the reassuring static surge of the radio transmission hitting the repeater on Bush Mountain.

"Three-eleven," came Paul Decker's familiar voice.

Much to her surprise, Anna began to cry. The relief of that comforting sound had momentarily undone her. Paul, the Frijole District Ranger, always answered. Always. On-duty or off. There was even a radio in his bathroom.

"Paul, Anna," she said unnecessarily, giving herself time. "I'm about an hour north of where Middle and North McKittrick fork. We've had an . . . incident. I'll need a litter and enough people to carry it out." She knew better than to hope for a helicopter. The nearest was in El Paso, two hours away. A body-basket could be dropped down from a helicopter but it would take a very long line; dangerous in such treacherous country. Never risk the living for the dead.

"The victim is . . ." Is what? Anna's mind raced for the radio-approved double talk for "dead." "Dispatched" was the word of choice when a ranger had had to kill a creature—human or otherwise. But an already dispatched ranger being consumed by turkey vultures? "The victim is non-salvageable," she said, falling back on her ambulance triage protocol.

An alarming silence followed. "Paul, do you copy?" she asked anxiously.

"Ten-four," came the automatic reply. Then: "Anna, it's

too late to get anyone up to you tonight. Can you hang in there till morning?"

Anna said yes and three-one-five clear. Wishing there was more to say, wishing the tenuous contact could be prolonged, she dropped her radio back into its leather holster.

At first light Paul would start out. In her mind's ear she could hear him digging his Search and Rescue kit out of the hall closet. Probably he would sleep as little as she did. He was that sort of man. Once, when alcohol and memories had kept her up late, she'd seen him creeping out of his house at three a.m. to count vehicles; making sure all his little seasonal employees had made it out of the high country and were safe in their beds.

Anna breathed deeply and leaned back against the pitted stone. At this height there was still sun to the west. Rich and red, it slipped toward Guadalupe Peak, the highest point in Texas. Texans, Anna thought, though she loved them with a pinch of salt and a lot of laughter, were full of shit. But when it came to the sky, they weren't just whistling Dixie. The Texas sky was something else. Sunsets of gold and crimson, stars to dazzle, clouds taller than the fabled Stetsons.

Thunderclouds were beginning to build to the north and west. There'd been lightning the previous night over Dog Canyon. Anna had watched it from her camp on the ridge between Dog and Middle McKittrick. It was the first storm of the season—all lightning and no precipitation. The weather pattern would continue that way till the rains came in July. Fire danger was high. Already fires burned half a dozen places in New Mexico and Arizona. Everyone in the park was on the lookout for smokes.

Red-gold fingers of light reached through the dry thunderheads, touching the desert with the illusion of living green—a green that would come with the monsoons.

"Seven-two-four Echo is ten-seven." The baby voice of

the Carlsbad Caverns dispatcher startled Anna back from the clean peace of the sky. Carlsbad was going out of service late; leaving the cave with the bats.

Fortunately, there was still plenty of light to work her way down to the creekbed. She had no food for supper but something had spoiled her appetite anyway.

Down was worse than up. Gravity, eager to help, dragged at her every misstep. But she made it, stood solidly on the smooth limestone, water at her feet, a corpse in the saw grass. Anna tried to call the Dog Canyon Ranger to mind: Sheila Drury, thirty-three? thirty-five?, female, Caucasian, park ranger, recently deceased.

The woman had entered on duty in December the year before. In the seven months since, she had caused quite a stir. There'd been a lot of repercussions when she had proposed building recreational vehicle sites at Dog, and she'd raised a lot of fuss and furor over a plan to reintroduce prairie dogs into the area.

Politics and gossip were all that Anna knew of her. Dog Canyon District was two hours by car from the Frijole District. They'd never had an occasion to work together.

Too late to get to know her now, Anna thought dryly. Heaven and the vultures only knew what would be left come sunrise. Not for the first time, Anna wished she'd learned more natural history. Did vultures feed all night? Would she hear the grumbling, plucking sounds in the coming dark?

She dug her headlamp from her pack and pulled it tight across her brow. CLUES: that's what the law enforcement specialists at FLETC, the Federal Law Enforcement Training Center in Georgia, had taught her to look for. CLUES: bloody fingerprints, cars parked in strange places, white powder trickling out of trunks. In the more populous parks like Glen Canyon and Yosemite, or those close to urban areas as were Joshua Tree or Smoky Mountains, crime was more prevalent. In fleeing Manhattan and her memories, Anna had kept to out-of-the-way places. So far all she'd had to deal with in the line of duty were off-leash dogs and Boy Scouts camping out of bounds. Still and all, she was a Federally Commissioned Law Enforcement Officer. She would look for CLUES.

However nauseating.

# CHAPTER 2

Anna fished two of the soggy lemon slices from her water bottle, mashed them to a pulp, and rubbed the pulp into her wet handkerchief. Tying it over her mouth and nose, she fervently hoped it would cut the stench of death down to a tolerable level.

Next she took the camera she'd been using on the lion transect and hung it around her neck. Switching on the headlamp, though it was not yet dark enough to do her much good, she waded into the saw grass.

The camera helped. It gave her distance. Through its lens she was able to see more clearly. Sheila Drury was parceled out into photographic units. As she clicked, Anna made mental notes: no scrapes, no bruises, no twisted limbs. Drury probably hadn't fallen.

Freaks of nature did happen now and then. Anna looked up at the cliff above, imagined Drury falling, dying instantly on impact: no contusions. Unlikely enough even if catclaw eight and ten feet high hadn't tangled close along the edge. Why would she fight cross-country through it in a full pack?

Anna turned her attention back to the corpse.

The skin of the face and arms was clear, smooth, the tongue unswollen. The Dog Canyon Ranger had not died of hunger, thirst, or exposure. Anna had more or less ruled those out anyway. Guadalupe Mountains National Park, though rugged and unforgiving, was barely twelve miles across. For a ranger familiar with the country to stay lost long enough to perish from the elements was highly improbable. Too, one presumed Drury had water, food—the stuff of survival—in her pack. A tent and sleeping bag were strapped on the outside.

No obvious powder burns, bullet holes, or stabbing wounds. Evidently the woman had not been waylaid by drug runners hiding in the wilderness.

Despite the tragic situation, Anna smiled. Edith, her mother-in-law, a veteran of the Bronx ("But darling, it was very middle class in the forties"), of the Great Depression, the number two train from Wall Street, and WWII, stood aghast at the concept of a woman camping alone in the wilderness. ("Anna, there's *nobody* there. *Anyone* could be there . . .")

Anna believed the truth was, alone was safe. A woman alone would live the longest. Criminals were a lazy bunch. If they weren't, they'd get their MBAs and rob with impunity. They most assuredly wouldn't walk eight hard miles to hide. They'd check into a Motel 6 on the Interstate, watch afternoon TV and hope for the best.

What did that leave, she wondered, her eye once again against the viewfinder. Suicide? A bit odd to do one's self in in full gear in a saw grass swamp. Heart attack? Stroke? Drowning? Lots of ways to die. Suddenly Anna felt fragile.

Evening was settling into the canyon's bottom. Soon she'd be wasting film. Three pictures left on the roll. Careful not to disturb anything, Anna leaned down and drew the curtain of heavy dark hair from Sheila Drury's face and throat.

There it was: another way to die. Oddly, the last and the first she had considered: lion kill. Claw marks cut up from Drury's clavicle to her chin. Puncture wounds—claws or teeth—made neat dark holes above the collarbone. Anna did not doubt that Sheila's neck had been snapped as well. It was the way the big cats made their kills.

For a long moment Anna stood, the dead woman at her feet, oblivious to the gathering darkness. Tears welling from deep inside spilled down her face and dripped from the square line of her jaw.

Now the lions would be hunted down and killed. Now every trigger-happy Texan would blast away at every tawny shadow that flickered in the brush. The government's bounty quotas on predators of domestic livestock would go up. Lions would die and die.

"Damn you, Drury," Anna whispered as ways to obscure the evidence appeared in and were discarded from her mind. "What in hell were you doing here?"

Steeling herself to accept the touch of dead flesh, Anna felt down Drury's jaw and neck, then lifted her arm. Rigor had already passed off. She'd been dead a while. Since sometime Friday afternoon or night, Anna guessed.

Her light trained on the ground, she moved past the body. Above Drury's head were two perfect paw prints. Behind them several feet were two more. Anna measured the distance with her eyes: a big lion.

Soon stars would begin to appear in the silver-gray ribbon of sky overhead. Before the shadowy tracks vanished in the growing gloom, she clicked a couple pictures of the prints and one last shot of the body.

There was no more film; no more to be done till morning. Aware of how desperately tired she was, Anna readjusted her headlamp to light her footsteps and trudged out of the saw grass. It seemed all she could do to drag one foot after the other.

The vultures did not drop down in her wake to resume their meal. Evidently the big birds did not feed at night. Anna was grateful. Notwithstanding her appreciation of the food chain, she wasn't sure she could've stood a night listening to its graphic demonstration. The sepulchral snacking would've been unsettling, to say the least.

Wearily, she wondered why the lion hadn't eaten more of its kill, eviscerated it as lions usually did. Something must have frightened it off. Perhaps a hiker unaware that less than fifteen yards away, a corpse lay in the grasses, a lion hunkered by. The canyon was closed but occasionally hikers did wander in.

Surely, in this dry season with game so scarce, the lion would return. It might be nearby, waiting. One of the forsworn gods' little jokes: to have Anna's long-coveted first lion sighting be her last sight on this earth.

Anna didn't know if she was scared or not. She supposed she was because she found herself groping through her pack to curl her fingers around the cold comfort of her .357 Smith & Wesson service revolver. It was hard to be philosophical in the night. There was something too primeval in the closeness of death.

To her surprise, she was hungry. Life reasserting its claim, insisting on its rights and privileges. There was probably food in Drury's pack but Anna wasn't that hungry. Vultures watching a lion watching her hunt for the food their food was carrying: the chain grew too tangled.

Sheila Drury, was she watching as well? Anna didn't have to believe in God to wonder where people's spirits went when they died. Wonder if hers would go there, too.

Ghost stories from childhood crept uninvited into her

thoughts and she found herself afraid to look toward the saw grass, afraid she'd see, not a lion, but a floating wraith.

With a physical shake of her shoulders, Anna pushed the night's terrors from her. Since Zach had died, and every night had been a night alone, she learned to put away fear.

Those nights, she remembered, she'd prayed for a ghost—a voice, a touch, anything. There was nothing then. And nothing now. Except a hungry night and, perhaps, a hungry lion.

Darkness closed on this rattling of thoughts. Overhead, the stream of stars grew deeper. Cold air settled into the canyon, flowed around her where she sat, knees drawn up, .357 by her side, staring into the melting mirror of the pool.

At some point Anna dug out the four Ritz crackers, the last chocolate pudding, and half a handful of gorp from her backpack and ate them. At some point after moonrise, when a light unseasonal rain began to fall, she unrolled her sleeping bag and crawled into it. At some point, though she would've denied it, Anna slept.

# CHAPTER 3

Wincing at the sting of water in the paper-thin saw grass cuts on her hands and arms, Anna slid down in the bath. Not a great bath by any means. Great baths had gone out with claw-foot tubs. The passion for showers that had replaced them with prefab white plastic boxes at the bottom of featureless stalls was incomprehensible to Anna.

In New York she'd lain for hours in the tub in the kitchen of a five-floor walk-up in Hell's Kitchen making pictures from the water stains on the ceiling and waiting for Zach to come home and make the wait worth her while.

Always he came home. Sometimes he made love to her. Sometimes he didn't.

Rogelio always did. Whether she wanted him to or not. Anna wondered what time it was, wondered if he would come, wondered if she cared and took another sip of wine. Mondavi Red, her vin ordinaire. It was cheap, came in big bottles, traveled well in a backpack, and didn't taste half bad.

Sipping again, she enjoyed the feeling of heat within and heat without unknotting her mind.

Piedmont sat just outside the bathroom door. His eyes glowed red in the light of the single candle. His thick, yellow-striped tail was curled neatly over his forepaws. Piedmont liked the sound of running water. Anna thought it was because he was probably born of a feral mother near the banks of the Black River somewhere down by Rattlesnake Springs. He would never come near the tub though. Perhaps because he'd half drowned in a flash flood. After the monsoon's worst cloudburst the July before, Anna had found him tangled in dead branches in the crotch of a tree.

The cat closed his eyes: going into his river trance.

Anna's gaze moved to the candlelight on the bath water, then, idly, down the length of her body. At thirty-nine she still retained her boyish figure but her skin didn't fit quite so snugly as it once had. Elbows, knees, neck, wherever the bending went on, there were wrinkles. Her muscles—better defined than when she was twenty—were beginning to look ropey. Still, it was a good body. Even in the face of the changing physical fashions touted in the glossy magazines, she had always liked it fine. A strong body: easy to maintain.

The water was unknotting her hair, unweaving the copper and the silver strands from the single braid she kept them locked in and spreading them around her shoulders like seaweed.

Ophelia drowned, Anna thought, or, in the New York theatrical agents' parlance of Molly's Friday ten o'clock: "An old Ophelia type."

A dead woman.

What was left of Sheila Drury had been wrapped in garbage bags. The park, bless its optimistic little heart, didn't boast a body bag. The green shiny bundle that had once been the Dog Canyon Ranger had been loaded onto a Stokes litter—a rolling wire-mesh stretcher—and trundled, carried, and wrestled down the stone-filled canyons.

Paul had been consummately professional. Anna had tried to appear that way though a hundred exceedingly tasteless jokes had stampeded through her mind during the long trek out. The seasonals—two naturalists and a ranger—who had come to assist were mostly quiet and sensible. The naturalists were both men—Craig Eastern and Manny Mankins. Cheryl Light was the seasonal law enforcement ranger.

A high percentage of National Park Service employees were summer seasonals. Winter found Guadalupe Mountains down to a skeleton staff. Most of the seasonals were highly educated. A number had advanced degrees. Some had families to support. Yet they left jobs and homes and husbands and wives for the privilege of living in a dormitory and working for six dollars and fifty-four cents an hour, no retirement, no benefits, and rent deducted automatically.

Many hoped, one day, to become permanent but the openings were few and closely guarded by tangled thickets of red tape. Anna knew Manny had been trying to get on permanently since his son was born four years before.

Craig Eastern's situation was a little different. He was a herpetologist on a two-year detail from the University of Texas at El Paso. Anna had been surprised Paul had brought Craig up Middle McKittrick. A shaky, easily alarmed man in his early thirties, Eastern was more at home with rattlesnakes, lizards, and toads than he was with people. He viewed most of humanity askance. The world was being destroyed by humans. The Guadalupe Mountains were the last bastion of untrammeled earth.

Anna had to admit that under pressure he bore up well, admirably even. Seeing Craig lift the corpse onto the Stokes, Anna had noticed how muscular he was. His nervousness made him seem like a little man, but he was far from it. Craig

Eastern had been working out with weights—for years by the look of him.

Manny Mankins was the opposite. The wiry naturalist was a man of small stature who seemed a great deal bigger than he was. "Bantam cock," Anna's mother-in-law would have called him.

Anna had fought fire alongside the skinny, sandy-haired man for seventeen days. He'd worked everyone into the ground. That was on the Foolhen fire in Idaho. They'd slammed fire line twenty-two hours straight. Manny was still cracking jokes, swinging a Pulaski when the rest of the crew was barely scraping theirs over the duff.

The bath was growing tepid. Anna pushed the hot water on with her big toe, poured herself another glass of cabernet from the bottle on the toilet seat. Settling back in physical content, she let the image of the seasonal law enforcement ranger drift behind her half-closed eyes.

Cheryl Light was new to the park, entering on duty only a couple of weeks before. Stocky—around five-foot-five and maybe a hundred and fifty pounds—with shoulder-length permed hair. Anna placed her age somewhere between thirty-five and forty-five. With woodsy types it was hard to tell. Their skin wrinkled prematurely from sun and weather but their vitality was ageless.

Usually Cheryl laughed a lot. The kind of laugh that made others laugh too, even before they knew what the joke was. There'd been no laughter that day.

Cheryl had carried Drury's pack and, over the rough spots, one end of the Stokes litter. The woman was powerful but that's not what stuck in Anna's mind. What had impressed her was the unobtrusive way Cheryl had supported, eased, bolstered, comforted, bucked-up everybody around her. Apparently she did it without effort or even knowledge that she was doing it. A well-timed smile, a touch, a proffered drink from her water bottle.

Anna envied it. Kindness—true, unadulterated kindness—was beyond her.

If Cheryl's kindness was legitimate, Anna's resident cynic interjected the customary sour note. Unadulterated, altruistic kindness? It went against the grain. Still and all, it was kindness.

"I think too much to be kind," she excused herself to a disinterested cat. Had Cheryl found a way to laugh about it by now? Though she and Craig and Manny were all business at the scene, there would be jokes tonight after a few beers and, maybe, for Craig, some nightmares. Probably Anna wouldn't hear much about it and Paul, nothing. Everyone pretended there was no wall between the permanent National Park Service employees and the seasonals. And everyone knew there was. A veritable bureaucratic Jericho with no Joshua in sight. Everyone was transient. Seasonals came and went like stray cats. Even permanent employees seldom stayed in one place more than a few years, not if they wanted to advance their careers. People who "homesteaded"—stayed in one park too long—tended to come to think of the place as theirs; they developed their own ideas of how it should be run. The NPS didn't care for that. It made people less tractable, less willing to follow the party line dictated from half a continent away.

Karl Johnson, the man who tended Guadalupe's stock, had been with the Park Service for fifteen years yet he'd never been promoted higher than GS-5, the grade of a beginning seasonal. His love of these mountains had cost him a lot. Sometimes Anna wondered if it wasn't worth it. Personally, the dashing from place to place made for unsettled lives; professionally, for duplicated paperwork and unfinished projects.

And the death of Sheila Drury, was it finished? Anna had been amazed at how little time the official investigation had taken. Benjamin Jakey, a sheriff out of El Paso and one of his deputies—a Pillsbury Doughboy look-alike who'd never stopped puffing from the hike in—had done some perfunctory poking around. "Yep. Lion got her. Surprised it don't happen more often," Sheriff Jakey said and the deputy puffed portentously. Jakey had looked through the grass, gone over the sketches Anna had made of the scene. The deputy shot a couple rolls of film and told Anna they wouldn't need hers.

That had been about it. The Feds would have it now—the park was federal land. But they would rubber-stamp it, Anna assumed.

Everyone would be surprised, here in the "wilderness," that lion kills didn't happen more often. "More often," Anna said aloud. More often than what? More often than never? Than once a decade? What? She must remember to find out come morning. And come morning, she had to write a witness statement for the county coroner, Nina Dietz.

It was she they had delivered the body to. Looking more like Aunt Bea than the keeper of the dead, she'd been waiting with the ambulance in the McKittrick Visitors Center parking lot. She'd ridden with Paul as he'd driven the body away.

No more Sheila Drury.

And, one day, no more Anna Pigeon. It was a sobering thought. Anna took a deep drink of her wine.

The front door opened, then clicked softly shut again. Piedmont slunk away to hide under the kitchen table. Anna heard a tape drop into the boom box: Guy Clark's "Rita Ballou."

Rogelio.

Now, for a while, there would be other things to think about.

"Ana." A tap on the bathroom door and it swung inward. Anna liked the way he said her name. The Spanish "Ana," soft, beseeching. She liked his rebelliousness. They'd met while she was on special detail for the US Forest Service in Pagosa Springs, Colorado. Anna had arrested him for chaining himself to the blade of a bulldozer scheduled to cut road into a timber sale. He'd smiled at her and he'd winked. She liked the way he looked. The candlelight glanced off the flat planes of his face, threw his eyes into deep shadow, and glinted off the rich brown of his curling hair. Roger Cooper. Rogelio. A displaced Irish/Israeli from Chicago conducting his own brand of desert warfare.

He slipped in, knelt by the tub with a childish grace. His hands dipped under the water, rested cool on her waist.

"No trouble this time. Just a lot of talking and drinking cerveza," he said. "The Border Patrol hardly stopped me. They must be getting used to my old bug."

"They don't have much of a problem with middle-class white men with Illinois plates sneaking into Texas," Anna said. The El Paso Border station was more concerned with illegal aliens than drugs. And something in his proud assumption of wickedness made her want to deflate him now and again. Eco-defenders had altogether too much fun fighting the good fight. They looked in the mirror and a little too often to overly impress Anna. "And the beer and the talk, that's the best part, isn't it?" Still, she was smiling and she'd moved her hands to cover his.

"Not the best part," Rogelio said, his voice liquid. "You are the best part."

The Clark tape came to an end and the player automatically clicked over to the second cassette. The Chenille Sisters singing, "I wanna be seduced." Anna laughed.

She did.

Anna did some of her best thinking after making love, curled warm and satisfied in the curve of Zach's shoulder. Of Rogelio's shoulder, she corrected herself without pity. The mind is clearer when the body is quiet.

"Rogelio, are you still awake?"

"Depends," came a slow answer and she felt the warmth of his hand at her breast.

She caught it and held it somewhere near the floating ribs—less distracting real estate. "I keep thinking about the Drury Lion Kill." Already, in self-defense—or natural callousness, Anna was not sure—she'd dubbed the death of the woman from Dog Canyon the "Drury Lion Kill." Though something about the phrase bothered her. "I wonder why she was messing around up there. She wasn't on transect. Middle McKittrick is closed."

"That's what rangers do," Rogelio replied and his smile warmed the darkness. "Go all the good places us mere mortals are shut out of. Everybody knows that."

"Seriously. Who in their right mind would drag a full pack down that canyon on a contraband lark?" Rogelio's hand was trying to wriggle free, his lips brushed her neck.

"Mmmm," he purred "you're doing it to me again. God but I'm crazy for you, Ana."

Anna tried to fix her mind on the saw grass, the vultures.

"One of your pet kitty cats ate a ranger," Rogelio said and his hand slid down to her thighs. "Lions do that, *querida*. They're meat eaters."

"Seriously—" Anna said and again caught his hands.

"Seriously," Rogelio replied and pulled her to him.

Even as she responded, she ached for Zachary, for some good, old-fashioned conversation.

First thing in the morning she would call Molly. First thing.

• • •

"Reality check," Anna said. She pressed her mouth close to the phone.

"I've only got seven minutes till Mrs. Claremont."

"I found a dead body."

"What's that sound in the background? Where are you?"

"At the pay phone by the washer and dryer in the Cholla Chateau in the Rec Hall. That's the dryer. It squeaks," Anna explained. Molly knew where she was. She was just being difficult.

"Get a phone. A real phone."

"I promise."

"Okay. A body. Human or otherwise?"

"A woman. I found her up Middle McKittrick Canyon yesterday on my lion transect."

There was a moment's silence. Anna waited through it. Molly was lighting a cigarette. Not for the first time, Anna was amazed that Molly's patients stood it. One hundred and fifty dollars an hour and they had to breathe tobacco smoke. "Middle McKittrick," Molly said. "That's one of those bloody awful washes you've got down there, isn't it?"

"That's right." Anna glanced at her pocket watch. "Four minutes till Mrs. Claremont."

"Mrs. Claremont will still be neurotic in fifteen. Tell me."

Anna told Molly everything, as she had since she was five and her sister was eleven. She told her of the vultures, the tears, the saw grass, the ghosts, the paw prints, the claw marks. Occasionally Molly interrupted with a question, clarifying, Anna knew, the very precise picture she was putting together in her mind.

Mrs. Claremont had been cooling her heels in the Park View Clinic's opulent waiting room for ten minutes by the time Anna had finished.

Another brief silence. Anna waited for the summation. Already, just from talking to Molly, she felt better.

"Okay," Molly said finally. "You didn't give a damn one way or another about this Sheila Drury. Right so far?"

"Right," Anna admitted. She wished Molly would sugar-coat things now and again, but she never would.

"Death, darkness, vultures munching, brought back the bad old days after Zach was killed. That's pretty straightforward. But what I'm hearing through it all is an outraged sense of injustice. Am I close?"

Anna felt around inside her brain, probed down her esophagus, took a left at her sternum, and peered into her heart. "I guess that's right." The surprise sounded in her voice and she heard Molly's foreshortened chuckle, almost the "heh heh heh" of the cartoons.

"Because some of the wrong people die?" Molly was fishing.

"Ah . . . Nope."

"That you weren't hailed a hero for finding her?"

"Nope."

"Because you had to be the one to find a stinking corpse?"

Anna thought about that for a second but it wasn't it, either. Horrible as it was, she loved a good adventure. "Nope."

"I give up," Molly said. "Gotta go. Call me when you hit on it."

There was a click and Molly was gone. Ushering in Mrs. Claremont without apology, Anna didn't doubt.

Craig Eastern came in with a blue plastic basket full of uniforms and white Fruit of the Loom underpants. He didn't look at Anna as he loaded the washer and put two quarters in the slot. Maybe he figured it would make less of an intrusion that way.

Anna realized she was still holding the receiver to her ear and replaced it in its cradle. "I'm done," she announced and Craig cranked in the quarters, starting the noise of the washer.

Outraged injustice.

Anna pondered it as she walked back to her residence. Molly had put her finger right on it. That was the feeling. Anna had mixed it with other emotions, not really even recognized it. Outraged injustice. It was an emotion for the young, for those who still believed in some pure, shining vision of absolute Justice, a virgin to be outraged. Anna had felt the outrage for years when she'd been simpler, blessed enough to see the world in clear, crisp black and white.

Over the years she'd been introduced to "mitigating circumstances." Everything had softened, muted into the more interesting but less dramatic shades of gray.

Why outraged injustice now? Anna rubbed the fine scratches on her arms. They were beginning to itch with healing.

Then it was clear, classic: the innocent wrongly accused.

The lion didn't do it.

# CHAPTER 4

"Anna, you saying 'The lion didn't do it' is like Jimmy Hoffa saying the Teamsters didn't do it."

"Paul, there were no saw grass cuts on Sheila. None. Lions wrestle their prey around, drag it. Even if it just chased her into the saw grass and killed her clean, she'd've had to get cut up some."

Paul sighed—a small one, barely audible. The sound of a patient man summoning up his reserves. Tilting back in his chair, he steepled his fingers. "Okay, let's go over this."

Anna felt irritation boiling up inside of her and took a couple of deep breaths to try to dilute it. Paul was about to manage her. Anna loathed being managed. She leaned back in her chair and steepled her fingers in conscious mimicry.

They were in the Ranger Division's headquarters, the old Frijole ranch house. It was a two-story home built near a spring just after the turn of the century. Even in the heat of June it was cool. The native stone walls were nearly two feet thick and pecan trees, brought from St. Louis in tins and carefully tended, were now fifty feet high. The shaded oasis was a haven for snakes, scorpions, mice, and rangers. But for an ongoing battle between the District Ranger and the mice, they all managed to live together in relative accord.

"Okay," Paul said again, looking like a man getting his ducks all in a row. "You saw lion tracks."

"Yes," Anna admitted. "By morning the rain had pretty much wiped them out in that silty mud, but they were there."

"Claw marks, puncture wounds, no sign of any other form of trauma."

"Right."

"Then what are you suggesting?" Paul looked across the fingertips he'd used to tap out each one of his points. The pale blue eyes were so open, so willing to hear what she had to say, that Anna felt like an idiot.

There wasn't much she could say. Like a three-year-old, she'd run to Paul Decker half-cocked, no hard facts. Just one anomaly and a gut feeling.

"I'm not sure. Maybe she had a heart attack, or a stroke, or something and the lion came later. I don't know." Anna spoke slowly, feeling her way through her thoughts. "A lot of stuff's been bothering me. Little things: no saw grass cuts, the body not eviscerated, why she was there in the first place, her hair was down and loose—nobody hikes with their hair flying around in their face—little stuff."

Anna petered out rather than stopped. Her eyes had been wandering around the room in a vague sort of way, now they came back to Paul's face just in time to catch the end of a smile slipping from his lips like the tail of a garter snake vanishing into high grass. Anna wished she'd not added the part about the hair. It was a joke that she never let her hair down. When she did at the rare social events she attended, she was met with a monotonous chorus of: "I didn't recognize you!"

"You've made some good points, Anna." Paul glanced at

his watch surreptitiously and suddenly it infuriated her that he was so damned nice, so unfailingly understanding. She knew from experience that he'd sit and listen to her "problem" as long as she felt the need to talk.

"It's not my problem," she said with more vehemence than the situation called for and rose to her feet. "Just thoughts." Anna knew she was overreacting, unwelcome emotions sharpening her tongue and shortening her temper.

"Sit down," Paul returned reasonably. "Obviously it's bothering you. That makes it important."

Anna sat.

"Maybe Sheila was hiking up from Pratt instead of down from Dog Canyon—on a day hike," Paul suggested.

Pratt Cabin was an historic stone house built at the confluence of North McKittrick and McKittrick creeks about two and a half miles in from the Visitors Center. It was a favored stop of visitors to the park and a logical jumping off place for backcountry hikers.

Anna shook her head. "Carrying a full pack? And that wouldn't change the fact that she had to pass through dense saw grass. No cuts." As she argued, she wondered what exactly it was that she was trying to prove.

Paul looked a little pained. "I don't know why she didn't have any cuts, Anna. I wish I did."

She believed him. He'd like to answer her questions, not because they were important or even particularly valid, but because she felt strongly about them and, to Paul, feelings needed to be dealt with.

Shaking off his kindness with a shrugging motion, she tried another tack. "There've been no incidents of lions attacking humans in West Texas for the last one hundred years. Not one. Zilch. Nada."

"Statistics," Paul said.

Lies, damn lies, and statistics, Anna thought. She nodded,

stood up feeling angry and defeated and heartily tired of both emotions. "Now Sheila Drury is a statistic."

"Anna, this is a federal matter. There'll be an autopsy as a matter of course. If they're not satisfied, the FBI will follow it up."

"Can I see the autopsy report?" Anna demanded.

There was a silence. There'd never been a death—accidental or otherwise—in the park's twenty-year history. Nobody knew precisely what to do or who should do it. As crime in the parks had grown, law enforcement had become increasingly important. Enforcement rangers were sent to ten weeks of training, were fingerprinted, drug tested, and had to carry handcuffs and side arms. But in the smaller, more remote parks there was little in the way of hard-core crime.

Paul jotted something down in the little yellow notebook he carried in his shirt pocket. "I'll ask about the autopsy. I can't see why there'd be a problem since you were the first officer on the scene, but you never know."

"It's governmental," Anna said and Paul laughed. Anna didn't. The bureaucratic delays so slowed work that government agencies had become a laughingstock. One day the bureaucrats would succeed in choking the parks to death. Already they'd so bound them with red tape that by the time there was permission and funding to save an area, an animal, it was usually too late. Death had its own timetable.

Paul tucked the notebook back in his pocket and Anna edged toward the door. "Thanks, Paul," she said, though she was unsure of what she was thanking him for. Everybody always said "Thanks, Paul." Maybe, she thought as she banged out the screen door feeling anything but grateful, one just felt obliged to him for caring.

Paul Decker cared that his people were happy.

Unfortunately there usually wasn't a damn thing he could do to ensure that they were.

"Be fair," Anna said half aloud, trying to temper her anger with words. Leave it alone, she told herself.

Mind racing too fast for her feet to follow, she found herself stopped under the pecan trees on the flagstone walk outside the ranch house. Overhead, the leaves made a pleasant clacking. Beyond the stone fence, where the overflow from the spring spilled out into the field, was a line of bright green. Grass following the moisture till it disappeared into the earth a hundred yards out. To the right were the small hay barn and roofed shed for the stock animals. Two big brown rumps were visible near the manger.

On impulse, Anna canceled her plans to spend the afternoon trying to make order out of the chaos in the Emergency Medical Supply cabinet. She vaulted the stone wall and let herself into the paddock from the side gate.

Karl Johnson, a currycomb lost in his enormous hand, was grooming Gideon, a big chocolate-colored quarter horse with one white foot. Karl looked like an almost classic ogre from out of a children's fairy tale. Six-foot-six inches tall, he weighed nearly two hundred and fifty pounds. Wiry reddish-brown hair curled out from nose, ears, the top of his uniform shirt, and sprang from his massive skull. His nose was pug to the point of absurdity, as if a button had been sewn on the square lumpy face when the real nose had been lost.

Anna guessed Karl to be thirty-one or -two at most but he'd been with Guadalupe forever. He'd worked trails, fought fire—he was even a clerk-typist for a couple of years. Up until eighteen months before, he'd held Anna's job. Then he'd been Acting Dog Canyon Ranger until Sheila had been hired on. After that Karl had transferred to Roads and Trails. The gossip was he was sulking because they'd not given him the Dog Canyon position.

Now he took care of the stock. Broad shoulders obscuring half the length of Gideon's back, he carefully curried the animal's hide. The huge man was whistling "If I only had a brain . . ."

Anna laughed, her impotent anger momentarily lost.

Karl jumped as if she'd poked him with a cattle prod and Gideon shied in sympathy.

"Sorry," Anna apologized, "I thought you'd heard me come up."

"I was thinking," Karl said as if that explained things. "You going riding?"

"I thought I would. Are you taking Gideon out?" She was just asking to be polite. Karl wouldn't ride. And he wouldn't say why. It was that that had probably cost him the Dog Canyon job. Like everyone else, Anna assumed he was afraid to get on the horses.

Karl shook his head. "Just combing him. They're still nervous. That lightning a few nights ago got 'em jumpy. It scared me too," he addressed the horse and Gideon rotated one ear back to listen. "It's nothing to be embarrassed about. Lookie here," he said to Anna and picked up Gideon's right front hoof. In Karl's hand it looked delicate, almost like a deer's hoof. A crack ran up from the bottom to half an inch below the quick. "It's been so dry. I'm putting Hoof Flex on but all the same you oughtn't be working him till it heals. You can ride him all right, but no packing."

Anna nodded. If the crack broke into the quick, Gideon would be bound for the glue factory, for Piedmont's cat food tin.

"I'll take Pesky," Anna said. Running a hand down Gideon's flat forehead, she shooed flies from his eyes and the corners of his mouth. The black cloud resettled behind her fingers and the horse blinked with what seemed to Anna, in her foul mood, a tired hopelessness. "You're a good old boy, Gideon," she said. "Yes, you are." From the corner of her eye

Anna thought she saw Karl smile. An event rare enough to focus her attention on him.

Maybe he's just passing gas, she thought and startled herself by laughing. There was something about Karl that was oddly innocent, babylike. It was why Anna liked him. And possibly why she didn't understand him at all.

"Pesky needs to get out, air himself off," Karl said.

Pesky and two of the pack mules were milling around the small paddock, fussing at each other and snatching mouthfuls of hay from between the pipe bars on the manger.

Affecting nonchalance, Anna walked toward the gate. The mules, Jack and Jill, caught on immediately and, amid rolling eyes and halfhearted kicks, ran out into the pasture beyond. Pesky was so torn between freedom and food, he stood too long dithering.

"Gotcha!" Anna gloated as she swung the gate shut. It was amazing how soothing it was to exert power over one's fellow creatures.

She haltered Pesky and tied him to the hitching rail. Karl had moved back and was painstakingly combing the tangles from Gideon's tail.

"You look like you heard already," he said as Anna wrestled with the cinch, trying to get it tight enough so the saddle wouldn't slip. Pesky was blowing up so he could loosen the strap with one mighty exhalation as soon as she got on. Pesky was the horse's earned name. His given name was Pasquale.

"Probably not," Anna grunted. "I never hear anything."

"About the hunt." The Norwegian's voice was bland, the careful neutrality of a cautious man.

Anna stopped what she was doing. The anger of minutes before was back, rising in her throat like indigestion. "Don't tell me," she said, but it was a question all the same.

"They're putting together a hunt. Paul and the Chief Ranger. Superintendent's orders."

"How can they know which one to kill?" Anna asked, knowing the answer, knowing the question was intentionally naive.

Karl just looked at her, then back to Gideon's tail.

Already rumors of a man-eater would be buzzing around the local ranches. Old stories would be flowing as fast as the Coors. Any excuse to drag out the hunting rifles was a good excuse in Texas. Texans were the best hunters in the world. They were born to it, believed in it, almost like a religion. Hunting and football, not opposable thumbs and the ability to laugh, were what separated man from the apes.

The killing of one cat wouldn't affect the health of the lion population as a whole. Maybe if the National Park Service sacrificed one animal, preferably shot near the area of the incident, it would buy off wholesale slaughter. That's how the argument would go. It would all sound so rational when Paul or Corinne Mathers, the Chief Ranger, explained it at the next squad meeting.

"But it's just a goddamned lynching party," Anna said aloud.

Pesky twitched as if her angry words were flies landing on his neck. Karl said nothing, just combed.

Outraged injustice.

Anna was choking on it. Nobody else would care. Not enough. If a human life were on the line . . . But no one would see the connection, no one would see that this wasn't any different.

No one would see.

Anna leaned her forehead against Pesky's broad warm shoulder and tried desperately to feel normal.

# CHAPTER 5

"Three-six-one; seven-two-five Alpha."

The radio woke Anna at nine-thirteen. She'd not slept that late in months. Her head felt thick and heavy with the wine she'd drunk the night before.

Lying on the hood of her old American Motors Rambler, she'd watched the stars deepen the endless Texas sky. She'd finished a bottle of California Chardonnay drinking to all lions living, all lions dead, and the lion soon to die.

Near midnight, while she'd still toasted those long-since vanished radio-collared lions, Rogelio had left, bound for Mexico, for a meeting of the Friends of the Pinacate. They were all converging at a little place he kept down there. Anna guessed he owned it. Rogelio had money from somewhere but he shied away from any specifics. She'd never been curious enough to pry.

"Three-six-one; seven-two-five Alpha," the radio bleated again and Anna swung her legs over the side of the Murphy bed to stare across the room bleary-eyed. Piedmont jumped up onto the bed and pressed his head into her ribs. Absently, she scratched the golden ears. "Three-six-one; seven-two-five Alpha."

"Answer your goddamn radio, Harland," she growled.

As if in obedience, Harland Roberts, Roads and Trails foreman, keyed his mike. "This is Harland. Go ahead."

Manny Mankins's voice, loud and clear from the Visitors Center base station, relayed the message that a visitor had seen a fawn caught in the fence a mile inside the park's boundary toward Carlsbad. It appeared to be badly injured. He asked Harland to investigate.

"Dispatch," Anna corrected. It was a part of Roberts's job to destroy problem animals. "Good morning to you, too, Manny." She rubbed her face hard. The skin felt loose and dry. "Remind me not to look in the mirror, Piedmont," she said to the cat. "Not till after I've had a shower at least." She scooped the cat up and dumped him and some Friskies near his bowl in the kitchen.

Tuesdays and Wednesdays were her lieu days, her days off. She'd call her sister, do her laundry, go into Carlsbad, shoot fifty rounds at the range, have a Prissy's Special and a couple of Tecates at Lucy's, take in a movie, do her grocery shopping. Then there'd be Wednesday to get through.

Anna flung the Murphy bed, unmade, up into its niche. While the water heated for coffee, she sat down at her desk. Her naked thighs stuck to the wooden chair. Already the day was heating up.

Opening the bottom drawer, Anna pulled out an eight-and-a-half-by-eleven envelope from under an untidy pile of bills—paid and unpaid.

"Don't do it," she said aloud. "Just don't do it." But she folded back the flap and pulled the pictures out anyway.

A tall, skinny man with fine eyes and clear pale skin looked out at her from a bridge over a little lake in Central

Park. Behind him was the top of the Plaza Hotel. Terribly earnest, he stood with his hands folded on the bridge's ornate metal railing, his sensual mouth composed in solemn lines. Except for the glittering purple insect feelers bobbing on his head, he might have been a stockbroker or a young senator.

But Zach was an actor. A classical actor. He was good. He might have made it. Then again, Anna thought wearily, maybe not. During their years in New York they'd watched an awful lot of good actors give up, go home and join the family business. Or worse, stick it out waiting tables and driving cabs, keeping their courage up with alcohol and boasts.

Anna looked at the next photo. Zach's head shot. So intense. A beautiful man in that sensitive, dying-of-tuberculosis, turn-of-the-century mold. Born too tall to play Hamlet.

"God, I miss you, Zach. It's beautiful here. But you'd've hated West Texas." Anna might have laughed but her throat was too tight. It was going to be one of those days. She put the pictures away and closed the drawer gently, as if they slept.

The water for her coffee had all but boiled away. Refilling the pan, she started the morning over.

On her way into Carlsbad, Anna saw the blue six-pac pickup the Roads and Trails foreman drove parked along the fence just inside the park boundary. He and Manny were standing near the fenceline with binoculars. There wasn't a dead fawn in the bed of the truck, so she pulled over.

"Hey, Manny, Harland," she greeted them as she climbed out of the Rambler.

Manny just nodded and kept looking out across the mesquite toward the escarpment.

Harland let his glasses fall down around his neck on their strap. They weren't government issue. They were finely crafted, expensive, birding binoculars. Many things about Harland Roberts were a little classier than the run-of-the-mill. In his early fifties, he had Stewart Granger gray streaks at his temples and aquiline good looks.

Anna'd worked for him on a couple of projects. Harland got things done. In government service that was saying something.

"I didn't recognize you with your hair down," Harland said as he leaned against her car and folded his arms.

Anna pushed the cloud of hair back from her face. Thinking of Zach, feeling sorry for herself, she'd blown it dry and curled it, wearing it as she had when she was younger.

"It looks good," Harland said.

The compliment both pleased and made her feel self-conscious. "What's happening?" She jerked her chin to where Manny still surveyed the countryside.

"This is where the injured fawn was reported," Roberts said. "There's hair and blood on the barbed wire, but it looks like the little guy got himself untangled and crawled off somewhere. We've walked this area for a quarter of a mile in every direction but no luck."

"Maybe he's okay," Anna said.

"Let's hope so."

They stood a moment watching Manny watching the brush.

"I don't see how you can do it, Harland. I wouldn't have your job for all the tea in China," Anna said suddenly.

He looked at her, mild reproach in his eyes. "I don't like destroying an animal. But I'd rather that than have them suffer."

Anna was sorry but she didn't say so. Letting her eyes wander, she hoped to fix on a new topic. In the rack across the six-pac's rear window was a seven millimeter Browning hunting rifle. "That your own?" she asked.

"Yes."

"I figured. A bit too fine for government work. Do you hunt big game?"

"I used to," Harland answered and Anna could tell he was uncomfortable with the subject. "I bought that line about it being a 'challenge.' When I found out a bull elk had an intelligence level equivalent to that of an eighteen-month-old toddler, I kind of lost my taste for it."

Anna smiled. Then remembered. "How's the hunt for the lion going?" she asked.

"No luck. We'll go up again today. I called old Jerimiah D. and he said he will lend us his dogs."

"Jerimiah D.?"

"Paulsen," Harland said. "He keeps hunting dogs."

"I bet," Anna said bitterly. "What does he get? The head? The pelt? Or just to be in on the kill?" Paulsen owned twenty-five thousand acres that bordered the park's northern boundary. He'd fought against every environmental issue in New Mexico and North Texas for thirty years. Usually he won.

"The animal will be salvaged for the display in the new Visitors Center," Harland said, overlooking her rudeness. "They can freeze-dry them so they look lifelike now. They're going to use it in an educational display. Corinne was glad to get it, in a way. That VC's her baby. If people are better informed, maybe this won't happen next time."

Anna doubted they could freeze-dry a "specimen" that large but she didn't say so. Instead, wanting suddenly to escape Harland and the conversation, she excused herself: "I better leave you to it."

"Wait." Harland laid a hand on her arm. "You didn't hear the big news." He was smiling, a boyish smile with a lot of charm. Making amends for her churlishness, it seemed. Letting her know there were no hard feelings.

Anna waited.

"We've got exotics on the West Side."

Resource Management spent countless hours and dollars eradicating exotic plant species that endangered native vegetation. "What?" Anna asked. "It's awful dry over there for tamarisk."

"Worse than tamarisk," Harland said, a twinkle in his gray eyes. "Martians. Tell her, Manny."

Manny looked their way a moment, the thin, pockmarked face showing a trace of humor but no inclination to join in the conversation. "You tell her, Harland."

"Craig Eastern was camped over there a couple nights back working on his snake studies and he saw a UFO. A greenish halo that danced over the ground and made noise like cosmic footsteps. A *putt-putt*. Sort of a celestial Model T. Manny said he was all shook up. Thought they'd come to take him home, I guess."

"Craig is a strange man," Anna said.

Harland moved slightly so he was between her and Manny. When he spoke, his voice was low, pitched for her ears only. "Craig Eastern is crazy," he said. "Seriously. He's mentally ill. This is not for public consumption. You're out alone a lot. You take care of yourself."

Before Anna could respond one way or another, he had turned away, was calling to Manny, giving up the hunt for the fawn.

As they climbed into his truck, Roberts looked back over his shoulder. "I like the hair, Anna."

Anna spent the next twenty miles thinking about Harland Roberts.

He had a talent for knocking her a little off balance. Talking with him she felt younger, more vulnerable, less sure of herself. Harland was of an age where men seldom looked at women as peers, coworkers. Always, however well concealed behind training or good manners, was the pervasive concept of women as the Weaker Sex.

The damned thing of it was, Anna thought, it made her behave like a "flawed vessel." She wasn't sure if it was knee-jerk, a nerve touched from early socialization or—and this was the creepy thought—because she liked it.

"Not bloody likely!" Anna said aloud and moved her thoughts on to other things.

Roberts had said Craig Eastern was crazy. Everybody said Eastern was crazy, but Harland meant it. "He's mentally ill." He'd used those words. And: "Take care of yourself."

Anna knew Craig was fanatic about keeping the park undeveloped. It was more than just the inescapable animosity one felt when forced to see what the human race was doing to the planet. With Craig it was personal, a betrayal of him as well as Texas and the world.

Craig had been one of the most outspoken opponents of Drury's proposal to develop recreational vehicle sites in Dog Canyon. In a way, his very vehemence undermined his cause. His rhetoric was so heated that none of the brass wanted to align themselves with him.

"You're out alone a lot. Take care of yourself."

Did Harland Roberts think Craig was crazy enough to hurt somebody? To hurt her? Craig talked a lot about shooting visitors. But all naturalists talked about shooting visitors. It was a way of letting off steam.

Was it different with Eastern? Looking at his nervous rantings through the curtain of suspicion Harland had dropped he did seem a little insane.

Anna's mind jumped to the nearest conclusion: Sheila Drury was dead. If the lion didn't do it . . .

It was absurd. She was clutching at straws, and melodramatic straws at that.

The autopsy would show something: congenital heart failure, brain aneurysm. Something that would prove Sheila was dead before the lion tasted her. But by the time the report came—if it ever did and wasn't simply lost in some FBI file—it would be too late. Not many days would pass before Paulsen's dogs would tree a cougar. It would be dubbed, after the required five minutes of deliberation, to be the cougar, and it would be shot.

"Damn! Damn! Damn!" Anna pounded the Rambler's steering wheel with the flat of her hand. The car swerved into the oncoming lane and a subcompact with Ohio plates honked, the driver mouthing obscenities.

"Think of something else, it's your day off," Anna ordered herself.

For twelve hours she managed to school her mind. Distract it, was more accurate: a Schwarzenegger movie, a couple of Tecates, a "new" Patsy Cline tape.

Near nine p.m., as she drove back to Guadalupe, Patsy singing "Too Many Secrets," Anna began again to worry at the edges of the Drury Lion Kill.

Beside her on the seat, atop an accumulated pile of rubble, were the slides she'd taken on the lion transect and of the Dog Canyon Ranger's corpse. Anna had taken them to Wal-Mart's one hour photo service and paid for the developing out of her own pocket.

Technically she should have turned the roll in to the clerk, filled out a form for funding, and waited the requisite eternity for the machinery to grind out one small task.

Patience was not Anna's strong suit.

Contemplating the envelope she had assiduously ignored all day, she wondered what it was she was so anxious to see.

Sheila Drury's intestines festooning the front of her uniform like macabre confetti?

Most definitely, she wanted to see the blood again. If she remembered correctly, there'd been very little. Surely that indicated the lion had clawed Ranger Drury sometime after she had achieved corpse-hood.

That might be an argument that would quicken some kind of interest in Paul. Then he would stop the hunt. If he could. Corinne Mathers wasn't known for her willingness to listen to her District Rangers. Mathers acted like a woman with a political itinerary. Guadalupe was a stop along the way.

"Be fair," Anna chided herself, but this time she expected she was being fair. Maybe even generous. Corinne was a woman on her way up.

Mankins was in the Cholla Chateau with Cheryl Light, watching television when Anna pulled in. She could see the blue-gray light through the windows. Manny would be three sheets to the wind by this time of night. Fleetingly, Anna wondered if his wife, Yolanda, cared that he drank so much beer. Guadalupe, like so many parks, was isolated, the employees living in rented government housing miles from anywhere. It became its own small, sometimes incestuous, society. Loneliness, boredom, and booze were occupational hazards.

The light in Craig's apartment was out. There was only the eerie purple glow of his snake aquarium light through the white curtain. Either he'd already gone to bed or he was camping on the West Side despite the invasion of the space aliens.

Anna smiled at the thought. Then she remembered Harland's warning. Feeling a fool, she locked her door behind her after she'd brought in the groceries.

The slides were tossed into the bag with the onions and the chocolate pudding. Leaving the frozen goods to hold their own for a few minutes more, Anna took them out and carried them over to the desk. The little slide viewer was in the top drawer with pens and .357 cartridges.

With hope but no expectations, she peered quickly through the transect photos, then dropped the first corpse shot into the viewer and held it up to the light.

Nothing had changed. The images that she held in her mind were accurate. The shots of the scratches and the puncture wounds were disappointing. The light was so poor when she'd taken them that the colors were faded. It was impossible to tell where the blood ended and the mud began. Not enough proof to impress Corinne Mathers with the lion's innocence.

Anna sat back. Piedmont had leapt silently to the desk top and was pushing the slide box back and forth between his paws. Soon he would grow bored and the box would be knocked to the floor with one sudden swat.

Was that the way it was with Sheila? Had she delicately made her way into the saw grass, protecting her arms and face, then, with the sudden swipe of one deadly paw, been struck down? And, before the lion dragged or worried at his prey, he was frightened away?

It could have happened that way. But, Anna didn't believe it. "Just being stubborn," she told Piedmont as she risked a skewered finger, rescuing the box of slides from his paws. She replaced it with another toy, a plastic ball with a bell encased inside.

The cat would have nothing to do with it. Anna had ruined everything. With a flick of his sausage tail, he jumped down.

"Be that way," Anna said peevishly. She dropped the next slide into the viewer and held it up to her eye. One of the last shots on the roll: a picture of the paw prints she'd found behind Sheila in the mud. If Anna remembered correctly the two sets had been about a yard apart It was hard to tell from the picture and she wished she'd had the presence of mind to put a pen or a dime in the shot at the time; something to give a size reference. The prints themselves were cookie-cutter perfect in the smooth surface of the fine-grained silt.

Anna put the second slide of the prints in and stared at it unthinkingly. With an uncluttered mind, the obvious became obvious. The difference between front and hind paw prints was minimal but she had spent a lot of hours with her eyes on the ground studying lion sign. The hind paw's central pad was more heart-shaped, the sides convex rather than concave. In these pictures both sets, front and back, were identical—even to the crease marks on the pads themselves.

Both sets of prints, the front and the hind, were forepaws.

"That can't be right . . ." she whispered, pushing her eye closer to the light source. She changed slides; studied the first one again. There were no prints from hind paws.

A lion with four front paws.

A lion that walked on its hands.

A lion eleven feet long that kept its hind paws on the stone.

A lion with its ass in a sling.

Anna listed the absurdities. "When is a Lion not a Lion?" she said aloud, putting her confusion into riddle formula.

When it's dead, she thought, and that's what this lion—or some lion—will be if the hunt's not stopped.

Again she looked at the slides. She was not mistaken.

Proof.

Proof of what, she wasn't exactly sure. Proof there was something fishy about the Drury Lion Kill.

"Proof we should look at this whole situation a little more closely before we go bashing around in the wilderness with dogs and guns killing off the wildlife." Anna sat in the Chief Ranger's office. She'd been waiting at the door when Corinne Mathers arrived for work at eight a.m.

Chief Ranger Mathers was a small woman but big breasted and big hipped, with short, iron-gray hair that curled naturally around her ears. Her face was round, suggesting both plumpness and softness. Neither was accurate. Corinne Mathers had come up the hard way. There were only a handful of women Chief Rangers in the National Park Service. She'd started when "girl" rangers wore miniskirts and were allowed badges exactly half the size of those the men wore. Mathers was smart. And she was harder than flint.

"Though I may not agree with your conclusions, you've been thorough, Anna. Good attention to detail, I'll give you that." The Chief Ranger tossed the slides down onto a yellow legal pad covered top to bottom with notes too small to be read upside down. Anna resisted the urge to rescue her fragile evidence.

"Then you'll stop the hunt."

Mathers took off her glasses—aviator style with gold rims—and pinched the bridge of her nose as if the little red marks there pained her. "It's not as simple as that, Anna."

"It's as simple as that. Just call off the dogs."

The Chief Ranger replaced the glasses and leaned across the desk. Her hands were folded on the legal pad, on the two ignored slides. "No. It's not." Deliberately, as if she wanted Anna to commit each word to memory, she said: "The cougar that we know to have killed Ranger Drury has already been dispatched."

# CHAPTER 6

Up on the Permian Ridge two miles north of Middle McKittrick Canyon a lioness had been shot and killed. Harland Roberts, Corinne Mathers, and two men from the New Mexico State Department of Fish and Wildlife had brought the body back to the park.

Anna's first lion had flies crawling from its mouth and blood, black as tar, matting the fur of its neck. The animal was five to seven years of age, weighed seventy-five pounds and was nursing at least one, possibly two kittens. The park's Public Information Officer released this information to the local papers suggesting it as the reason for the attack.

The kittens were not found.

The following day Anna rode Gideon up the four-mile trail to the ridge. As long as the light lasted she combed the area looking for the den. Near dark, when she knew her time was running out, she hobbled Gideon in a grassy place and climbed part way down the slope into Big Canyon, a wild area just to the north of the park's boundary over the Texas/New Mexico border in the Lincoln National Forest.

Perched on an outcropping of limestone, she called down into the forested recesses of the ravines. "Come on kittens, here kitty, kitties. Come on."

The pathetic absurdity of it stung her eyes but she hoped, her heart in her voice, it would trigger some response; a sound from the cougar kittens. For an instant, as the call died away, swallowed by the trees, she thought she heard something. Not mewing, but a strange bird's call, or the wind on a stony bottleneck: four notes from a half-remembered song.

Again and again she called but never heard the sound a second time. Finally she came to doubt she'd really heard anything. Hope was such a creative companion.

Till the moon rose to light their way, Gideon had to pick his way down the mountain in darkness.

That had been nearly a week past. The moon was waning now, the nights dark till after midnight, the moon still up at nine a.m.

Anna could see it, pale against blue sky, over El Capitan. She forced her eyes back down to the 10-343 Case Incident Record she was typing up on the Drury Lion Kill. Offense/Incident #50-01-00: DEATHS/ACCIDENTAL. Five copies. Five copies of every typographical error she made. This 343 had to be perfect, no strike-overs. This would be the official report requested by Sheila Drury's insurance company. Anna knew she'd end up redoing it half a dozen times unless she could con the secretary or the clerk-typist into typing it for her.

Carpeted half-walls corralled the two clericals in the central area of the administrative offices. The rooms with windows were parceled out to the higher-ups. Government Service and Private Industry did not differ in all respects.

Marta Freeman, the superintendent's secretary, was in the area farthest away. Marta, a determinedly blond, well-endowed woman in her fifties, was given to cleavage, knowing looks, and innuendo. Anna had never felt comfortable with her.

In the next corral, Christina Walters, the clerk-typist, bent over a computer terminal. Her pale brown hair, nearly the color of the oak veneer on the desk tops, fell in a curtain hiding her face. Anna wondered if she dared ask Christina. She scarcely knew the woman. Christina Walters had entered on duty a month or so after Sheila Drury. Most of Anna's time was spent in the field and they had different days off so their paths seldom crossed.

Anna knew she had a little girl who rode a pink tricycle around the housing area on Saturday mornings, wasn't married at the moment, and seemed competent enough. But this was the first time Anna had really noticed her, really looked at her.

Walters was good-looking with a brand of prettiness that was rare in the Park Service. She looked soft. Her hair curled softly, arms and neck and breasts rounded with a softness that somehow fell short of fat. Her muscles weren't corded from carrying a pack, her hands not callused from shooting or riding or climbing. Her skin wasn't burned brown and creased by the sun and wind.

Urban, Anna thought. Christina Walters had a traditional urban femininity. Strangely, Anna liked it. On another woman it might have set her teeth on edge, but on the fair-haired clerk it looked good. Perhaps, Anna explained the phenomenon to herself, because Christina didn't push it: she chose it.

It crossed Anna's mind to put on a little lipstick and perfume when she got home that night. There'd been a time she'd lived in the stuff, a time she'd required it to feel attractive. With a sudden sense of achievement, she knew she could go back to it now just for fun, just for the sheer sensual pleasure of the commercial feminine luxury.

"Do you need something?" Christina was asking in a low voice with a hint of a drawl and Anna realized she had been staring.

"Do I look that desperate?" she answered with a laugh.

Christina Walters studied her gravely. "Yes."

"I'm afraid I'm fouling up in triplicate here." Anna almost said "fucking up" but there was something about Christina that made her want to seem a gentler person than she was.

"Let me see." Christina walked around the low wall and looked over Anna's shoulder. Delicate perfume drifted from her hair. White Linen, Anna guessed. It suited her.

"It's the 343 on the Drury Lion Kill," Anna said. She half turned in her chair and saw the fleeting freeze on Christina's oval face. An aging, a minute dying, as if for a moment pain—or hatred—had jabbed deep.

"Sorry," Anna said with abrupt embarrassment. "I didn't realize you knew her that well."

Christina straightened up, her hair falling to hide her eyes. When she smoothed it back her face was working again. "I didn't know her that well. Here—" she pulled the form out of the typewriter "—it'll only take me a minute." Smiling with what looked like genuine warmth, she fluttered a manicured hand. "Magic fingers."

Anna's radio butted in before she had a chance to say thank you. "Three-one-five; three-eleven."

"Go ahead, Paul."

"Are you near a phone?"

"Ten-four."

"Call me at Frijole. Three-eleven clear."

Anna dialed the Ranger Division's extension and Paul picked up on the first ring. "Mrs. Drury is here," he said. By the formal measured tones, Anna knew Sheila's mother was there in the room with him. "She's come to retrieve Ranger Drury's belongings. Would you accompany her to Dog Canyon and see to it she gets all the help she needs?"

"I'll need a vehicle. I'm in that damned jeep."

"Take mine," Paul said. "Leave the keys in the jeep. I'll use it."

Anna smiled. Paul wanted out from under this chore in a bad way. He was trying to buy her goodwill with the new one-ton Chevy with the fancy arrowheads and striping, flashing light-bars, air-conditioning, and radio console.

"I'll be there in about ten minutes, Paul."

"Ranger Drury's pack will be in the back of the truck. And thanks, Anna." Gratitude warmed his voice.

Perhaps Paul was an empath, she thought as she put the cover back on the abandoned typewriter. Like in the science fiction movies. Maybe other people's pain actually hurt him, even when they were strangers.

"Well, I'm off to Dog Canyon," Anna said to Christina's back. "Mrs. Drury's here to collect Sheila's things. Thanks," she added. "I owe you a beer."

The clerk waved a "*De nada.*"

This beer was a social debt Anna actually considered paying. There was something intriguing about Christina Walters.

Probably just a classy flake, Anna thought uncharitably as she threw her satchel into the jeep. But she was looking forward to that beer.

Mrs. Drury—Mrs. Thomas Drury as she had corrected Paul when he'd introduced her—was in her late fifties or early sixties. Makeup, carefully applied, gave color to her pale skin and muddied her age without making her look younger. Her short, permed hair had been dyed a light brown. Anna assumed the shade was chosen to color the gray but not seem flashy or "fast." Mrs. Drury wore an inexpensive polyester pantsuit of sage green. A purse of the same white leatherette as her low-heeled pumps was clamped tightly beneath one arm. Respectable but not rich, Anna summed her up.

During the two-hour drive to Dog Canyon—twelve miles on foot over the high country, nearly a hundred by road around the park's perimeter—Mrs. Thomas Drury told Anna more than she'd ever wanted to know about the Drury family in general and Sheila in particular.

Sheila's father had died when she was ten ". . . but in the sixth grade, not the fifth. Sheila may have been odd but she was always bright." Mrs. Drury had gone to work as a secretary then at Minnegasco in St. Paul, Minnesota. It was a good job. She still held it. During the drive from the Dark Canyon turnoff at Highway 62/180 to the Wildersens' goat farm six miles in, she listed the employee benefits.

At twenty-nine (Anna had been way off on Sheila's age. "She'd never use a decent night cream, though heaven knows I bought her enough jars—" Mrs. Drury explained), Sheila had still been on the company's life insurance plan. $108,000 would now come to Mrs. Drury. Five years' salary.

Anna had agreed that Minnegasco had an excellent employee benefit plan and Mrs. Drury's monologue moved on to new subjects. Sheila was an only child. Mrs. Drury's second pregnancy had ended in miscarriage and she hadn't the heart to try again, though she'd often thought it might have been better for Sheila if she had. Sheila was an odd girl, headstrong and wayward.

From the scraps of information dropped amidst the drawn-out recitals of people whose names and indiscretions meant nothing to Anna, she came to believe that Sheila's "waywardness" consisted mostly of a refusal to get her hair foiled though it was ". . . impossibly dark—almost like a Jewish person's"; her nails manicured "—though I offered to pay for it, and in the Cities manicures aren't cheap—"; and her steadfast refusal to date "nice boys."

By the time they reached the Queens Highway turnoff, Anna found she liked Sheila more in memoriam that she would've guessed. For the first time since she'd stumbled across the body, she felt a personal sense of loss. She wished she'd gotten to know the Dog Canyon Ranger better. They might have been friends.

As they drove down the miles of winding road cutting back west through the Lincoln National Forest, Mrs. Drury asked: "Are we in the park now?" She was pointing to the fenceline on both sides of the road. It was the first time Anna had noticed the new fencing edging nearly all of the Paulsen Ranch. "That's Jerry Paulsen's property. He owns forty sections. Not really a big place in this part of the country. It abuts the park on the northern boundary outside of Dog Canyon."

The fence cut down the middle of a lot of man-made divisions: it marked the border between Texas and New Mexico, between public and private lands. Deer jumped it, toads hopped under it, and birds and clouds floated over it without a downward glance. But in the petty depths of humanity it was an important line.

Paulsen had spared no expense: new green metal posts, shining silver wire with four-pronged barbs half an inch long, and, every fifty or sixty feet, a brand-new sign reading NO TRESPASSING.

Paulsen was dead serious about private ownership. STAY OFF JERRY PAULSEN'S LAND was Xeroxed on every page of the Boundary Patrol Report Forms to remind rangers riding fenceline. Anna wished he'd return the favor. The next time he flew his shiny new helicopter over so much as one corner of the park she would go to the Federal Aviation Agency.

There'd been bad blood between the park and the local

ranchers from the beginning. The Guadalupes had been their backyard for generations. They hunted and camped, drew water from the springs, grazed cattle and goats in the high country. Then suddenly in 1972 it was off-limits.

Though they had been quick enough to accept the sale money when the government bought it, some ranchers refused to accept that it was no longer their private preserve.

Anna knew Paulsen had been suspected on more than one occasion of shooting the park's elk.

"Paulsen," Mrs. Drury nursed the name between her lips as if it tasted familiar. "Oh. Sheila wrote of him. He sounded like a very nice man."

Anna blinked her surprise, but said nothing. It was possible Sheila had gotten along with him. More likely Mrs. Drury said it to express her approval of the conservative way of life. To Anna's ears it sounded vaguely like a snipe at Sheila. Tired of the constant dripping of Mrs. Drury's voice, she switched on the radio. Paul had it tuned to a country western station out of Carlsbad. Travis's "Diggin' Up Bones" was playing.

Anna turned it up hoping she might silence Mrs. Drury without actually appearing rude.

Near noon they pulled into Dog Canyon. The terrain on the northern edge of the Guadalupe Mountains was very different from that on the Frijole District side. Small hills rolled away to the north in tufted golden grass and juniper trees. Once there'd been prairie dog colonies; hence the name Dog Canyon. They'd long since been exterminated by ranchers. Now and then there was talk of reintroducing them into the park but so far no superintendent had been willing to antagonize the local landowners over such an unglamorous species. And Drury'd been dead set against it. The little creatures were too destructive when loosed on "improved" campsites.

Rogelio had talked for a while of smuggling in a few breeding pairs and turning them loose, see how they fared. Rogelio talked of a lot of things. When Sheila Drury had started pushing for a recreational vehicle campground in Dog Canyon, he talked for a while of pipe bombs and monkey-wrenching bulldozers.

All just talk on both sides. Neither the RVs nor the prairie dogs had ever materialized, though the RV camp might have become a reality had Sheila Drury lived.

"This is it," Anna said. To the left of the road was a campground. Hardened sites were sprinkled amid big old cottonwood trees above a dry creekbed. Ahead several hundred yards the road ended in a loop at the barn and machine shed.

Sheila's trailer was to the right, set back from the road. Her battered Subaru wagon was parked in the scant shade of a juniper near the end of the trailer. Anna pulled the truck in behind it and climbed out, glad to straighten her legs and stretch her back. Mrs. Drury didn't move. It crossed Anna's mind that, despite her complaints, she must have loved her daughter. At least at one time. Going into her house, seeing all of her things left behind, would not be easy. Anna walked around the truck and opened the passenger door. "This is it," she said again.

Mrs. Drury took Anna's proffered hand and allowed herself to be helped down from the cab.

Anna preceded her up the scattered white gravel that served as Sheila's front walk. A pot, cheaply painted in a pseudo-Mexican motif, stood beside the metal steps. In it was a thoroughly dead geranium. Anna expected a remark from Mrs. Drury, but the heart really seemed to have gone out of the woman.

Anna climbed the steps and unlocked the door. The cluttered living room was a mare's nest of magazines, old newspapers, books, folders, memos with coffee rings on them.

Everywhere there were snapshots: in shoe boxes and envelopes, piled in ashtrays. Under the sofa's one end table was a basket two feet high and half that wide almost full of them.

Leaving Mrs. Drury to come to terms with the relics of her daughter's life, Anna busied herself opening windows and turning on fans. The trailer was hot as an oven but not as bad as Anna had anticipated. At least it didn't stink. The dishes were done and the garbage taken out. Given the mess the living room was in, this tidiness was surprising.

When the day came for her to die, Anna wondered if she'd have as much foresight. Zachary hadn't. He'd left the stereo on and a steak defrosting on the kitchen counter. But Zachary had meant to come back. Had Sheila? Again Anna considered a suicide. Again she rejected the idea.

Opening the refrigerator, she saw a jar of dill pickles, three Old Milwaukees, a shoe box lid full of film, half a stick of margarine still in its paper wrapper, some processed American cheese slices, half a loaf of bread, and a shriveled carrot. A bachelor's refrigerator. The freezer wasn't any more appetizing. There was a bag of frozen french fries and a pint of ice cream, open with a spoon with a bamboo handle and one serrated edge stuck in it.

Anna went back into the living room. Mrs. Drury still stood just inside the door but at least she had put her handbag down. "We'll start with her pictures," the woman said, a weary eye traversing the boxes and bowls and piles of photographs. "I expect most will have to be thrown away but there may be a few I'll want to keep. Or you might want some." She looked at Anna hopefully, as if wanting her to be Sheila's friend.

"Yes," Anna said, unsure what Mrs. Drury would want to keep—would want her to keep. Anything with Sheila in it, she decided.

Since Sheila was the photographer, Anna had thought there

wouldn't be many of those. Evidently Drury had had a camera with a tripod. She'd put herself in nearly half the pictures.

The snicking sound of snapshots shuffling and the hot, still air quickly dulled Anna's mind. The photos, for the most part, were not interesting enough to offset her growing drowsiness. There were two shots of Craig Eastern that Anna studied with more care than the rest. Both were of him crouching beside a snow-dusted prickly pear. He was smiling. It must've been in December or January before the RV site proposal and the ensuing smear campaign he'd launched.

"Someone has already been through my daughter's things," Mrs. Drury said sharply.

Anna's head snapped up at the accusing tone. "Not that I know of, Mrs. Drury," she replied soothingly. "No one's been over here to do it until today."

Sheila's mother just glared.

"Just you and me," Anna added helplessly.

Mrs. Drury seemed to think that over, her lips pursed, wrinkles radiating from beneath her nose like a cat's whiskers. After a moment, she shook her head. "No," she stated flatly. "Not just you and I. Look." Grabbing the edges of the basket between her feet, she gave it a shake. Anna looked. Like everything else in the room, it was tumbled full of snapshots. "You of all people should have noticed," Mrs. Drury said and Anna knew that in the woman's mind she had been turned into Sheila's dearest friend.

"What?" she asked politely.

"There's all different things in here," Mrs. Drury explained with exaggerated patience. "Look: horses." She threw two snapshots onto the coffee table. "Flowers." A picture of blooming cholla was tossed on the pile. "Here's some kind of dog." A long shot of a coyote looking back over its shoulder was thrust into Anna's hand. "Sheila was not tidy, but she was organized. She kept her pictures according to subject. Even when she was little, she'd take pictures with her Brownie Instamatic. Then when they came back, she'd sort them into things and put each thing in a box."

Tears were running down Mrs. Drury's face, runneling her makeup, dripping spots of pale orange onto her jacket. Anna liked her better at that moment than she had since they'd met.

"I should have noticed," Anna agreed, knowing she should have. The pictures were canted at funny angles. Some of them were super close-ups—so close it was hard to tell what they were of. Lots were shot through things: knotholes, doorways, cans with both ends cut out. Attempts at Art, Anna surmised. But every container she had looked through had been of one subject: rock pictures in the mason jar, birds in the ashtray, Sheila in uniform in the candy dish.

A wooden shoe, a ceramic vase made to look like a paper bag, and several other containers stood empty on the coffee table. Someone had dumped their contents into the basket.

"Is there something to drink?" Mrs. Drury asked plaintively.

"I'll get you a glass of water," Anna said, glad to have something to do.

"No," Mrs. Drury said. "To drink."

"Beer?"

"That would be all right."

Anna got two beers from the refrigerator. There was a six-pack under the counter. She put it in to cool. Later they might need it. Bringing the beers and one glass into the living room, she sat beside Sheila's mother on the couch.

They drank in silence, Anna from the can, Mrs. Drury pouring the beer into the glass half an inch at a time like a woman measuring out medicine.

"Why would somebody go through your daughter's pictures?" Anna asked finally.

"I don't know," Mrs. Drury said. "They weren't any good."

They finished the beers. Anna carried the cans into the kitchen, rinsed them, and crushed them into neat circles under her heavy boots. Beneath the sink, where she guessed it would be, was Sheila's recycle bag.

"Might Sheila have taken photographs of something someone didn't want her to see?" Anna hunched down to look under the cups and across the Formica counter that separated the kitchen from the living area.

Mrs. Drury was shaking her head. Her face sagged with confusion and fatigue. "I couldn't even see why she took any of the pictures that she did. They weren't ever of anything. Just things you see every day. She might've, I suppose. Sheila took pictures of everything and she wasn't ever socially ept."

Anna didn't know if Mrs. Drury meant socially apt or if she believed "ept" was the opposite of "inept." But Sheila did, from the looks of it, take pictures of everything. "Everything" might include something someone wanted to go unrecorded.

By late afternoon they had finished sorting through the photos, collecting boxes from the two bedrooms and even the bath. They found nothing suspicious. No sinister types exchanging packages, no car license numbers, no middle-aged men in motel lobbies with blondes. Either they'd been found and removed or never existed.

Mrs. Drury had a surprisingly little pile she'd chosen to keep. Mostly to be polite, Anna had selected three or four of Sheila to take home.

Mrs. Drury made toasted cheese sandwiches for supper. They washed them down with a second beer. Mrs. Drury turned on the television and they listened to Channel 9 predict more hot and dry for West Texas and New Mexico. At least, tonight, there would be no lightning.

After the news, Mrs. Drury left the set on to watch a rerun

of an old *Andy of Mayberry* and Anna went out to the truck and brought in the backpack Sheila had been carrying the day she was killed.

It smelled faintly of decay and there were specks of dark brown on it that Anna chose to think were mud. The police had wrapped a yellow "Police Line Do Not Cross" tape around it.

Probably not the police, Anna thought. Probably the puffing deputy.

Having lain the pack on the living room rug, she sliced through the tape with the blade of her Swiss army knife. "I need to go through Sheila's pack, if you don't mind, Mrs. Drury. Most of the gear is NPS stuff. There may be some personal effects, if you'd like to help me . . ."

Mrs. Drury rose obediently from the table, her eyes on Andy Griffith's comforting face until her body had turned so far, her head finally had to follow. Sitting on the couch, she fixed her attention on the soiled pack.

Anna took it as a signal she could begin. There wasn't much to see: freeze-dried food for one supper and one lunch, a first-aid kit, a change of clothes, a few toilet articles, a stove and cook kit. Anna separated out the items marked GUMO. As uneuphonious as it was, national parks often went by the name formed by the first two letters of the first two words in their title. Carlsbad Caverns was fated to be known as "CACA." When all the gear from the GUMO backcountry cache had been removed all that remained was a little pile of rumpled clothes. Anna pushed them toward Sheila's mother.

Not much, Anna thought. Not enough. What was missing? Something wasn't there that she expected to see. It nagged like a forgotten name. "What's missing?" she demanded sharply.

Too spent to take offense at the tone, Mrs. Drury concentrated on Anna's question. "Sheila's camera?" she ventured after a moment.

"Must be," Anna said, surveying the contents spread out over the carpet. Pictures rifled, a camera missing: a puzzle was forming but one made not of pieces but of pieces missing, of holes.

Anna stuffed the park's things into the pack and zipped it closed.

"We may as well do the rest," Mrs. Drury said resignedly. "Then we can go home tomorrow and forget about the whole thing."

The phrase jarred Anna. She wished Mrs. Drury could afford Molly. The woman obviously had some emotions that needed sorting out.

Collecting Sheila Drury's belongings took very little time. She didn't have much, and half of that was still sealed with tape in moving boxes she'd never gotten around to unpacking. As Mrs. Drury packed the kitchen utensils into a lidless plastic foam cooler, Anna packed Sheila's clothes—mostly uniforms—into one of two identical suitcases that had been pushed out of sight under the bed.

A gray canvas daypack was dumped in the corner of the closet. Anna grabbed it to put the boots and shoes in. The pack wasn't empty. When she poured the contents onto the bed one hole of the fledgling mystery was filled: Sheila's camera, a pocket 35mm, was in the bottom of the pack with a pair of NPS binoculars and the remains of a salami and cheese sandwich. Sixteen of the thirty-six pictures on the roll had been taken.

A noise made Anna look up. Mrs. Drury stood in the bedroom doorway, a dish towel between her hands.

"I found it," Anna said, holding up the little camera. On impulse she said: "I'd like to keep the film if I may."

"Those little cameras are worth a lot of money," Mrs.

Drury said and Anna was both irritated and embarrassed. She wasn't going to steal the damn thing.

"Not the camera," she said evenly. "Just the film. Maybe it will tell me something."

Mrs. Drury nodded. She'd lost interest. Flicking the dish towel in the direction of the uniforms, she said: "You can have that book-bag thing, too, and her park outfits. I'd just throw them out." Without saying what she had come for, she left and it crossed Anna's mind that she'd just been checking up on her. Quickly, she clicked through the last twenty pictures and tossed the exposed film into the daypack.

All of Ranger Drury's worldly goods fitted easily in the back of Paul's patrol vehicle, a fact Mrs. Drury remarked upon unfavorably more than once. She seemed to think a person should leave a bigger pile of consumer goods behind when they died.

Anna declined comment. In the hope it would take the edge off the night, she drank a third Old Milwaukee as she lashed a tarp down over the back of the pickup. It wouldn't rain, probably not for weeks, but it was an excuse to stay outside for a few minutes more. Mrs. Drury had retreated to the solace of Channel 9.

It was after ten p.m. when Anna came in. The beer was a failure: the Drury Problem was not alcohol-soluble. Mrs. Drury was pale and crumpled-looking. Anna took pity. "We'll stay here tonight. I'll drive you back first thing tomorrow."

The old woman—for now she looked older than her years—nodded. "I'll sleep in the little room," she told Anna, meaning Sheila's spare room.

Anna fetched the suitcase full of linens from the truck and made up the bed. Mrs. Drury seemed to expect it. And it was something to do.

When Mrs. Drury finally went to bed, Anna was relieved.

Not wanting to leave her alone, Anna had stayed up watching a late-night local talk show with her.

It felt like a reprieve to go into the bedroom and close the door. Anna realized she had not spent that much time with anyone—other than occasionally Rogelio—in years. It was exhausting.

Having unrolled Sheila's sleeping bag—a new North Face from the cache—she lay down on the double bed. Her muscles twitched she was so tired but she was hardly sleepy at all. Staring up at the acoustical tile ceiling, she let her mind wander.

Somebody was looking for pictures. Somebody had either found them, not found them, or somebody was a figment of her imagination.

If the pictures were dangerous, Sheila would have hidden them. Everything she owned had been dismantled, packed into boxes, and removed from the trailer. There were no alarming photographs found.

Where, Anna asked herself, would she hide something in a mobile home? Mattress? Under the wall-to-wall? Behind the fake wood paneling? The ideas bothered her till she got up and checked them out. The carpet was glued down tight, the paneling all of a piece.

Even with the windows open, the trailer was hot. Anna divested herself of all but her underpants—lacy peach confections, the last vestige of a former clotheshorse. Having folded her uniform trousers over the pipe in the closet, she lay back down.

"Pretty damn mysterious," she said to herself and laughed. "No shit, Sherlock. Go to sleep." Clicking off the lamp, she closed her eyes.

When she was in college, she remembered trying to hide her stash from the fabled Narcs. Every place she put it would suddenly seem glaringly obvious and, in a fit of paranoia, she'd move it.

Some enterprising authors had described the phenomenon perfectly. Anna wracked her brain but she couldn't recall their names. They'd written a clever book about marijuana cultivation. Anna recalled very little of it, only the introduction. "We've never tried marijuana," it said—or words to that effect. "We got all our information from our friend, Ernie. Ernie keeps his stash in the shower rod. Sorry, Ernie, we don't need you anymore."

Shower rod.

The clothes rod.

Anna clicked on the light. The clothes rod in the closet was a length of iron pipe dropped into two U-shaped brackets. She padded over and lifted it out. Her trousers slid to the floor as she peered in. A roll of paper corked one end.

Careful not to tear anything, Anna coiled it smaller and eased it out. A dozen snapshots, curled from their incarceration, sprang apart. She carried them to the bed, knelt on the rug, and spread them in the circle of light.

These were the pictures that had been sought. A naked woman laughing, her hair soft around her shoulders, posed on the slickrock in Middle McKittrick about a mile downstream from where the body had been found.

Christina Walters, her white breasts full and round, catching the sun, her knees coyly together, invitingly apart.

Sheila had set the timer for the last three: she and Christina making love, the tight brown wire of Ranger Drury's body close against the soft cream of the other woman's.

Anna gathered them up, sorry, almost, to have pried. The pictures did not repulse her. They were, in their way, beautiful. Certainly Sheila Drury's best effort.

They might be a reason to kill. Anna didn't know. It seemed melodramatic. But sometimes people died. And sometimes people killed them. People killed people for all sorts of reasons.

Like many rangers, Anna chose Law Enforcement not because she wanted to bust perpetrators but because the Protection Divisions in most parks did all the search and rescue and emergency medicine. The serious cop stuff most rangers preferred to leave to the police.

This was beginning to smack of serious cop stuff.

Fear licked around Anna's ankles. She wished she had brought her .357. Rangers were required to carry defensive equipment whenever on duty. Not for the first time, Anna wished she paid a little more attention to the rules.

# CHAPTER 7

Anna closed the heavy binder. Her back and neck ached but she couldn't straighten up. Piedmont was draped around her neck fast asleep. Picking up his tail, she brushed its feathery-soft tip across her eyelids.

There'd been nothing much of help in her Law Enforcement notes from FLETC. All the Scene of the Crime materials—evidence gathering—had presumed the officer knew there'd been a crime committed. Lots of detailed diagrams for roping off the area, controlling the flow of traffic, protecting the chain of evidence so it wouldn't get thrown out of court.

Nothing pertained to half-eaten rangers in saw grass swamps.

I should have gotten suspicious earlier, Anna thought. She comforted herself with the idea that Jakey, his deputy, and Paul hadn't been suspicious either.

They still weren't.

As far as anyone else was concerned a crime had not been committed and the culprit had been caught and executed.

"Not dispatched, executed."

Piedmont opened one orange eye at the sound of her voice but he was not awake, his third eyelid remained half closed.

"Somebody done her in, Piedmont. Miss Scarlet did it in the library with the pinking shears. Colonel Mustard did it in the kitchen with a cougar."

The snapshots from Sheila Drury's clothes rod were face-down on the desk. Turning them over one by one, she looked through them slowly. They'd been taken not far from where she had found Drury's body. Less than a mile downstream where the creek flowed from one emerald pool to the next over a wide smooth floor of stone.

Did that mean anything? Had Christina killed her lover in passion? Or just to get back the photos? Was Sheila Drury blackmailing her? Some might think it a form of poetic justice to do in their blackmailer at the scene of their indiscretion. But a mile upstream through rough country? And what was the pack all about?

Could Drury have been blackmailing anyone else?

"Slow down, slow down," Anna murmured. Pressing Piedmont's tail to her upper lip, she twirled the tip as if it were the end of a blond mustache. "We must use the little gray cells."

The few left I haven't drowned, she thought. Against her better judgment, she took another sip of Sauvignon Blanc. Clearheadedness, desirable as it might be, couldn't compete with habit.

On the back of an announcement of an equal opportunity meeting Anna wrote: WHO HAD REASONS TO KILL SHEILA DRURY and underlined it.

Christina Walters. She'd already been through that.

Craig Eastern. He hated Drury—if "hated" wasn't too strong a word—for her attempts to develop the camping area for RV sites. Harland Roberts thought Craig was crazy enough to hurt her, why not Sheila?

Mrs. Thomas Drury. She'd mentioned something about insurance money. There'd been problems between mother and daughter. That had been fairly obvious. Try as she might, Anna couldn't picture Mrs. Drury more than four feet off a paved trail.

Who else? She stared at the blank sheet of paper. Rogelio? Because Sheila was opposed to reintroducing prairie dogs?

"My mother-in-law," Anna said dryly. "Because Ranger Drury had such appalling manners as to eat ice cream with a grapefruit spoon?"

Piedmont was not amused. Anna laughed, a snort of silent amusement. What now? Form some intelligent theory then set about questioning the suspects? "Where were you at such and such a time?"

A knock startled her from her musings, startled Piedmont from her shoulders. Automatically she checked her radio, turned up the squelch. It was working. If there was an ambulance run or a problem in the campground they'd've radioed—for a ranger's $20,000 a year, she was on call twenty-four hours a day. Who would come to her door? It occurred to her that emergencies were more common than social calls anymore. The thought made her suddenly lonely.

"Come in," she hollered. The door rattled and she realized she'd locked it. Embarrassed at her newly suspicious nature, Anna bounded across the room to open the door.

Christina Walters was on the top step. Just as Anna jerked the door wide, she was turning to go. Looking a little shamefaced at being caught creeping away, the woman turned back.

Given her recent speculations and the color photos that were lying on her desk, Anna could think of nothing to say. Even the old standbys of "Good evening. May I help you?" and "Won't you come in?" had deserted her.

"I came for that beer," Christina Walters said shyly and looked up at Anna with eyes as dark and unfathomable as

Zachary Taylor's. The same velvet brown that Anna'd lost herself in so many times. "May I come in?"

"Sure," Anna answered ungraciously and stood aside more like a doorman than a hostess.

Christina walked in, seemingly over her shyness of a moment before. She studied the few postcards Anna had taped up on the wall with an apparently unfeigned interest. Piedmont came out from his skulking place under the table and twined himself around her ankles as if she were a long-lost cousin.

Anna watched, still with no words in her brain, as Christina picked the cat up and coiled him around her neck as if she'd been doing it all her life. She was wearing a jersey dress. The elongated tank top clung to her from shoulders to hips, then flared long, ending at mid-calf. On her feet were rubber thongs. The dress was kelly green, the thongs lavender. Somehow Christina made it look fashionable. Piedmont, gold and shameless, completed the picture by draping himself like a fox fur across her shoulders.

Anna could smell the faint scent of White Linen.

Christina turned and smiled. Anna closed the door. Was the woman trying to seduce her? Or was it simply the knowledge that the possibility existed that preyed on her mind?

Wanting to destroy the silence, Anna punched the PLAY button on the tape player. The Chenille Sisters. Auto-rewind had brought them back to "Seduced." Anna punched it off.

Christina, Piedmont slithering down in her arms to be held like a baby, was working her way around the single room that comprised all of Anna's living quarters. Pleasant, not prying, merely polite, she was taking in the fragments of Anna's life. Soon those dark eyes would stray across the desk top, across the snapshots.

"A beer," Anna said. "I've got wine. I'm drinking wine. Would you rather have that?"

"White wine would be nice," Christina replied, sounding genuinely delighted.

"You can sit." Like a traffic cop, Anna pointed to the armchair. Besides being the only chair, it had the advantage of being on the other side of the room from the desk. Not only was Anna unsure whether or not she wanted Christina to know she had found the pictures—if, indeed, it was Christina who had been in Drury's trailer searching—but there was something about Christina Walters that made Anna want to spare her any shock, any unpleasantness. Though they were of her, the snaps seemed too explicit for Christina's dark eyes.

Anna did an awkward dip scooping up the offending photographs, and retreated to the kitchen area. Hidden behind the refrigerator door, she stuffed them into the hip pocket of her Levi's. Shortly thereafter, she emerged with a liter bottle of wine. Hoping she looked innocent but managing only to look relieved, she said inanely: "I got it."

Christina laughed. "One glass will do for starters—I'm a cheap date."

"I doubt that." Words came before thought. Though they sounded harsh, Anna meant them as a compliment. She waited a second to see how Christina would take it.

The woman smiled easily, crossed her long legs. Piedmont jumped to the floor. Lovely as it was, it was not a good lap for curling up in.

Anna poured a glass of wine for her guest and, returning to the desk, she topped off her own. The bottle she set on the floor by the kerosene lamp.

"Light it," Christina said. It sounded like the eager request of a child and not an order.

Fumbling with matches, Anna lit the lamp.

Christina Walters dropped gracefully to the floor and began looking through the tape collection Anna kept in shoe boxes beneath the coffee table. Seemingly she had more poise sitting on a stranger's carpet than Anna could muster in a straight-backed chair in her own home.

As she read the spines of the cassettes, Christina chatted comfortably of music. "I used to sing in the church choir when I was growing up in Tennessee," she said and she laughed. A nice round rich sound from somewhere deeper than nerves or politeness. "Momma thought I was such a devout little thing till she found out I only put up with all the talk about Jesus so I could have the music. There was a stop to choir after that, though not to church."

Anna smiled, handed Christina her wine. She took it in long tapered fingers, nails polished but not sharp or unkind-looking.

"To old friends and better days," Christina said. Sadness touched her face, warmed the brown eyes.

Anna felt her throat constrict. "Old friends," she repeated and drank to other dark eyes and lamplit nights.

"How about this? Sophistication in the wilderness. I love it." Christina held up Cole Porter's *Anything Goes*.

"One of my favorites," Anna replied, pleased that Christina had chosen that instead of a modern popular musician. "I sing some of those songs to Gideon to keep us both awake on the trail."

"I'll bet he loves it." Christina dropped the tape in.

Anna suspected she was trying to put her at ease. What surprised her was how well it was working. "I think Gideon misses the good old days when rangers whistled 'The Streets of Laredo.'"

Piedmont, creeping along the sides of the room, skulking under the furniture, sprang out to pounce on the hem of Christina's dress. Putting her hand under the fabric, she moved it around creating a mole for him to kill.

It impressed Anna that she put Piedmont's amusement before the well-being of her garment.

"I want to get Alison a kitten," Christina said. "She needs to learn to be kind because she is bigger, more powerful than something. She needs to have some little life depend on her now. I don't expect she'll ever have a little sister to practice on."

Sadness weighed on Christina's voice and Anna, who'd never much cared for children, found herself wishing Christina could have another. "Alison's the little blond girl on the pink tricycle, isn't she?" Anna asked and the other woman nodded, looking pleased Anna had noticed. "She's a pretty little girl."

Christina said nothing but there was something in her look that made Anna laugh at herself. "Listen to me," she said. "I'm carrying on the tradition. As if pretty were the best and most important thing a little girl could be."

Christina refilled her own glass, then poured Anna more wine. Anna accepted her taking the role of hostess as easily as Christina had assumed it.

"Let me try again," Anna said as she slid down on the floor, her back against the desk, her legs stretched out. "She looks like a sharp, determined, organized little girl. How's that?"

"Perfect!" Christina said, and she actually clapped her hands. Somehow it wasn't phony or coy or childish or any of the things Anna might have thought had the gesture come from someone else. It was charming.

"Alison is terrifyingly organized and she's just turned four last month. Why did you say 'organized'? It's an odd word to describe a child."

"I can see her thinking," Anna explained. "See the little wheels and cogs and gears turning as she plots out her course through the houses."

"She is my light," Christina said. "Everything that is good and worthwhile about me has surfaced in that little person. All the bent and broken bits were left out. Alison means the world to me."

There was an edge of desperation—or determination—in Christina's voice that made Anna think now she was to hear the real reason for the visit. Disappointment—minor, Anna told herself—ached behind her sternum. She wished this had been just a social call. The ache deepened as she remembered the snapshots in her pocket.

The tape clicked to an end. Neither of them moved to turn it over. Christina was looking into Anna's face and, though Anna wanted to look away, she found she couldn't.

"You found the pictures, didn't you?" the woman asked softly.

"Inside the clothes rod in the bedroom closet," Anna replied.

Despite the situation, Christina laughed. "For Heaven's sake!" she said. "I'm impressed. You must be a regular Miss Marple."

She was impressed, Anna could tell. She liked it. And she felt a fool for liking it. "You . . . went into Ranger Drury's and looked through her collection."

"We broke in, yes."

"We?"

"Alison and I."

In spite of herself, Anna smiled. It hardly seemed a deadly duo, this gentle woman and her child. A thought struck Anna: "The dishes and the garbage. You cleaned up."

"The heat made it smell," Christina said simply, as if Sheila could come home and be offended by it.

Anna had more questions, but it seemed if she waited Christina would fill the awkward silences as she had been doing since she arrived. Truth or lies, Anna was curious to see what she would say.

As if I'd know the difference, Anna said to herself. But she thought she would.

"Could I see them?" Christina asked.

Wondering what kind of a cop she was to hand over her best and only evidence to the prime suspect, Anna took the snapshots from her pocket and gave them to Christina. Two women sitting companionably talking of children and music over a glass of wine: it seemed absurd to refuse a request on the grounds of suspected murder.

There were twelve pictures. Christina looked through them slowly. Her eyes filled with tears. Anna got to her feet and fetched a wad of toilet paper from the bathroom. When she came back she didn't settle again to her comfortable place on the carpet but perched vulture-like on the edge of the straight-backed chair. "I haven't any Kleenex," she apologized as she held out the tissue.

"This is fine. Thank you." Christina blew her nose.

Anna was speculating whether or not she had murdered her lover, but when Christina looked up there was such loneliness in her brown eyes Anna found herself saying with honesty as well as compassion: "Those are beautiful photographs."

The simple kindness seemed to undo Christina and the trickle of tears became a river. Anna knew from experience that tears made men nervous. Though she certainly enjoyed them less, they bothered her no more than laughter.

In a minute or two the sobs subsided. Christina took a deep drink of her wine and sighed as if she were breathing out her very soul.

"I thought maybe she was blackmailing you," Anna said. "Though who'd care these days is beyond me. But maybe you wanted to go to seminary, become an Episcopal priest, run for Congress, or Mrs. America. Was she?"

Christina shook her head. "She threatened sometimes. Half

kidding you know, wanting to make me 'come out of the closet.' I like it just fine in the closet. But Sheila'd never have done it."

"Because she loved you?"

"No. I don't know that she did love me. Because she was a very ethical person. Painfully so. She used to boast—and it was true in a lot of ways—that she had no morals but she did have ethics. To tell someone else's secrets would not have been an ethical thing to do."

"Why did you break in, search her picture collection?"

"I was afraid if the pictures turned up in her effects they might be made public in some way. Then Erik would find out like he finds out everything. He would use them to prove I was an unfit mother. He'd take Alison from me."

"Erik is Alison's father?"

"Legally."

Anna looked at her questioningly. It had nothing to do with Drury or lions, and she couldn't bring herself to voice mere curiosity.

"After Erik and I had been trying a while we found out his sperm count was too low—practically nil—and what few little guys there were were pretty poor swimmers. 'Weak specimens' the doctor called them. Alison's daddy is the turkey baster. High tech, though. We had it done in a fancy clinic in San Raphael."

"I take it it was not an amicable divorce," Anna ventured and Christina laughed bitterly.

"No. Erik was having an affair with his corner office and his mahogany desk at an investment banking firm in San Francisco, and I was having an affair with the woman who came to do the stenciling in the nursery.

"Erik had been pretty upset over the sperm count thing even though it really didn't matter much to me. I guess having his wife run off with another woman was more than he could take. He even threatened to kill her. He actually waited at her off-ramp and rammed Linda's car with his Toyota. He was just trying to scare us, I think. It worked. Linda moved to Seattle. I lost touch with her after a while."

"Why didn't he get Alison then?"

"He tried but I went on the stand and lied my way out of it. There wasn't any proof. And I guess I didn't look like the judge's idea of one of 'them.' He'll never give up, though."

"He loves Alison that much? Or hates you?"

"Both in his way, I guess. But what he really loves is winning and what he can't stand is losing."

A moment passed in silence. Christina looked through the pictures again but this time there were no tears. When she'd finished, she held them out to Anna.

"Keep them," Anna said.

"You loved somebody!" Christina sounded faintly surprised.

"Did you think of me as the Snow Queen, a heart of ice?"

Christina was quiet so long, Anna thought she wasn't going to reply.

"I suppose I did," she said finally. "You seem so tough, so together, lifting heavy weights and driving big trucks. It's easier to believe other people are tough—unfeeling—then you don't have to be careful of them. You can go right on along being careful only of yourself. If you have a heart," Christina said gently, "it's made of gold." She held the corner of the bundle of pictures over the chimney of the lamp. Flames bloomed green and blue from the developing chemical.

"It's a shame," Anna said. "They were really the only pictures Sheila ever took that were worth a damn."

• • •

Christina left at nine-forty; eleven-forty New York time. Anna decided to risk Molly's displeasure, gambling she'd still be up watching Jay Leno.

For this call, Anna went to the pay phone down the road half a mile at the Pine Springs Store. The laundry room in the Cholla Chateau was too public.

"It's me. Did I wake you up?" Anna asked.

"Nope. This is the City That Never Sleeps. Tonight I know why. The people in 3C won't let it. I knew I should have moved when they took up clog dancing." There was a sudden silence in the listening darkness of the phone lines, a hushed breath, a sense of palpable relief.

"Still smoking?" Anna asked.

"Still drinking?" Molly returned.

"Like a fish."

"Like a chimney."

"By sixty-two you'll be dead of emphysema like Aunt Gertie."

"By seventy-four you'll fall drunk in the upper pond and drown like Gramma Davis."

"Come to West Texas. At least mix your smoke with some real air," Anna said and, as always, she felt a fluttering of hope that this time Molly would say yes. And wouldn't cancel out at the last minute.

"Too many crazy clients," Molly said with a laugh.

"Speaking of crazy," Anna blurted out, "I think I may be gay."

"Woman to woman love? Politically correct. Low risk of disease. High chance of getting grant money for artistic endeavors. That'll be a hundred and forty-five dollars."

"Molly . . ."

"You're serious. Okay." There followed a silence through which Anna could hear her sister changing gears, dropping the banter. Now they would talk. Relief welled up like a warm spring.

"And Rogelio?" Molly asked.

"Rogelio is . . ." Anna searched for the words that would sum up the man who had appeared in and disappeared out of her bed for the last eight months. "Rogelio is every inch a man."

"Nine," Molly said dryly.

"Give or take."

"Your occasionally torrid past indicates a degree of heterosexuality that I, as a licensed psychiatrist, cannot overlook," Molly said.

"Tonight I think I felt myself leaning toward a torrid future with Christina."

"Christina?"

"Every inch a woman. Christina Walters. She's the clerk-typist here." Anna heard Molly sigh—or light a cigarette. "What?" she demanded.

Two beats of black silence pounded through the phone wires. "What do you feel about all this?" her sister asked.

The doctor was IN.

"Mostly confusion."

"Okay. Tell me about Christina."

Anna was glad to talk of the woman. She was surprised at her eagerness. Was it the same as the girlish longing to tell her friends of the new boy in her life?

For over three-quarters of an hour, way past midnight eastern daylight time, Molly listened. When Anna had squeezed out her last thought on the subject, Molly listened ten seconds more.

"Christina sounds like a nice woman," she said at last and Anna felt disappointed.

"Is that all?" she demanded.

"Anna, I don't want to throw cold water on your new career as a lesbian. Lord knows it would increase my status in therapists' circles if I could produce a sibling who was a bona fide gay woman, but how long has it been since you've made a friend?"

"I have friends," Anna retorted.

"I don't think so. I think you used to have friends. After Zach was killed—and you finally sobered up—you took off out of New York City like all the demons of hell were after you. You became Smokey Bear's right-hand man and you've never looked back. When I run into your old friends at Saks they're wearing black arm bands. Everybody thinks you died, too."

"None of my friends could afford Saks," Anna snapped.

"All right," Molly said. "When I'm at Saks, I see them through the window waiting for the bus to the Lower East Side. But you get my point."

"Maybe I don't."

"Maybe you do. Maybe you need a girlfriend. Maybe you're overwhelmed that this woman was warm and kind and female. Maybe you're gun-shy of attachment because Zach left you. Maybe you miss Zach's feminine side."

"You're shrinking me," Anna complained.

"You're the one with the sexual identity crisis. What do you want?"

"Rogelio has a feminine side," Anna countered.

"From what you've told me, Rogelio has a weak side. Not at all the same."

"I'll think about that," Anna promised. "I never know whether you're being commercial or merely profound."

Molly laughed, unoffended. "Hey, one's as good as the other these days. Maybe you are turning gay. That's well and good. I just wanted to give you some other things to think about. Powerful need for affection, identification—all that underrated and overexploited sisterhood stuff—is visceral. Feels almost sexual to those not in touch with themselves."

Anna started to protest that she was in touch with herself, but the lie was too bold for her. "One more complication," she said and felt a wicked pleasure in having a real bomb to drop. "Christina Walters is my prime suspect in what I'm increasingly sure is the murder of the Dog Canyon Ranger."

There was a most satisfying silence on the other end of the line. Anna smiled.

"When I told Mother and Dad I wanted a playmate, I was hinting for a kitten," Molly said. "I liked being an only child. Do you hear this?" There was a shushing sound, then Molly's voice again. "That was me pouring myself a medicinal scotch and soda. You have till I finish it to fill in the rest of the story. Then I'm going to bed. Ready? Go!"

Anna told her largely conjectural story of love, lust, blackmail, and murder.

"How?" Molly asked flatly when she had finished. "Lured her lover upstream like a demented salmon and coshed her with a cactus?"

"Maybe," Anna said. "I've not done 'how' just yet. I'm working on 'why.' Christina Walters, my . . . friend . . . is the only real good 'why' I've got so far."

"Work on 'how,'" Molly advised. "Take my professional word for it: everybody's got ten good reasons to do away with everybody else. It's just nobody knows how. Do 'how.'"

There was an odd little clink, like a tiny distant bell. "That," said Molly, "was the last ice-cube hitting my teeth. Goodnight."

"Goodnight," Anna returned but the line had gone dead.

# CHAPTER 8

"Look at the bright side, Gideon," Anna addressed the grouchy-looking ears as the horse dragged his feet, stumbling with childish ill grace up the Frijole Trail away from the barn. "Even with tack I probably weigh less than you'd be packing if you were working for Harland."

It was Thursday and Harland had his mule packer using Pesky and the mules to haul coolers full of food and beer into the trail crew where they were spiked out on the Tejas Trail in the high country.

Paul had sent Anna to ride the Guadalupe Peak Trail. Usually hot Thursdays in June were quiet. With temperatures creeping near the hundred-degree mark and no water available at any of the backcountry campgrounds, only the hardy and the foolhardy were packing in. But this Thursday was the annual Pentecostal Church's fund-raising hike up the highest peak in Texas.

Churches from all over Texas, New Mexico, and as far away as Oklahoma participated. Every year somebody got hurt, half a dozen people broke park rules, and nearly everybody littered.

Anna began whistling "Nearer My God to Thee," and the horse pricked up his ears. "Gonna be a good day, Gideon," she said. "It's not every day you're guaranteed to be hailed as a hero or the anti-Christ or both by sundown."

The beauty of the Chihuahuan Desert had been smoothing the wrinkles from Anna's mind since she'd saddled up at eight a.m. The winds had finally stopped. There would be a reprieve from their incessant scour until probably November. Cholla—the skinny cactus that grew up in angular, spine-covered branches—was beginning to bloom. Festive pink blossoms the size of teacups and looking for all the world like they had been fashioned from crepe paper enlivened the uncompromising cacti. Mexicans called them *Velas de Coyotes*—candles of the coyotes. Prickly pear pads carried one, two, ten yellow blooms, and the grasses were rich with wildflowers.

In the midst of all this spiritual plenty Anna was annoyed to find herself once again thinking of death. "Molly said we must concentrate on 'how.' Think, Gideon, think." Anna spoke to keep Gideon awake. On the familiar trail from the Frijole ranch house to the Pine Springs campground—three miles he'd done a hundred times—Gideon tended to doze off while he walked. Then if anything—western diamondback rattler or monarch butterfly—woke him suddenly, he'd jump right out from under his rider.

"Okay, Gideon," Anna conceded. "I know you've only got horse brains for brains. I'll think. You listen.

"Quick 'whys.' Maybe in New York everybody has ten good reasons for killing everybody else but in West Texas we are somewhat more civilized. We like the personal touch.

"Water bar, old buddy . . ."

Gideon's hoof crashed into the stone set crosswise on the

trail and Anna patted his neck reassuringly. "Such a Nureyev you are, a veritable Baryshnikov.

"Okay. The 'whys' in short. Christina's still first with love, lust, and blackmail to her credit. Second, the mysterious Erik of legend and lore who kills with a Toyota. Karl coming in third with job envy. We'll squeeze Craig Eastern in in fourth place because he's crazy and maybe crazy enough to kill to keep the moneylenders out of the temple—the developers out of Dog Canyon. Fourth and a half: Mrs. Drury with her insurance money. Rogelio fifth with his homeless prairie dogs." Gideon cocked one furry ear.

"What?" Anna demanded. "Who did I forget? Okay. No family favoritism. Last but not least, mother-in-law Edith, spurred on to violence by Emily Post over the grapefruit spoon in the ice-cream incident.

"Pretty slim pickins', Gideon, my little hay-burner. All my suspects are your basic Caspar Milquetoast types."

Gideon snorted, blowing the flies and dust from his nostrils.

"Right," Anna conceded. "We were to do 'how.'"

For a while they rode without speaking, Gideon heaving great complaining sighs, Anna ignoring them. Two military helicopters out of Halloran Air Force Base flew over and Anna shook her fist at them. The airways over the wilderness were supposedly regulated but it seemed all the flyboys fancied themselves the new Tom Cruise.

"'How' for Christina." Gideon started as if he'd been goosed with a cattle prod. "Aha! Caught you napping," Anna crowed. "Christina could've lured Sheila into the canyon any number of ways. A simple invite even. Sheila, being the stronger of the two, would carry the pack. Then . . . Then what, Gideon? Help me here. Aren't you a highly trained police horse? Knocked her over the head? No sign of head trauma. Poisoned her? That's got possibilities. Wait for the autopsy. Frightened her to death? Too farfetched. Drugged her, slathered her with catnip, and waited for a lion to finish the job?"

Gideon stopped, relieved himself in the trail, grunting with unself-conscious equine satisfaction.

"Fair enough," Anna admitted. "We'll drop the catnip angle and leave it at Christina/Poison. Who's next? Ah. Erik. Ditto Erik—if there is an Erik."

Anna fell silent. Had Christina spun her story from scratch, banking on the fact that Anna, a middle-aged woman, more or less alone, a widow without any close friends, would be an easy mark? A few compliments, some laughter, and she'd be so thrilled just to be paid attention to she'd bite anything, swallow it hook, line, and sinker?

"Wouldn't I feel a total horse's ass. Nothing personal, Gideon." The scene she'd painted made Anna cringe but she didn't believe it, not entirely. From long experience she knew that she wore her loneliness like armor. Very few people ever recognized it for what it was. To the casual observer it looked very much like arrogance.

Sometimes it was.

"So: Erik, in a jealous rage, talks Sheila into coming to this secluded spot and: one; breaks her neck. Is Erik a big man? Two: injects her with poison. Is the ex–Mr. Walters a chemist or pharmacist?" Anna remembered Christina's mentioning investment banking. "Bored her to death with Ginny Maes and Fanny Maes? I've got it! Smothers her with his down sleeping bag, lays her gently in the saw grass figuring by the time she's found the water will obscure prints, tracks, and marks. Smothering's got possibilities. Wait for the autopsy.

"Karl's next, Gideon. Maybe you want to tune out so you don't have to hear your buddy slandered." Gideon wouldn't dignify that with an answer and Anna went on with her musings. "Karl could've gotten her up there on any of a dozen pretexts: undiscovered pictographs, rare plants. He's powerful. Smothering, neck snapping, it'd be a piece of cake. He wouldn't even break a sweat. Then carry her into the grass.

"Wait!" Gideon stopped, looked back over his shoulder. "That doesn't work. Anybody in the park would have known I was on lion transect down Middle McKittrick on the seventeenth. In Guadalupe's eighty thousand acres it would be any thinking villain's last choice as a place to hide the body." Unless someone wanted the body found; wanted her to find it on a lion transect. That was where people assume the lions were. In reality, lion transects were simply places chosen to look for lion sign to find out, often, where the lions were not. If someone wanted the body to be found and wanted it to be found on a lion transect it followed that they wanted it to appear that a lion had done the killing.

Which meant the lion scratches, the strange tracks, were not a coincidence made after the fact by an opportunistic cougar. They had been put there for her to find.

Anna pulled the death scene into her mind. The paw prints—could they have been made by plaster casts or rubber, like children used to make paw prints in the Touch and See Museums? If so, they were the finest casts she'd ever seen. But it was not beyond the realm of possibility.

And the scratches and bites? Could they have been dug into Ranger Drury's flesh with something other than a feline claw? Knife? Ice pick? Fondue skewer?

Gideon, showing sudden energy, trotted down the dry bank of the creek that cut through Pine Canyon. Already, half a mile away from Guadalupe Peak, they could hear shouting. For the moment, Anna shelved the subject of murder. She clicked her tongue against her teeth. "Come on, Gideon, let's go find us some Pentecostals."

• • •

People of all ages were swarming up Guadalupe Peak. Overweight men, women and girls in dresses, nobody in hiking boots, very few carrying food, many carrying no water at all or a quart to be shared by a family of four when every man, woman, and child would need at least a half gallon to make it comfortably—and safely—the ten miles and 3,000 feet to the top of the mountain and back.

"Half gallon," Anna said time and again. Time and again a smiling face nodded, a hand held up a pittance of water. "We have plenty, sister, praise the Lord."

The opiate of the people was fueling the righteous.

By noon, after she had given nearly all her water away to feverish-looking children dragged along in the religious fervor, Anna found herself hoping for an Old Testament God to visit the peak with one of His famous scourges: a lightning storm that would blast the rock clean of cloying humanity.

Near three o'clock, as she led Gideon down the trail, a thirteen-year-old girl with a sprained ankle rigid in the saddle, as pale as if she rode on the back of Lucifer himself, Anna gave the last of her water to a red-faced woman, obviously pregnant and obviously overheated.

"Praise the Lord," the girl said.

"Go down," Anna returned. "Forget the peak. Remember that baby. Turn around now. Go down."

"If we suffer, we'll offer it up. Christ suffered on the cross for us," her husband said. He looked to be all of nineteen or twenty.

Anna stood for a moment, Gideon nuzzling her hand where it held the halter rope, and marveled at the beatific stupidity that radiated from the two flushed faces.

"There's no safe way for you to get past this horse," Anna said finally. "He's got a thing about anybody crowding him on the trail. Turn around and go down."

"Honey . . ." The girl laid a hand on her husband's arm.

Anna could tell she was glad their pilgrimage was to be cut short.

The boy looked up from his wife's face.

"No way," Anna lied. "Hooves like sledgehammers. Scares me even to think about it."

"Next year," the boy promised.

"Next year," Anna repeated.

With a truly beautiful smile, he handed her back the empty water bottle. "Thank you for the water, sister."

"You're welcome," Anna said mechanically. She was suddenly transfixed by the squared, white, one-quart, government-issue water bottle in its canvas holster. They were ubiquitous at GUMO: in fire packs, in pickups, on saddles, on belts, in car seats. But not in Sheila Drury's backpack. It wasn't the missing camera that had set off the alarms in Anna's head. It was the simple fact Sheila had been carrying no water.

In June, in the desert, no one, least of all an experienced hiker, carried a heavy pack eight miles without water. It couldn't be done. Not in June. Not with the heat and the wind. Anna had drunk three-quarters of a gallon that day.

Sheila had not been lured down Middle McKittrick. She had been forced. Or carried. Probably on short notice. The pack was just a prop—like a stage prop—to make it look as though she'd gone on her own.

"Holy smoke!" Anna breathed.

"What's wrong? What's happening?" the girl squeaked from Gideon's back and Anna was sorry she had frightened her.

"Nothing, Mary. You're okay. I just remembered something I need to do." Anna turned and smiled reassuringly. "Another twenty minutes and we'll be down. Hang in there."

• • •

"That's an interesting theory, Anna," Paul was saying. Anna had delivered the girl into the hands of her church group leader, and given Gideon four carrots and a quarter-cup of horse vitamins he was particularly fond of. Now she sat in Paul's cool cluttered office in the old Frijole ranch house. "For the sake of argument, let's say you're right on all counts. Who do you think forced Sheila to hike up out of Dog Canyon and down Middle McKittrick?"

It had been on the tip of Anna's tongue to tell him: Karl. Karl wanted the Dog Canyon District Ranger position, he resented Sheila for getting it. He had the strength. He knew the park better than anyone. But Paul was looking at her shrewdly. Not unlike a psychiatrist testing the waters to see just exactly what kind of crazy the patient was. Under that gentle, blue gaze she said only: "In a closed area, without water, strange paw prints, no saw grass cuts. I think we should get our hands on the autopsy report ASAP."

"The FBI—" Paul began.

"Fuck the FBI!" Anna snapped. "They've no idea what lions do or don't do. Unless there are bags of cocaine on the corpse they don't give a damn."

Paul said nothing.

"Sorry," Anna said. She almost meant it.

"I know you're wound up over this thing, Anna. It's not going to get any better. You may as well know some of the ranchers are lobbying for the right to hunt lions in certain areas of the park that border their lands."

Anna didn't know what it was she was going to say but Paul stopped the words with an upraised hand before they gusted out of her.

"I don't think that's going to happen, Anna. It's just talk by a few people. There's no precedent for it in this park. Corinne and I have talked it over and we're of the opinion it will all blow over. These things usually do.

"Much as I admire your concern, I don't think your pursuing this is going to help, Anna. I think you might even end up doing more harm than good."

Anna waited a moment, trying to let her anger pass. It didn't. It backed up in her throat till it felt like her chest was going to explode.

"Did Corinne decide that?" she asked finally.

"We both did, Anna. This time, I think Corinne's right."

"What if—"

"What if," Paul cut her off, his famous patience finally exhausted, "I get you the autopsy report. If it says lion kill, no poisons, no signs of other violence, then you let go of this thing and get back to the business of being a park ranger?" The phone rang and he snatched it up. "Frijole," he barked.

Anna guessed she was dismissed. Determined not to look contrite, she slid out of her chair and left the room, back straight.

Small triumph, she thought as she stopped outside under the pecan trees, listened to the soothing chatter of a spring that had whispered the incomprehensible secrets of the desert for a thousand years. She was becoming a thorn in Paul Decker's side. A boil on his neck. A pain in his butt. Not a good way to beef up one's year-end evaluation.

A gopher, pushing two fistfuls of soil, poked his little brown head out of a new-made hole among the roots of a pecan. "Hi guy," Anna greeted him. With a look of alarm, the little face vanished. "Et tu," she muttered.

From the barn came the sounds of metal on metal. Karl pitchforking manure into the wheelbarrow.

Why not? Anna thought. I've already alienated everyone else. May as well go for broke.

Karl had an audience. Pesky and Gideon looked on adoringly as the big man mucked out their shelter. Pesky kept nudging Karl's behind. Anna supposed he sometimes carried sugar or carrots in his hip pockets for the animals. The mules were not so easily won. They stood back by the manger, wary of Pesky's hooves, waiting for some serious food.

Under his breath, Karl was whistling, "Let's be quiet as a mouse and build a lovely little house for Wendy," from *Peter Pan*.

Anna watched for half a minute. She figured she'd like Karl even if he did kill a ranger every now and again. "Gideon's hoof is looking a little better," she said for openers.

"You been putting Hoof Flex on it," Karl returned. "That's good. Nobody else bothers."

"You bother," Anna replied.

"It's no bother," Karl said.

Anna couldn't help but wonder what Karl's mind looked like inside. She pictured an attic full of well-used, well-cared-for toys where the sun always streamed in through gabled windows.

"I thought you'd be off today."

"Tomorrow and Saturday."

Anna knew Karl's lieu days but she'd wanted to hear him say it. Sheila had died on a Friday night thirteen days before. "What're you going to do on your days off?"

"Nothing," Karl said. "Maybe I'll go to town. Go to the show."

"Not much playing. I went weekend before last. Saw the new Schwarzenegger film. Did you see that?" Anna was fishing. Karl looked up from his manure. There was no telling whether she'd gotten a nibble or not. Maybe he was alarmed or wary or annoyed or maybe just thinking in his effortful way.

"Weekend before last I went home to Van Horn," he said. Van Horn was a little town an hour south on Highway 54. "My mom wanted me to lift things down from the shelf in the garage. She's got a garage." Karl started to whistle again, lifting the handles of the full wheelbarrow easily and wheeling it toward the gate.

Pesky butted his head against Anna, rubbing the flies from his face. Absently, she scratched his forehead with her knuckles.

ALIBIS.

They came right after CLUES.

# CHAPTER 9

Time to have another "beer" with Christina Walters. Anna fervently hoped she had spent all that deadly Friday with at least seven nuns who never slept. Or, better yet, in jail.

Rubberbands clamped in her teeth, she rebraided her hair. "Stalling?" she asked her reflection in the bathroom mirror. "Or primping?" For the fourteenth time she glanced at the clock: 6:17. When did one drop in on a mother-and-child? When did four-year-olds eat supper? Anna didn't feel up to interrogating Christina while her little girl looked on, round-eyed, over her bowl of SpaghettiOs. Not that Christina seemed a SpaghettiOs type of mother.

Not like me, Anna thought. Christina would be a four-major-food-groups kind of mother.

6:21.

Anna combed the braids out with her fingers, left her hair loose and crimped. Annoyed at herself for caring, she purposely—or spitefully—pulled on ragged jeans and a faded sweatshirt Rogelio had salvaged from some Goodwill box in

El Paso because it had Mickey Mouse on it. Still and all, she was wearing perfume—"Heartsong" from the Tucson Co-op—and she carried a nice Pinot Noir she'd been saving.

Christina and Alison lived in one of the two-bedroom-with-garage houses sprinkled down the curving roadway from where the seasonals, Anna, and two bachelor maintenance men were housed. Housing was always at a premium in the parks and usually substandard. Anna was lucky: she didn't much care. The Walterses lived in what Anna referred to as the "real" houses: houses with washers and dryers and telephones and televisions and families.

The unmistakable racket of plastic wheels on pavement let Anna know supper was either over or not yet called. Alison was riding her pink tricycle in tight circles on the smooth cement pad in front of the garage.

"Hi," Anna said. "Is your mother home?"

It was a stupid question. Alison probably knew it but, being a well-brought-up child, chose to overlook it. "Momma's in the back," she announced. "I'm not to go on the black."

Anna stared a second before she realized what Alison meant. She was not to ride her tricycle off the white cement slab onto the black asphalt and into the road and traffic. Hence the tight circles. "Good idea," Anna said and: "The backyard?"

Alison nodded, starting up her trike again with burring engine noise blown out through pursed lips.

Christina, wearing white painter's overalls and a pale yellow tank top, knelt near the chain-link fence weeding a flower bed rich with the colors of marigolds and snapdragons.

"Exotics," Anna said, "take a lot of water to maintain in the desert."

"Good evening," Christina returned, mocking Anna gently. "Did you just drop by to abuse me?" As she stood, she smiled and held open the gate.

"More or less," Anna replied truthfully. "But I brought an anesthetic."

Christina nodded appreciatively as she read the label on the wine bottle. "I like reds better than whites. Even in summer I like the warmth."

Anna laughed for the sheer pleasure of hearing one of her pet thoughts voiced by someone else.

"It'll be better aged an hour or so." Christina set the wine just inside the porch door. "Ally and I were going to come by and abduct you this evening. We need your expert advice.

"Honey? Ready to go?" she called, shooing Anna out the garden gate as the tricycle clattered down the walk beside the house to meet them. In mild but not unpleasant confusion, Anna waited as Christina supervised the putting away of the trike.

"Do you want to tell Ranger Pigeon where we're going?" Christina asked as the three of them walked out the drive and turned up past the seasonal housing.

"Anna," Anna said.

Alison bounded away ahead of them, then walked backward several yards in front. "Dottie's neighbor's cat had kittens. Momma said I could have one and that you knew how to pick the best one because you had an orange cat."

"Dottie Bernard lives up at the highway camp," Christina explained. "She sits with Alison weekdays."

Anna was flattered—all out of proportion to the event, she told herself—but still, she enjoyed the feeling. Maybe Molly was right. Maybe it had been too long since she'd had a friend. Too many years spent looking at other human beings as merely creatures the wildlands needed to be protected from.

In the end Christina may have been sorry she asked Anna

along. To Alison's great delight, Anna's expert advice was two kittens, so they could play together when she was away at the sitter's all day.

"Piedmont doesn't have anyone to play with," Christina said half accusingly.

"Piedmont was an only child," Anna returned.

"Like Ally." Christina looked sad for an instant then banished it with a smile. "Two kittens," she said.

Alison picked out two black kittens, one with a white mustache, one with two white front paws. They carried them home in a cardboard VCR box. Under Anna's supervision it was converted into a litter box and food and warm milk set out to make the kittens feel at homc.

"You mustn't play with them too much," Anna warned, echoing words she remembered her mother saying over the furry heads of the many kittens she and Molly had dragged home over the years. "Or they'll get sick. And you must be especially gentle with them for a few days because they'll miss their momma."

When they'd all three been settled in front of the TV, Alison watching *Cheers* and the kittens curled together asleep on her lap, Christina made microwave popcorn and opened the Pinot Noir.

"My hair is so mousey!" she said with an implied snort of disgust. "I'm thinking of getting it permed or streaked or something. What do you think?"

Girl-talk. God! how Anna had missed it without ever knowing she was. Much-maligned girl-talk: sweethearts and hair, new clothes and getting your colors done, movies and books and music and gossip. But not the backbiting and undercutting that stung like a canker through all levels of the Park Service. Real gossip; gossip about why people did the bizarre things they did, said the outrageous things they said, believed the improbable things they believed. Gossip to ferret out what people must be thinking, what made them tick. So much more satisfying than the mannish "I told the so-and-so, I said by God" variety that had buffeted Anna's ears for so long.

They talked through two television shows, through putting Alison to bed, through the last of the wine. Anna forgot the reason she'd needed to talk with Christina in the first place.

Cups of decaf in their hands, they had moved out onto the back porch and were sitting in darkness watching the heat lightning flicker on the horizon over Van Horn sixty miles to the south when she remembered.

Then she only wanted to forget it again, for all time, but she knew she couldn't. Rightly or wrongly, she felt she'd come to know Christina too well to creep around about it.

"I've been thinking a lot about Sheila's death," she said without preamble. "Some new things have come up that make me think she was murdered, then the murder was covered up by somebody wanting it to look like a lion killed her."

There was a long silence, deepened by the distant sound of thunder. Anna wished she could see Christina's face but the darkness under the porch roof was too deep.

"Oh my Lord. To kill her . . . That can't be right. It takes such hate. Watching the life go from someone . . . Forcing it out. No, Anna, that can't be right. Why would anyone kill Sheila?"

All Anna's answers froze on her tongue. So long had she been contemplating this murder, she had forgotten it would be a shock to Chris, would ruin her sleep and haunt her when she was awake. Unless she had done it. Especially if she had done it.

The wordless darkness began to feel empty, accusing.

"The pictures. You think I killed her." The words dropped

into the silence like stones into deep water. Christina's voice was so devoid of emotion, Anna knew she was angry or hurt or both.

"Not really," Anna said lamely. "I'm just covering all the bases. Filling in squares. Checking alibis."

"Alibis! Oh for Heaven's sake!" Christina laughed but it was not a pleasant sound. "How could you possibly think so poorly of me? How could you sit here drinking coffee and watching the sky with me thinking I might be a murderess?"

Anna thought about that one. It was a question she would've asked herself sooner or later. "Just because you might've had reason to kill someone doesn't mean you're not a nice person," she said at last.

"I'd better check on Alison," Christina said abruptly and Anna was left alone on the dark porch. With the first faint stirring of fear, it occurred to her that Christina had gone to fetch a gun, a hypodermic needle, a rolling pin—some implement of destruction.

The soft darkness seemed to harden, become menacing. "Damn," she whispered, lamenting the death of the camaraderie.

A pitiful mew sounded from the unlighted living room. Picturing Christina lurking Anthony Perkins–like behind the china cabinet or inside the hall closet, axe poised, Anna decided to stay where she was. She moved her chair so her back was not to the inside of the house.

Again the plaintive, unconvincing mewing. Nothing else: no lullabies, no footsteps in the hall, no "nighty-nights."

"Damn," Anna whispered a second time. With her eyes, she measured the distance to the porch door. Eight feet. If she bolted from her chair she could be through it and clear of the garden in four seconds, halfway home in ten, and safe in less than a minute. Of course, if she were wrong, she would look like a complete ass in that same amount of time. Foolish or dead? Which did the average human being fear the most?

A needle pricked into the back of her calf. Half swallowing a yelp, she jerked clear, slid to the floor and, pivoting on one knee, came to her feet, the chair she'd been sitting in held between her and her attacker.

The overhead light glared on. Momentarily, Anna was blinded.

"Playing at lion tamer?" Christina stood in the sliding glass door that divided the porch from the house. Between her and Anna, held at bay by the four legs of the chair, was the tiny black kitten with two white paws. It had tried to climb Anna's leg.

Relief and absurdity rolled out on laughter. Fear, the ultimate magician, the perfect puppet-master, had made for her a monster. Anna set the chair back in its proper place, sat down, and picked up the kitten.

Christina still stood framed by the aluminum doorway.

"I have no intention of explaining that little scene, if that's what you're waiting for," Anna said, suppressing a giggle as the tableau of her and the chair and the infinitesimal lion flashed through her mind.

Christina shrugged. She sat in the rocker she'd occupied before. The light was left on, harsh, throwing shadows, aging her face. "Alibis," she said. "That's 'where were you on the night of January twenty-fifth at seven p.m.' stuff, isn't it?"

Anna just nodded. The night had grown significantly cooler.

"But you want Friday night the seventeenth of June, the night Sheila died, don't you?" Christina laughed, a bark of sound. "Oops. How did I know she died Friday night and not Saturday morning? UNLESS I KILLED HER!

"Drumroll there—or whatever it is they are using these days. Friday was a guess, that's all. For what it's worth, I was doing the inventory for the books and so forth at the McKittrick Canyon Visitors Center. I worked late. I was there by myself from five p.m. till nearly ten. Manny saw me at six when he came to close the canyon. He brought me Paul's key to let myself out."

"Did you return it to Paul that night?"

"No. The next day."

McKittrick Canyon access road ran four miles out from the canyon mouth to Highway 62/180. Every night at six somebody drove in, made sure all the visitors were out of the canyon, then padlocked the gate at the highway.

"Karl may have seen me. The Roads and Trails truck he drives was parked there when I arrived. He may have seen me through the window . . . No." She looked disappointed. "It was still there when I left. He wouldn't've seen me, I guess."

"Did you see anyone else? Was anyone else in the canyon that night?"

"No. Nobody."

"At least we know for sure Sheila didn't come in from this end. Manny ran the Visitors Center that Friday till five and he said Sheila'd not been by. That means she had to come over from the Dog Canyon side." For a minute neither woman spoke. Anna was lost in her own thoughts.

"Why so glum?" Christina asked.

Anna looked into the clear brown eyes. So innocent. Studiedly so? "Karl said he'd gone home to Van Horn that weekend."

Christina rubbed her fingertips on her eyelids. "It's getting late."

"Time I was going home." Anna rose, gave the kitten to Christina. She wanted to say something more. To say: "I don't think you did it." But sometimes she did. "I'll check out Karl's truck before I go into the backcountry tomorrow."

"You do that," Christina returned and, though she sounded more weary than angry, Anna figured the friendship was over before it had truly begun.

People tended to take it personally when they were accused of murdering their lovers.

# CHAPTER 10

Usually Anna's morning walk from the housing area to the Maintenance Yard where the NPS vehicles were kept was a pleasant part of her day. The air was clear and cool. The desert's perfume, released by the morning dew, was at its most heady. Cottontails, mule deer, and, if she was lucky, a coyote, flickered through the gray branches of the rabbit brush.

This morning all those ingredients, save the coyote, were in place but her mind was so filled with the rubble of human emotions, she never saw them.

Life changed the moment one began to stalk one's fellow man. Apparently in much the same way it would if one were to take up a life of crime. Perhaps because that, too, was a form of stalking. Someone had stalked and killed Sheila Drury. Now Anna stalked them, dug through their secrets. Murder required so many secrets and secrets were isolating things.

How lonely a life of crime must be, how tempting to tell

someone—anyone—just to break the icy silence. How one might find oneself hinting at the possibilities, talking in What-Ifs and hypothetical questions. The world was designed for people who had no secrets, nothing to hide. One would go through life paying cash, telling lies, and twitching every time the doorbell rang. And, surely, feeling as transparent as glass.

Anna marveled that anyone would choose to be so vulnerable, so nervous. Then it crossed her mind that perhaps it came about not by choice, but simply by failing to say "no" to each sweet and terrifying betrayal till finally there'd be no turning back. Always wanting a little more and a little more till the deed was done, the Rubicon crossed, the die cast.

After a while the crime would take on a life of its own, grow, form partnerships, expectations, financial dependencies until, even should one want out, the sheer inertia would carry them on.

And Anna knew there was a breed of men—and women—who craved the challenge, the adrenaline rush of night actions. The way Rogelio loved ecotage: partly fighting the good fight, partly playing at commandos. There was a breed of criminal who got high on the smell of fear, the warm wet touch of blood.

She stepped off the asphalt and walked the narrow dirt path toward the chain-link fence that surrounded Maintenance.

Was Craig Eastern that crazy? Anna dismissed him from her thoughts. This morning's mission was to investigate Karl Johnson—or, at any rate, his truck.

Karl felt he had been cheated out of the ranger position in Dog Canyon, believed he had been betrayed, that something he had earned and deserved had been snatched away. The National Park Service had very few women in middle or higher management. Women held the lower-paying clerical and seasonal jobs. Word had come down from on high to promote women and people of color whenever possible. The Good Old

Boy contingent thought Karl was just another victim of the plot against white males. Maybe Karl thought so too.

A lot of people went through life feeling they'd been ripped off. The money, the good jobs, the beautiful women, the rich husbands, had been snatched away from them, given to the wrong people.

How many crimes were committed because somebody felt the need to get "some of their own" back? Just to feel, for once, that they had a little control, were a little smarter than the rest?

Human crimes seemed more sordid, yet at the same time infinitely more forgivable, than crimes that were just business as usual; all the profits neatly laundered, washed clean of the victim's blood and vomit before reaching the lined pockets of the three-piece suits.

As she slipped through the gate into the Maintenance Yard, her mind set on a little breaking and entering, Anna wondered if there was a crime she wouldn't commit under the right circumstances. Murder certainly. In fact she was keeping a list of Those Better Off Dead. If she were hungry she would steal. There were betrayals of the heart.

She'd never be cruel to an animal and she wouldn't litter.

"That's as good as it gets," she said to the sun, just edging above the eastern desert; to whatever powers might be listening.

Just after six-thirty a.m. she let herself into the Maintenance building through the shop door. The Roads and Trails crew wouldn't come on duty till seven.

The place smelled of new paint and automotive oil. A smell that she usually found comforting. It put her back in her father's auto shop where she'd played endlessly with nuts and bolts and cotter pins. This morning it only served to remind her she was on alien ground. Technically she had a right to be in the building. The key she'd been issued was an indication of that. Half a dozen times a week she was in and out of Harland's enclave. But this time she'd come to rifle through his files. That shed a different light on the matter. One she didn't much care to be seen in.

Soundlessly, Anna crossed the concrete floor of the shop and tried the door to Harland's office. It was locked. Squinting to cut through the gloom, she peered into the crack between the door and the jamb. The bolt was not thrown. Quick as a cat, she ran to the scrap bin in the carpentry shop and dug through the bits of wood and metal. A triangle of tin caught her eye. Anna grabbed it out of the heap and trotted back to Harland's office.

The tin was better even than a credit card for slipping the catch. In less than a minute, she was inside. There was no point in closing the door behind her. The two windows of Harland's interior office looked out on the auto shop to one side and the carpentry shop on the other. He worked in a fishbowl. Fortunately there were only two filing cabinets. Anna pulled open all six drawers. Too dark to read. "In for a penny . . ." she whispered and flipped on the overhead light.

Harland Roberts was an organized man and Anna blessed him for it. Each hanging file was labeled and color-coded. Aptly enough all pay, overtime, annual leave, and sick leave requests were under money-green tabs.

Anna pulled out the overtime file. The requests, signed in Harland's neat, military hand, were in chronological order, most recent first. She flipped back through them to the seventeenth of June. Nothing. On the fifteenth the mule packer had worked six hours overtime packing fence materials into the backcountry and on the twenty-first Karl had worked two and a half hours overtime fixing a broken water main. No one had worked the night of June 17. There were no extenuating circumstances, no last-minute changes. Karl was in McKittrick Canyon that night on personal business.

Leaving everything as she'd found it, Anna left the office and relocked the door.

Johnson drove a small blue half-ton pickup with metal toolboxes on either side. The truck was parked across the yard near the building where the ambulance and fire truck were housed.

Staring at the mundane little vehicle, Anna realized she wasn't exactly sure what she'd come to look for. Buttons? Threads? Flakes of skin? Soil from Dog Canyon? Hairs? Given the hand-me-down nature of government vehicles, the truck was bound to be a regular treasure trove of human artifacts.

The temptation to turn around, go home, and have another cup of coffee before starting up the Tejas on backcountry patrol was strong. But she had promised Christina she would check it out and she'd risen ninety minutes early to do it.

"Just look," she told herself. "Don't look to find."

Armed with half a dozen plastic sandwich bags she'd grabbed on the off chance something promising did turn up, Anna started with the bed of the little truck.

For a vehicle used primarily for hauling garbage, Karl's truck was quite clean. As she peered at the collection of aluminum pop-tops, cigarette butts, and plastic tent pegs her sweep had turned up, she tried to picture how the pickup, seen—allegedly—in the McKittrick Canyon parking lot from five to ten p.m. on the night of Sheila Drury's murder, the night Karl said he was in Van Horn lifting things down from garage shelves, could have been used.

Sheila, already unconscious or dead, might have been hauled in the back hidden from sight under a tarp or bags of garbage. A small-framed woman, she might have been squeezed into one of the toolboxes. Or she could have been forced into the cab, her pack thrown in the back.

Of the various situations there remained only a few constants. If the truck had been used in the crime and had been used to transport Drury, Anna could look for anything that might indicate the presence of an iridescent green backpack, Sheila herself, or any signs of a struggle.

The truck bed indicated neither the first nor the second possibility and was so battered from years of use that any trace of the third would blend right in.

Anna moved to the cab.

Karl's tidiness ended at the door. From the evidence that met her eye, Anna could have made a case for the man living in his vehicle. Loose papers and empty Gatorade containers covered the seat. The dash held compass, maps, sunglasses, sticky cups, and two monkey wrenches. The floor on the passenger side was ankle-deep in papers and crumpled soda pop cans.

Again Anna considered going home. There was still time for that second cup of coffee.

"Just look."

Careful not to arrange Karl's heap into any tell-tale orderliness, she began picking through the piles. The dash provided nothing more damning than an empty tin of Red Man chewing tobacco. If that were the extent of Karl's sins against society he would go unpunished. At least in West Texas.

Not wanting to slide through the flotsam of Karl's life, Anna got out and went around to check the glove box from the passenger side. She glanced at her watch: 6:45. Soon she must give it up or leave it for another day.

The glove box produced the expected pencils with broken leads, pens without caps, and registration papers. And a hypodermic syringe without a needle.

Anna sniffed at it delicately but only because she'd seen cops on television do it. Unless it was filled with Jean Naté or Windex she doubted she'd learn anything. Hoping Karl wouldn't miss it, that he wasn't diabetic and would die from lack of a syringe, she dropped it in one of her sandwich bags and stowed it in her shirt pocket.

Law Enforcement rangers had only ten weeks of training to a regular cop's sixteen. In the old days, before crime had moved into the parks, it had sufficed. This morning Anna found herself missing that month and a half. Maybe that's when they'd covered Sniffing Suspicious Substances.

With one potential "find" to her credit, the search took on more interest. Scooping up the mess on the seat one section at a time, Anna checked the upholstery. Near where the driver sat was a dark stain on the vinyl. At one time seven or eight drops of red-brown liquid had fallen on the seat. Most of it was smeared away but some had caught in the fabric where the smooth surface had been worn and frayed. If a victim had been stretched across the seat, head on or near the driver's lap, blood from face, neck, or shoulder wounds would have dripped just there.

Excitement trembled in her hands as she scraped up some of the frayed cloth with her pocketknife and stowed the shreds carefully in a fresh sandwich bag. Anna was having fun. Intent upon the hunt, she had forgotten about the big kindly man who gave carrots and sugar to the horses.

Neither the rest of the seat nor the floor offered up any more promising items. On the passenger door, just above the handle, were two long smears of mud. If a victim had lain on the seat as Anna imagined and if she had struggled, the mud from her boots could've smeared the door at just that place.

Feeling like Sherlock Holmes on a good day, she began scraping the mud into a third Baggie. Maybe there was a difference between Dog Canyon dirt on the park's northernmost edge and dirt from Frijole or McKittrick on the southern borders.

"Sorry Miss, but rangers aren't allowed to carve their initials on Roads and Trails vehicles." The voice so startled Anna, she actually squawked like a duck.

Smiling, Harland was looking down through the window glass to where she squatted. His thick dark brows asked the question he seemed too polite to phrase: "What the hell are you doing?"

Anna had no answer. The bag, the knife, the time of day—none could be explained away by even the most ornate lie.

"Good morning, Harland." Straightening up, she folded the knife and slipped the Baggie into her trouser pocket. Anna wracked her brain and drew nothing but blanks. Except for the truth, there was no good reason she could come up with for scraping dirt from the inside of a Maintenance vehicle's door. Harland was waiting while she decided which was the lesser of the two evils: telling him nothing or telling him something—anything.

"There has been a little matter that's been concerning Paul," she began, feeling her way. "Nothing serious. I was hoping a look at the truck would clear it up. Just guesswork and speculation at the moment. If I find out it's a real problem you'll get a full report. If, like I expect, it's just gossip, I'll tell you the whole story over a beer and we'll at least get a good laugh out of it." Hard-eyed, Harland waited for a better explanation. Anna smiled in a way she hoped looked as sheepish as it felt. Nothing is more disarming in a woman than incompetence.

"I'll hold you to that beer," Harland said finally. "And especially that laugh. But right now chivalry's dead. You get to handle Karl all alone. He hates anybody messing with 'his' truck." He nodded toward the gate where Karl, looking like a storm about to break, was hurrying in from the parking lot. Harland gave Anna a wink and, whistling, sauntered across the yard to his office.

Investigative paraphernalia safely tucked out of sight,

Anna had a little more presence of mind. "'Morning, Karl," she said easily. "I left my sunglasses in the barn yesterday. I thought you might have picked them up for me. They were on top of the oat bin."

Karl stared at her for a full three seconds, his face utterly blank, and Anna felt her belly grow cold.

"No," he said. "They weren't there. I gave the mules some oats with their dinner. I'd've seen them."

Anna had no idea whether Karl had been fooled or not but the fun had gone out of the morning as quickly as it had come into it. "Thanks anyway," she said and made her escape.

"Anna, headed back to housing?"

It was Harland. Anna hoped she'd not been obviously hightailing it out of Maintenance.

"Yup. Getting my pack. Backcountry patrol."

"I'll walk with you, keep you safe from the forces of evil." He smiled, his gray eyes taking in the hundred yards of peaceful road between the yard and the housing area. The great threats were a desert cottontail the size of a small boot and two buffer-colored butterflies. "I forgot my radio," he confided in a stage whisper as he fell into step beside her.

Anna laughed. "I do it all the time." She was mildly impressed that he walked. Most of the staff seemed to drive their private cars the quarter-mile to the Maintenance Yard where they traded them for a government vehicle.

"Perfect day for the high country," Harland said wistfully. "I wish I was going with you. Don't ever let them promote you to GS-11," he said earnestly. "You'll be trapped behind a desk forever after."

Anna looked up at the green and brown hills, then the pale cliffs of the escarpment. The tops were fringed black with evergreens robbed of color and shape by distance. "I won't," she said, and meant it.

Harland smiled. His teeth were straight and white but they looked like they were his own.

Fifty is not old, Anna found herself thinking, and wondered why.

Harland reached down, picked up a cigarette butt and put it in his hip pocket. "What has Karl done to get the Ranger Division's notice?" he asked.

Having no credible answer, Anna asked him a question in return. "Speaking of notice, the other day you said something about Craig Eastern being . . . well . . . not quite all here."

"Mentally ill," Harland said bluntly.

"Yes. And to take care of myself. I've given that some thought. Not much, because I don't know what in the hell I'm supposed to make of it. Care to elaborate?"

"Not really," Harland replied.

For a minute, or nearly so, they walked without talking. When they were at the seasonal housing where Anna lived, Harland stopped. She deliberated whether this was some gentlemanly hint that the walk was over or if he'd thought better of keeping the rationale behind his cryptic warning a secret.

It was the latter.

"Please say this will stay between you and me," Harland said, not looking at her. "Because I'm going to tell you anyway and I'd just as soon sleep sound at night."

"It will," Anna promised, hoping she could keep it.

"Craig suffers from paranoid delusions. He's been institutionalized twice for it. He's on medications but he has had violent episodes in the past. You know how he feels about human beings in general, how protective he is of the land. But maybe you didn't know that he particularly fears women. Especially women he is sexually attracted to. He feels women use sexual politics to outdistance him. Just something I wanted you to be aware of, take care about. That's all."

"How do you know?" Anna was embarrassed at how suspicious she sounded. Suspicion was becoming a habit.

"Craig was at the mental institution where my wife lives," Harland said simply. "In Austin."

"Oh," was all Anna could find to say.

Harland Roberts laid a hand on her arm. "It's okay," he said kindly. "They've got trees and flush toilets, chicken on Sunday—everything. It's a far cry from Mrs. Rochester's attic."

Anna nodded and echoed, if a bit weakly, his smile.

"Give my regards to the high country," he said and strode off toward the "real" houses.

"I will," Anna called after him, wanting to give him some return for the confidence.

There was no time for that second cup of coffee. Anna packaged the samples and the hypodermic and sent them to the police lab in Roswell, New Mexico, care of Timothy Dayton. They'd gone to law enforcement school together. He would do it as a favor, eschewing channels.

"Three-eleven; three-one-five en route up the Tejas." Anna radioed in her position then zipped her radio into the side pocket of her pack. It would be good to get into the high country again, up where it was clean. Too many days had been spent down among people.

With each step up the glaring limestone of the Tejas Trail, she felt a thread break; one of the peevish tethers of social and professional minutiae snap. Alone, in the backcountry, politics, sex, murder, and all their derivations would fade. They never vanished entirely; mostly the clamor just dulled, like the roar of trucks on 62/180 that poured endless trailer-tank loads of natural gas into Mexico.

One day, Anna thought, she would walk far enough, go

deep enough, stay long enough, that the toxins of humanity would finally work completely out of her system, leaving her mind new again. That would be the trip she would never return from. Molly would find her living on roots and berries, wearing nothing but a loincloth and humming a mantra in some mountaintop cave.

Anna smiled at the picture. Molly in Italian pumps and a Giorgio Armani suit standing in the mesquite, cigarette in hand.

Someday.

Bucolic splendor, peace of mind, oneness with Nature, all the elevated thoughts buoying Anna up the endless switchbacks of the Tejas, evaporated as she rounded the sharp bend above Devil's Hallway.

Shaded from the rays of the morning sun by a fist of wind-carved stone, Craig Eastern sat with his back to a rock and his legs across the trail. The bill of a white baseball cap with the green fist of the EARTH FIRST! logo emblazoned on it covered his eyes. Muscular neck and shoulders, displayed nicely by a gray tank top, sloped down from small flat ears.

Anna stopped several feet from him and waited. Of course he had heard her crunching ascent. One did not sneak in lug-soled boots and a heavy pack. Head down, he was scribbling in a little yellow notebook. When he'd finished he snapped it shut with a gesture reminiscent of Captain Kirk snapping shut his communicator.

"Howdy, Anna," he said solemnly, looking up. He smiled and it was as if an elf or a child suddenly took over the man's body. His dark eyes glowed, his lips curved in a sweet smile exposing small, even, very white teeth. One cheek dimpled.

Because of this man—or, more accurately, because of what Harland had told her about him—Anna had been locking her door nights. At that moment Eastern couldn't have looked less like an antisocial psychotic or more like an appealing boy. His thirty-six years had scarcely marked his face and, with the cap, the thinning hair was hidden.

Surely, she thought, no one with that choirboy grin would do any real damage.

"Howdy, Craig," she echoed. She wanted to be friendly, easy with him, but she knew too many things she had no right to know. Things that made her look past the smile and the dimple; made her look for the insanity that Roberts assured her lurked behind what they'd all accepted as yet one more form of the desert lunacy that made the Southwest a place of heroes, tall tales, and strange truths.

"Backcountry patrol," he informed her of her mission, then tapped the zipper pocket of his daypack where the rubber antennae of an NTS Motorola protruded. "I heard."

"Carrying a radio on your day off. I'm impressed." Anna shrugged out of her pack and squatted in the trail, her butt on her heels. She'd learned to balance flat-footed like that for hours. A cheap seat, better than the bleachers, a visitor from Cairo with whom she'd hiked briefly had assured her. "On my days off I hide out," she said, making conversation.

"No," Craig contradicted her. "I've heard you going with Paul on ambulance runs. Do you like saving people?"

The question was almost a challenge. The dimple flashed but Anna had been reminded that Craig had an edge. How sharp that edge was she had yet to find out. Because the question interested her, she gave it serious consideration before answering. "I like being good at it," she said carefully. "I don't feel much one way or another about the people. Maybe because it's easier that way."

"Maybe because you don't care?" Craig asked shrewdly.

Anna just smiled. "What's this I hear about UFOs on the West Side?" she asked, hoping to lighten the conversation.

Momentarily, he looked confused, then his face clouded. "Harland?"

Anna didn't reply.

"I'm real sick of his bullshit," Craig fumed. "I saw something and everybody makes this big joke. I saw green lights, moving low, and heard these thumping sounds, like footsteps. I was a mile or so away, I couldn't see clear. They'll be back. So will I. With a camera. Harland's a bastard."

His anger had effectively silenced Anna. For a while she stared down the mountain to the straight-sided stones of Devil's Hallway, trying to think of a graceful way to escape.

"Paul told me about you and the lion hunt," Craig said abruptly, clearly wanting to change the subject as much as she did. "Corinne's pissed. You're not playing the game, Anna."

Again he smiled. He gave them out like earned sweets. Despite what Anna had once called her "better judgment," she was charmed.

"You won't climb the NPS ladder that way." The smile winked out, the choirboy, the elf vanished. In their place was a young man wound a little too tight, eyes glittering too brightly, muscles strung too taut. As he spoke, the slight ducking of the head, the defensive twitch of the shoulder that Anna always thought of when she pictured him returned.

"Don't climb, Anna," he said. "They're hypocrites: Corinne, that damn Christina, Roberts, Karl with his good-old-boy act. Especially Corinne. She'd pave the whole park if she thought it'd get her the nod from the Regional Office. She's using Guadalupe to get a superintendency somewhere. She'd kill every cougar in Texas for a line on her resume."

Though it wasn't entirely unexpected, his outburst startled Anna. Rocking back on her heels, she watched the working of his facial muscles. "Institutionalized for paranoid delusions," flashed though her mind.

Probing, experimenting with the effect of words, of ideas, on Craig's volatile emotions, Anna said: "The Park Service has its share of losers, no doubt about that. It makes the loss of Sheila Drury the more tragic. She was a first-class ranger. The Park Service needs more like her."

Her eyes fixed on him unwaveringly. For an instant she thought she'd gone fishing in a dead lake. Then the calm masking his features began rippling like the surface of a pond when, deep in the waters, creatures are struggling.

Finally the underwater beast broke free and it was Rage. "Drury was a whore!" Eastern spat the words out as if each was formed new, hot, bitter for Drury's condemnation. "She'd've carved up Dog Canyon, turned it into a Safeway parking lot just to advertise herself. She didn't care about this place. She never hiked or camped. If she couldn't ride her horse in, forget it. She was on her way up. She was a whore. To her everything was sexual. She used it. She was one of Corinne's 'little girls'—"

Craig seemed to notice then that Anna, more than merely listening, was studying him as an entomologist might study an exotic insect. Abruptly, he ceased speaking. In a quick, scrabbling motion, he scooped his book into his daypack and stood up.

Anna stayed in her squat, aware that on the steep-sided trail she was safer with her center of gravity close to the ground.

Craig squeezed his bulky shoulders into the pack's straps. "They'll sell out the park," he said, his voice subdued, sad. "Like they sold out Big Bend, Big Thicket. It's just a matter of time. There's not many places left to run to. They're selling out the world."

With that, he shambled past and around the bend out of sight. For long moments Anna remained where she was.

What stayed with her was the sadness and the elfin smile.

"The high country," she said aloud. Rising, she shouldered her pack and, celebrating each step that she put between herself and the seemingly all-pervasive psychosis of humanity, began to climb.

# CHAPTER 11

In the pines, pygmy nuthatches and mule deer for companions, the breezes blew away thought and Anna achieved the peace she'd come to depend on the wilderness for. In place of doubt and suspicion came yellow butterflies feeding incongruously at fox dung. Unself-conscious as a bird, she whistled, lending human notes to the sweet cacophony of the woods.

Perhaps planted there by Karl Johnson, maybe in her mind since childhood, Anna found tongue and lips forming the music from the score of *Peter Pan*. Haunted by the nursery melody, again and again she whistled the notes, the words floating through her mind as she walked the trails. "Tender shepherd, tender shepherd, let me help you count your sheep. One in the meadow, two in the garden, three in the nursery fast asleep." The song tickled some memory. Far from being nagged by it, Anna enjoyed a sense of elusive comfort.

On the third day the comfort was remembered.

The melody she had heard—or imagined she had—in Big Canyon when she was searching for the orphaned lion cubs, was the first four notes of "Tender Shepherd." If she didn't think but only felt, she could almost believe a kindly cosmic shepherd looked after the lost kittens.

On the third day, happier than she'd been for a while, she radioed in her itinerary and began the sixteen-mile hike out. She'd chosen the long way: across the Bowl on the Tejas then south on the McKittrick Ridge Trail.

McKittrick Ridge was a favorite walk of hers. The rugged trail wound for miles above the south fork of McKittrick Canyon. A mile to the north, hidden behind wooded hills, was Middle McKittrick, where Drury had died. And, once she began the long descent, she would catch glimpses of the white escarpment above North McKittrick, the third prong of the three-tined canyon fork.

Near four o'clock, she came out of the trees and looked down the three thousand feet into the bottom of McKittrick Canyon. The creek sparkled suddenly silver where it surfaced, left a white stone trail when it vanished underground. Big-tooth maple, ponderosa, gray-leaf oak, Texas madrone, and juniper veiled the canyon floor. Above, where North McKittrick forked off, she could see great ribs of the Permian Reef, pocked with sotol and yucca, pushing into this water-fed paradise. White bones at the oasis.

"I'm starting down the ridge," Anna radioed Cheryl Light, the ranger on duty in the canyon that day. "I should be at the Visitors Center at about six-thirty. I'll need a ride back to the housing area."

"Somebody will be there," Light returned.

"Thanks. Three-one-five clear." For a couple of minutes more Anna enjoyed the view. Then, shouldering her pack, she started down again to the battering, badgering world of people.

The trail carved a descent in rocky switchbacks, dropping through biomes with delightful rapidity. The air grew perceptibly warmer. In places the trail was so steep a crew, now twenty years gone—probably pediatricians and ranch hands, mechanics and alcoholics by this time—had blasted steps from the living stone.

Moist and alive with grasses and succulents, the flank of the mountain protected Anna's right shoulder as she walked downhill. To her left a cliff dropped away for three hundred feet. Madrone and juniper, stunted dwarves of their highland selves, clung courageously to the few small ledges. Another thousand feet of scrub and brush then below that was water: the splendor of the desert.

Trees grew in the creekbed and up ravines that would pour their floodwaters into McKittrick come the monsoons. By the end of October the maples—rare but for this water-blessed enclave—would turn crimson. The ravines would be as red as if they ran with blood. Then, for two brief weeks, the Guadalupe Mountains would be overrun with Texans starved for fall colors.

Periwinkle blue sky, sparkling white thunderheads beginning to form, heat, and insect buzz formed a dream around Anna as she walked down the rocky incline, boots sure and flat on the stone.

Then the stone was gone, sky and cliff face reeling. She had stepped from the trail into nothing. Her left boot had struck sky instead of earth and she was pitching sideways. With a sickening sense of the world gone awry, she fell as if in a nightmare. "Damn," she whispered, her mind not yet grasping the hideous reality.

For ninety feet or so the cliff was not sheer but sloped steeply away in a limestone slide. From there it dropped two hundred feet to another wooded section. Anna twisted in air, tried to regain the safety of the path but the thirty-five pounds on her back threw her over the edge. She flung her arms out but the pack kept her on her back like an overturned beetle. All she could do was flail.

The slick nylon on the limestone reduced friction to almost nothing and Anna slid down toward the drop. Pressing hands and heels into the stone, she slowed her skid. Rock tore the flesh from her palms. On some level she was aware of the damage but not the pain.

Below, over the toes of her boots, she could see a gray horizon. The end of the slope. The end of the world.

With an effort that tore a scream from her lungs, she shoved out with left leg and arm. Fueled by adrenaline, it seemed as if every muscle in her body contracted and the sudden spasm flipped her over onto her belly. Spread-eagled, the pockmarked limestone ripping her clothes, Anna tried to stop her slide. Her shirt was dragged up, her flesh caught and burned. Screaming now, her fingers were stiff as claws scrabbling at the rock.

Then the claws caught. A bone or joint snapped in her shoulder and sudden pain almost loosed her fingers but she held on. A ledge, scarcely an inch wide where the limestone had cracked and the weather had heaved a part out ever so slightly, provided purchase for her fingers.

For a moment, Anna hung there, her bleeding chest and belly pressed against the sun-warmed stone, her torn finger-ends driven against the tiny ledge. Below her she heard the sweet simple call of the canyon wren. She was aware of the sun on the back of her legs and the sheer bliss of simply being still, suspended above death. Gradually she became conscious of the drag of the pack on her shoulders, the searing pain in her left arm socket.

It was dislocated. Soon, bone pressing against the soft tissue of nerves outside the socket, the arm would grow numb, she would lose control of her fingers, and she would fall.

Die from a dislocated shoulder, Anna thought and wondered how strangely a mind worked under pressure to think such things.

Carefully, not knowing how much her belabored grip would bear, she began to feel blindly across the rockface with the toe of her boot. Each small swipe of lug sole over the stone threatened to dislodge her precarious grasp. Her fingers began to uncurl, the strength draining out of them, turning to pain and pooling in her shoulder joint.

Then her foot found something: a root an inch or two high pushing out of a crack. Enough to hold her without breaking.

"Hang on, hang on, hang on," Anna chanted silently as she began to look for footing for her right boot. This time the search was not long. A narrow crevice ran vertically down through the stone eight or ten inches to her right. With a short stabbing kick she drove the toe of her boot between the jaws of stone. Slowly, pound by pound, she lowered her weight to her feet. Her right foot slipped then stopped, resting on a natural step within the crack.

Braced on her feet, Anna pressed herself into the rock and uncurled her fingers. They moved stiffly as if the joints had rusted in their clenched attitudes. Freed, her left arm fell and Anna screamed with the pain. Gripping tightly with her good hand, she prayed she wouldn't overbalance or faint.

Behind her eyelids red dots danced and she felt again as though she were falling. Squeezing against the rockface, she leaned to the left, letting her arm hang. If the dislocation weren't too severe the limb's own weight might pull it back into the socket. She tried to remember how long her Emergency Medicine instructor said it took, but her mind would not fix on the past.

With her arm lowered, Anna could see where she was. Above was the trail. Sixty feet below, the mountain dropped away. She could see the bright backs of violet-green swallows swooping high above the canyon floor. The crack she'd wedged her foot into ran from the trail to the drop. Near the top it was only an inch wide, widening as it descended until it was several feet across where it broke on the lip of the cliff.

Anna heard rather than felt her humerus bone go back into the socket, heard through her skeleton and not her ears. The pain subsided. "Thankyoubabyjesus," she murmured, and for once she wasn't being irreverent.

Awareness of the one pain was replaced by another. Blood was oozing from the scrapes on her belly and breasts. Fervently she hoped it would dry like glue, stick her fast to the rock. What chance, she wondered, was there to pluck herself from this rocky crucifix without losing her grip and falling?

Still, she was alive. That one fact made all the difference. Her mind started working again.

Fifty feet of nylon cord and a good long-bladed knife were in her pack. They made up part of the weight that was trying to drag her from her fragile fingernail grip on life. The cord would be just about behind her neck coiled neatly through the handle of her first-aid kit. The knife was in the kit. A half a dozen feet above and to the right a couple of yards a dwarfed gray-leaf oak had shoved roots deep into the crack in the rock. The tree was only three or four feet tall but if the spring winds and the summer rains had not dislodged it, Anna guessed it would hold her weight. With the knife and the cord she might, with luck, rig a safety line.

But the knife and cord, four inches behind her right ear, might as well have been at home on the top shelf of the closet. If she released the buckles of the pack it would fall away, down two hundred and forty feet and the kit with it. If she tried to manhandle it, both she and the pack would fall. Soon, she knew, she must cut the pack loose. Her own weight would be more than she could support in the not too distant future.

Mentally, Anna frisked herself, searching for other tools. All she came up with were lip balm, a watch, and her tiny pocketknife. The knife was less than two inches long, weighed nothing: no good for throwing, wedging, or clawing. If she had an envelope that needed opening it would be just the thing, Anna thought acidly. It occurred to her then that, in a way, that was just what she did have. The muscles of her calves were beginning to tremble. She must do something while she was still able.

Working her hand into her pocket, risking no movement that would shake her precarious foundations, Anna fished the little knife out and opened it with her teeth. The small blade, kept razor sharp, cut through the nylon of the pack just above the shoulder strap fairly easily. When the slash was half a foot long, Anna pocketed the knife and pushed her hand over her shoulder through the material. The kit was there. She worked it out though the hole and clamped its soft handles in her teeth.

With infinite care, she pulled both shoulder straps free of their buckles and, holding them so the pack would not roll back and drag her with it, she undid the buckle of her hip belt. The instant it snapped free, she released the shoulder straps and dug her fingers into the ledge.

The pack fell back, bumped her legs, slid down the stone, and was gone.

Anna remained. For the first time she dared to think she was really going to make it. This hope of survival made the prospect of any mistake so terrifying that for a moment she couldn't move, not even to open her eyes.

From above, the sound of gravel grinding underfoot caught her up with sudden wild relief. "Help, help me," she called around the canvas straps between her teeth. The crunching changed tenor. It wasn't the footfall of a timely savior. The stone-on-stone ringing was caused by a rock the size of a cantaloupe rolling down the slope.

"Fuck!" Anna yelled and pressed her cheek tightly against

the limestone. The rock struck her behind the ear; a fist punching her from consciousness, from life. As the blackness took her she felt her fingers slipping from the ledge, her feet from their pathetic supports. In the millisecond before she lost herself, Anna was aware of a great and futile anger.

Then that, too, was gone.

# CHAPTER 12

Somehow Anna thought death wouldn't hurt this bad. She'd always pictured the Great Beyond as an unfathomable nothing; like trying to see from the tip of one's finger or smell with one's knees.

This was pain, the old familiar earthly variety.

Quite a lot of it.

For what seemed like a long while, less than quick but more than dead, Anna lived around this ache. Slowly it came to her that she could open her eyes. There was light, gray uniform light, but no shapes or colors. Vague images of a cloud-filled Heaven taken from childhood Sunday-school books drifted in her mind; images incomplete and faded.

But Heaven would be cool and it wouldn't hurt.

A shadow marred the cloudscape and Anna turned her face. Stone grated against her mouth. An ant, small and black and six-legged, crawled across the universe. Anna knew then that she lay facedown on the limestone and that she probably had to die all over again.

It had been too damned hard the first time.

She forced her mind clear. "Primary survey," she whispered. "I'm breathing. I'm conscious. I'm bleeding." There was a dark stain on her shoulder and her braid painted thin red lines on the pale rock. Her left arm wasn't working too well. The shoulder joint felt as if it was full of broken glass, but it did function. Collarbone cracked, she thought; tissues damaged from the dislocation.

Moving as little as possible, she looked around her. She had fallen to the bottom of the slope. No more than a yard, two at the most, separated her from the two-hundred-foot drop. She lay at a forty-five-degree angle on a natural lip, a meager flaring of stone, that marked the cliff's edge. A rock or root—something protruding from the limestone—had kept her from sliding over the edge when her heavy leather service belt caught on it. It felt as if the protrusion had pierced and ripped her abdomen, but she wasn't sure.

Pain and fatigue were calling her back into darkness but she refused to go. Focusing on the ant, making bets—if he reaches that shadow, I'll live; if he goes around that blade of grass I'll wake and find it was all a dream—Anna stayed conscious.

The ant went around the blade of grass and she didn't wake. A blade of grass. Grass had to have something to grow from: soil, a ledge, a crack. As her mind focused on that, she began to see more clearly.

The blade of grass was growing on a little flat space three or four feet wide. This step had been cut into the cliff when the rock above had fallen away. A crack ran upward from it forming a chimney of stone several feet deep and as many across.

The platform at the bottom of the chimney was less than a yard from where Anna hung. If she could reach it she could rest, safe on the floor of this tiny, three-sided, ceilingless room.

She stretched her right arm out. Her fingers just curled around the sharp edge of the broken rock, but it was a solid grip. The toe of her right boot reached to the crevice floor. Gingerly, she tried dragging herself toward safety but the belt that had saved her life now held her fast and the pain in her gut threatened to overwhelm her.

She lay still wanting to cry but unable to focus even on self-pity. Giving up was seductive: a moment of fear, then an end to fighting. Fleetingly, she wondered if death were a narcotic, if inside her death and adrenaline waged a small-scale chemical war, fighting for her will.

Involuntarily her left foot twitched and several pieces of gravel were sent down the mountain. An instant of sound; an eternity of silence. Anna was not yet ready for the eternal silence.

Adrenaline won.

Twisting her injured arm, almost welcoming the clean ache of grating bone, she crawled her fingers along the stone until she had worked her hand underneath her belly. She could feel the smooth metal of her belt buckle. It was hung up on what felt like a post. Once free of it, she would have one chance to jerk her body the two feet to the crack. If she slipped or her strength failed or her clothing snagged, she would slide off the edge.

Two hundred feet.

A cold rush of fear froze her as surely as an arctic wind and for a moment Anna could neither see nor breathe. When it passed, it left her weakened.

Now or never, she thought. Bucking away from the stone, she pushed at the buckle with cramped fingers. For an instant it remained caught. Then with awful suddenness she was free and slipping. With strength born of desperation, she dragged the weight of her body across the limestone. When her face cleared the vertical lip, she saw an upright slab within, a powerful handhold. Seizing it, she tumbled into the crack in the rock.

"Oh God, oh God, oh God," she heard herself saying when she became cognizant and she laughed. "Oh God for a chamber pot." The inevitable adrenaline reaction was setting in.

Nausea was next, then trembling weakness. Then pain reasserted its dominion. Anna took stock of her situation. Looking out, back across the smooth limestone she could see the protrusion that had broken her slide: a knob of iron ore an inch and a half high. The natural ore, harder than limestone, remained like an upthrust thumb when the rock had eroded away. Anna's NPS belt had snagged on it.

Delicately, she unbuckled her belt and unzipped her hiking shorts. The iron had not broken the skin but a dark red welt ran up her abdomen. Where the iron had caught under the buckle her flesh was already turning dark purple. With torn fingers, she palpated her belly. There was pain but no rigidity. A good sign there was no internal bleeding. Training started to take over, Anna falling into the secondary survey pattern she'd been taught to use to assess for injury.

She stopped herself with a snort. No one would find her where she was, halfway down a mountain, hidden in a hole, her pack tumbled into the thickets a couple hundred feet below. Shouts would not carry up the cliff nor down to the canyon floor. What difference did it make if she were badly injured or not? Her belly hurt, her head hurt, her left shoulder was killing her and so what? She must climb.

Bracing one foot against each wall of the stone chimney, she began working her way up. Ten feet and she was singing "Itsy bitsy spider" to blank the pain from her mind. Fifteen and her legs began to tremble. Fear of falling slowed her inching progress. Thirty feet up there was a narrow shelf she could brace her butt on and, the weight off her legs, she rested.

Afraid to stop too long lest her strained muscles begin to cramp, Anna pushed herself on before many minutes had passed. Blood was dripping down her neck on the left side but the drip was slow. She had no idea how much was blood and how much sweat. Salt burned deep into the scrapes on her chest.

"That which does not kill us, makes us strong," she repeated. It was her mother-in-law's favorite aphorism, but she didn't believe it. "That which does not kill us, does not kill us," she amended and squeezed upward foothold by foothold, her body the wedge that kept her from falling back down.

Forty-five feet and the crevice began to narrow. For a little while the going was easier. Then the chimney was gone. The stone above, weakened from weathering in the cracked surface, had fallen away. A gigantic chip of limestone had broken off leaving ledges, like shelves, tapering away from the chimney's top. A shallow crack several inches wide was all that remained of the chimney. It ran the last three yards to the trail.

Anna braced herself and let her breathing slow. There was no advantage in going back down, even if she could have. Up then. Eight, maybe nine feet. Close enough she could call for help and be heard. But there was no help and Anna doubted she had the strength to stay braced for more than an hour at most.

This is probably it, she thought, I will probably die. "I may die," she said aloud to see how it sounded. Absurd but true. "Don't think about it."

She worked one foot up onto the tiny ledge then drove her hand into the narrow crevice and made a fist. The flesh jammed tight and she pulled herself up till she was standing one foot on the ledge to either side of the chimney.

Ignoring the pain in her injured shoulder, she drove her left hand into the crack above her right and made a fist, a wedge of finger bones. Pulling herself up, she scrabbled for footholds. The stone, broken here, less weathered, gave better purchase. Hand over hand, skin scraped away by the rock, Anna dragged herself up.

A snapping sound beneath her left shoulder shot fire up into her brain, but her right hand was on the bole of a small tree at the trail's edge and her feet were solidly placed. With an effort that dragged a grunting cry from her, Anna rolled onto the welcome cradling rocks of McKittrick Ridge Trail.

It was good to lie still, to hurt in peace, to be alive. Soon, though, the kindly rocks of the trail grew sharp, digging into her back. Flies swarmed around the oozing scrapes on her body. Thirst dragged her back from drifting dreams of rescue.

Anna shoved her useless arm into her shirt front and buttoned it there with the three remaining buttons. Step by step she stumbled down the familiar trail. Somewhere near the bottom, a round face under the shapeless cloth brim of a fishing hat swam into view. Beneath it, Anna was dimly aware of a woman with pure white curling hair wearing a lime-green T-shirt.

"Pardon me," Anna said and was surprised at how human she still sounded, "but could you do me a favor?"

Evidently she could. When next Anna opened her eyes it was Cheryl Light's face she saw.

"You're doing good," Cheryl said, her square, seamed face as comforting as some generic mom's. "We're taking you out. We'll be to the first water crossing in a minute. You're doing good."

"Good," Anna repeated. Tree branches flowed overhead. She was in the Stokes litter being trundled home. Anna was glad it was Cheryl Light. She hadn't anything against Cheryl. As consciousness drifted away again, Anna wondered what it was she had against everyone else.

# CHAPTER 13

Widespread but not deadly was how the doctor at the Carlsbad Hospital had described Anna's injuries. Her collarbone was cracked, her abdomen badly bruised, she had a slight concussion and severe contusions on her hands, legs, and torso.

Two days in the hospital for observation and she could go home. The first day she was called a "lucky girl" and a "brave girl" so often she was ready to punch somebody. When Rogelio appeared, a cold quart of Ballena and two flat loaves of Mexican sweet bread in a paper bag, Anna began to feel a little less vicious. When he kissed her and said: "Jesus, but you're one hell of a strong woman," she began to feel downright cheerful. At least till the tears came. But they were slow and healing. The kind she could laugh through and mean it. She was not utterly alone. Life no longer hung by a fingernail.

Rogelio pressed her bandaged palm to his lips. Beneath her fingertips she could feel the rough stubble on his cheek. "All the perfume in Arabia couldn't sweeten this little hand," he said and smiled. "See. Not a complete illiterate."

Anna laughed. "Because, like Lady Macbeth's, it is drenched in blood?"

"Whatever," he said. He dipped his finger in a tear caught in the corner of her mouth. Delicately, he dabbed it behind his ear and, though she would've liked to cry for another hour—another day—to flush the fear and helplessness from her soul, she found herself smiling.

Rogelio brought the Ballena and the bread to her table. They looked rustic, real in contrast to the formidable efficiency of the stainless-steel tray. Anna took some of the bread but shook her head when Rogelio passed her the beer. "I'm on drugs."

"Ah." Rogelio didn't seem displeased to have the beer to himself. "Seen God yet?"

"Wrong kind of drugs," Anna replied. "But then I don't feel like hell anymore. I'll take that and be happy."

"You're pretty beat up, Anna. We'll make love like porcupines for a while."

At present she felt she'd never again want to be touched anywhere on her person with anything more forceful than a feather duster. Even through the painkillers, she knew she hurt. Knowing the feeling would pass, Anna smiled and said nothing.

"Tell me what happened," Rogelio said.

Anna pushed her thoughts back to McKittrick Ridge. Her mind's eye was not seeing too clearly. "Not much to tell," she said after a moment. "I got careless. Just stepped into space is what it felt like. With the pack I couldn't recover my balance and fell over. Then a rock busted loose and hit me." She tried to remember the exact sequence of events and failed. "Then Gertrude died and Hamlet died and Laertes died and everybody else lived happily ever after," she finished.

Rogelio kissed her gently as if she were made of glass. "Whatever they're giving you, save some for me."

What sounded like the report of an automatic weapon rattled outside the window and Anna started. "Firecrackers," Rogelio explained soothingly. "The kids are gearing up. Tomorrow is the Fourth of July."

The third of July: Anna's mind turned on the date.

"What is it, *querida*?" Rogelio asked. "Why so sad?"

"Today Zach would have been forty." Usually Anna forbore speaking of Zachary. Not just to Rogelio, but to anyone. The drugs had lowered her defenses.

For a while Rogelio said nothing. He finished the Ballena, stared out of the second-story window. Beyond, where the low hills north of Carlsbad met the sky, afternoon thunderheads were beginning to build.

"My birthday was a week ago yesterday," he said finally. "June twenty-fifth."

"Happy birthday," Anna said and: "I didn't know."

"You never bothered to ask," he said evenly, his eyes still on the thunderclouds. "I turned thirty-two." Anna hadn't bothered to ask about that, either. "To get your undivided attention, it seems a person has got to die. I'm not willing to go quite that far." He rose, put the empty beer bottle in the front pouch pocket of the Mexican-made cotton pullover he wore. The hospital could not be trusted to recycle the glass.

"I'm glad you came." Anna felt lost and guilty and tired. "I'll try to pay more attention."

"Don't knock yourself out." He kissed her and left.

Anna promised herself she would take better care of him. She would make a plan. First, though, she must sleep. "Happy birthday, Zach," she whispered as the drugs took her back.

She dreamt of trying to call him, of standing in a phone-booth at the corner of Fifty-second and Ninth, but the street gangs had spray-painted over his number and the holes on the dial phone didn't match up with the digits.

Anna was awakened to eat a supper not worth being conscious for and again, later, to take a sleeping pill. By the next morning when a nurse, a woman in her fifties who managed by some miracle of personal grooming to make the white polyester nurse's uniform look chic, poked her head in to say: "Want a visitor?" Anna did.

The drugged sleep had obliterated the memory of much of Rogelio's visit but Anna was left with a vague sense that she needed to make amends.

She was not to have the chance. It was Christina and Alison. Alison had a hand-drawn get well card with a camel on it. She'd wanted to draw Gideon to keep Anna company while she was sick, but she was better at camels so she drew a camel with "Gideon" carefully lettered in a cartoon bubble coming out of its mouth.

"I fed Piedmont. Your door was unlocked," Christina said.

"You lifted down the sack. *I* fed Piedmont," Alison corrected her mother.

Christina winked at Anna. The gesture seemed rakish on her serene countenance.

"Credit where credit is due," Anna said. "Thank you both."

"We stayed and petted him for one half of a hour," Alison added. "I kissed him on his head." That seemed to finish the subject in the child's mind. The top of her head disappeared from Anna's sight below the foot of the bed and sounds of rummaging ensued. Something ordinary being converted into a toy, Anna guessed.

"Thank you," she repeated, this time for Christina's ear alone.

Christina had brought a change of clothes, a comb and

brush, hand mirror, colored hairbands, and some "Safari" cologne. "It seemed more fitting than 'White Shoulders,'" she explained.

Again, Anna started to cry. "Damn," she cursed herself and immediately regretted the fist she pounded into the coverlet in accompaniment. Pain shot up her shoulder and neck and into her skull. "I'm turning into a weeping willow," she complained.

"Heaven forbid!" Christina returned with easy laughter. "We can't have Anna Pigeon The Great And Terrible in tears. What is the world coming to? Here," she arranged Anna's pillows and, standing beside the bed, began to brush out her hair. "Hold this."

Anna held one pigtail in her hand while Christina French-braided the other side into a neat plait. "Already I'm feeling healthier, more together. The next braid might perform miracles. Where did you learn to do that?"

"Well, you can either go to beauty school or have a four-year-old daughter who is a little V. A. I. N."

"Vee, ay, eye, en: vain," Alison chanted by rote from the floor, where she'd dragged Anna's hiking boots from the closet.

Anna laughed. It hurt.

"Well, well," Christina said. "We learn something every day. So. Learn me. What happened? I thought you were Ms. Backwoodswoman, able to leap tall trees at a single bound."

"Fell off the trail," Anna replied. "Heavy gravity area." She was rewarded for the feeble and plagiarized witticism by the warmth of Christina's smile. She enjoyed even its reflection in the hand mirror where she watched the other woman's porcelain fingers weave her hair. "Will you come do my hair every morning till my collarbone heals?" Anna teased.

"Yes," Christina said simply and Anna believed her. "You

don't whine half as much as Alison does when I pull too hard."

"Comb too hard, Momma," came a correction from the floor. "You make groves in people's heads."

"Grooves," Christina said mildly. "Gee, are, oh, oh, vee, ee, ess: grooves."

"Grooves," Alison repeated obediently and added: "In people's heads. Look! Magic! Alley shazam!" She stood. Anna could just see her head over the foot of the bed. The little girl held her finger out, a rock balanced on the tip. Slowly, she turned it over. The rock didn't fail off. "A sticky rock," she explained, as if to free her mother and Anna from unbearable suspense. With her other hand she plucked the magic rock from her finger and stuck it on her tongue.

"Alison!" her mother cried. "Stop that. For heaven's sake! You know better." If she hadn't held three strands of half-plaited hair strung through her fingers, Anna didn't doubt that she would have vaulted the bed and made the little girl spit the rock into her hand.

Unperturbed, Alison lifted the bit of gravel carefully off her tongue and stuck it on the bed's footboard. "Tastes like the paste in Dottie's toy box," she said.

Christina wrapped Anna's braids into a graceful figure eight and pinned them in place. As she put away the comb and mirror, Anna dabbed on a little cologne. She hoped Rogelio would come back. But not just now. She looked in the other woman's guileless face. The dark eyes were opaque today. "After the lion-taming episode, I was afraid you wouldn't ever speak to me again," Anna said.

"I thought about it," Christina admitted. "Sometimes you are such a pain in the pasta fazzouli, Anna!"

"Why did you come today?"

"I don't know. To clear my good name?" Christina smiled as she folded herself gracefully into the uncompromising right angles of the red plastic visitors' chair. "You're hurt. I like you. I'm here."

"Thanks," was all Anna could manage but it was, at least, sincere.

"I wouldn't take that kind of abuse from a lesser person, you know," Christina said. "I hope you're duly flattered."

"I hope you never take any abuse from anybody, ever," Anna said seriously. Christina looked a little startled at her vehemence, and Anna wondered if she'd hit a nerve.

"Will you come shoot anyone who tries?" Christina teased.

"No problem."

"Why, Anna Pigeon!" Christina said lightly. "I do believe you care. Say you'll come visit me in prison after you put me away for killing my lover."

"It's a promise. I'll bake you a cake with a file in it every year on your birthday."

Then they talked of baking, both glad to change the subject.

Christina and Alison stayed another hour, an hour that passed quickly for Anna. She was sorry to see them leave.

When she was again alone, she looked at the mail that Christina had brought. Too tired to read but not sleepy, she flipped through bills and credit card offers. Near the bottom of the tidy bundle was a phone message from the police lab in Roswell, New Mexico, where she'd sent the samples scraped from Karl's truck. All the note said was Tim Dayton had called and the number.

The next item was a blue, sealed, For Your Eyes Only envelope. Inside Anna found a copy of the four-page autopsy report on Sheila Drury. Paul had finally come through. She set the report aside to be read when her mind was sharper.

Last in the pile was a packet of photos. The pictures Anna had sent in a mailer to Kodak from Ranger Drury's camera. She opened the package. There was nothing of interest:

photos of cholla in bloom, several shots of Gabe—the Dog Canyon horse—being shod by Karl, and four pictures of lightning over the hills north of Dog Canyon all taken from funky, artsy angles.

Rogelio didn't come and Anna began to feel depressed. Merely the drugs wearing off, she told herself. Partly, at least, that was true. From the crown of her head to the soles of her feet, she hurt.

Irritably, she rang the nurse and demanded more painkillers. She was given two Advils.

Simply to spite consciousness, Anna tried to sleep. She had almost attained her goal of temporary oblivion when she was pulled from the confused dreams of half-sleep by a tap on the door. Optimism kept her eyes closed for a second; in her drowsiness she hoped Zach would be standing at the foot of her bed.

Reality came with its usual quick brutality. Zach vanished. Anna opened her eyes, fully awake.

Harland Roberts stood in the doorway. He leaned against the doorframe. The setting sun, slanting through the hospital windows, dyed the white streaks at his temples a rich gold and glowed on his sunburnt skin.

Surprise cleansed Anna's mind of the lingering cobwebs of dreams. Two emotions filled her, neither of which was particularly welcome: an annoyingly girlish pleasure at the sight of the hothouse flowers held negligently down by his thigh, and a sudden rushing love of Christina Walters for dressing her hair and giving her cologne.

"A bribe," Harland said. When he smiled the resemblance to Stewart Granger was startling. He held up the flowers. Yellow roses. "Can I buy your silence?"

"I'm easy," Anna said.

"I doubt that," he returned and there was that in his voice that would've made Anna blush if she'd been the blushing kind. He confiscated her water pitcher and began arranging the flowers with an expert domesticity that seemed natural to him. "My wife is a decorator— was a decorator," he amended and ducked his head to his work so Anna couldn't read his face.

"Yellow rose of Texas," Anna said. She could see the smile wrinkle the skin high on his cheekbone. "What am I to keep quiet about?"

He stopped his deft fiddling and looked straight at her, his gray eyes unwavering. "That stretch of trail above Turtle Rock should've been brushed and leveled. I've been meaning to send someone up to do it. I put it off. You could've been killed. It's fixed now. Nothing like shutting the barn door after the cows get out."

Anna was touched, tears again threatening. Damn the drugs, she thought, choosing to blame chemistry rather than psychology. "I've been around the block, as they say. If I haven't learned to watch my step by now it's nobody's fault but my own."

"Anyway," he drew the word out like a man anxious to change the subject. "I was in town and, I must confess, I couldn't resist the temptation to have a conversation with someone who, politically speaking, is somewhat to the left of Yippi Ti Yi Yo."

Anna smiled. It still hurt. "A Texas liberal. I thought that was a contradiction in terms."

Harland sank down on the foot of the bed. Even that small jolt sent an ache reverberating through Anna's bruised innards. Still she hoped the nurse wouldn't come and shoo him into the red plastic chair.

"I'm not from Texas," Harland said.

Anna was surprised. "You drawl," she accused, raising a speculative eyebrow. That hurt, too.

"Pensacola, Florida. Navy brat."

"You've been around the block and around the world?"

He laughed, a rich male noise that warmed Anna's cracked bones like good brandy. "I've done this and that," he admitted.

"Tell me," Anna said. "I could use a good bedtime story."

He obliged with tales of "wrassling 'gators" and serving as general dogsbody at a roadside SEE OUR DEADLY POISON SNAKES attraction in Florida to work his way through college; of going to Vietnam to fight for democracy and spending three years procuring Japanese kimonos and Russian vodka for officers and their wives; of kicking around the States trying his hand at leading canoe trips, hunting expeditions, working for the YMCA; of finally finding a home with the Park Service.

Harland stayed nearly an hour. Anna was sorry when, shortly before supper, the nurse shooed him out.

Mechanically Anna ate a color-coordinated meal consisting of the four basic food groups, all of which tasted pretty much the same. She asked the LVN—a high school girl with overprocessed hair and a sweet, slightly vacant face—if the food was vacu-formed by Mattel. For her attempt at levity, Anna got an empty smile. However, the girl was willing to smuggle in a cup of coffee with honest-to-God caffeine so Anna forgave her her shortcomings.

Fortified by food and stimulants, she opened the autopsy report on Ranger Drury. Much of it was chemical analyses that meant little to her. After a cursory look through, she turned to the summation and comments on the last page.

Ranger Drury had died between seven p.m. and midnight on Friday, June 17. The cause of death was perforation of the spinal cord between the fourth and fifth cervical vertebrae. The puncture wound, one and a half inches deep, was found to have traces of animal fur at the opening and, one inch down, a fragment of a tooth from a large carnivore. There were three other puncture wounds three-quarters to one inch deep in a pattern consistent with the size of an adult lion's bite. Several animal hairs were found in the scrapes along the shoulder. There were no broken bones or other signs of trauma. Stomach contents included an incompletely digested pear and salami and cheese.

The only other item of interest was a trace of a hallucinogen which had been found in Sheila's blood. Possibly LSD.

In college Anna had dropped some Window Pane acid at Avila Beach. The world became a totally different place. Backpacking without water, in a closed area—all could become logical seen through that distorted glass. There was no knowing what rainbow the Dog Canyon Ranger had been chasing or what demons she had been running from.

Paul had underlined the final sentence: "Death accidental: killed by a mountain lion (*Felis concolor*)."

Anna laid the papers on her lap and leaned back into her pillows. No plaster casts to make prints, no garden tools masquerading as lion's claws, no wilderness Moriarty planning the perfect murder; just one lady ranger with an overheated imagination and an affinity for cats.

"Killed by a mountain lion (*Felis concolor*)." Anna read the words again, then let the papers slip to the floor. She hurt. She was a fool. Her collarbone was broken. She was skinned up from neck to knees. She was old and alone.

"Goddamn, but I'm tired," Anna whispered. Though it was only seven thirty-five, she switched off the bedside lamp and closed her eyes.

# CHAPTER 14

"Paul told me to take all the time I needed," Anna said into the phone receiver. "1 hate to seem paranoid but from the way he said it, I think he wants to be rid of me for a while."

Feet tucked under her like a teenager, Anna was curled up on Christina's bed. One of the midnight kittens was asleep on the pillow between a fuzzy polar bear and a doll dressed in flounces and a picture hat that would have put Scarlett O'Hara to shame.

Anna's left arm was in a sling and both hands were lightly bandaged. She held the receiver of the peach-colored Princess phone against her ear with her fingertips.

"Take it," Molly commanded. "Two weeks at least. Get the hell out of there. I knew bucolic splendor was bad for the health. Come to New York. We'll send out for deli, take in some shows. We'll avoid stairs, take only elevators. There won't be anything for you to fall off of."

Molly sounded annoyed. Every time Anna hurt herself her

sister got mad at her. "Maybe I will," Anna said but she doubted it. She was feeling too old, too beat-up to face Manhattan even on her sister's income. Probably she would go to Rogelio's place in Mexico. He'd invited her often enough. Perhaps now was the time to go. Maybe bake him a birthday cake. Thinking of him, Anna's promise to pay better attention crossed her mind.

"Molly," she said on impulse, "how are you doing? Are you happy and everything?"

The moment of stunned silence embarrassed Anna more deeply than any recrimination her sister might have made.

"I'm all right, I guess," Molly said at last. There followed the pregnant pause of a match finding tobacco, the sigh of relief. Molly laughed. "My fees have gotten so high I can't afford to ask myself how I feel."

"I'll ask again," Anna promised. "On the family discount."

After they'd hung up, Anna sat a while in the quiet of Christina's room. Outside the high window of the government-issue house the sky had grown gray with evening. A star flashed, giving away its identity as a 747.

The room was very feminine, traditionally so, with ruffles and stuffed toys, dresser scarves, bottles of perfume on a mirrored dressing table, framed Arthur Rackham prints on the walls. But Anna liked it. All the things: the silver-backed hairbrush, the basket full of potpourri, the glass jewelry box with the unicorn engraved on the lid, all the toys and tchotchkes seemed honest. Items with meaning acquired throughout a life. Not decor purchased in bulk and sprinkled to effect.

Anna scooped up the kitten. Being limited to the use of one hand, she dangled him a bit and he woke, but within seconds on her lap curled back into his catnap. Soft and trusting, the warmth of the little body under her hand soothed her.

She'd been out of the hospital two days. She was healing fast. Painkillers helped her sleep. Real food was giving her back her strength. She'd even managed to go into the ranger station for a couple of hours.

It was the same damn thing, Anna thought wearily. Bureaucracy, petty power struggles. Corinne in her office muttering behind closed doors, chewing up some unfortunate underling. Paul, already chewed, looking harried and grim and—God damn him, Anna thought uncharitably—understanding. Just once, maybe twice, she'd love to hear him tell someone to bugger off, to take a flying fuck at the moon. Marta sniping, always within safe limits, always with the same sly, smiling, sideways glance, asking solicitously after Christina. Chris had called in sick the day Anna fell. Marta made it clear she didn't believe it for a minute. The superintendent gone to a function. Craig Eastern shrugging and twitching his way through a plan to camp on the West Side with night photographic equipment next full moon. He would record the aliens, then nobody would laugh.

There were days Anna doubted she was in West Texas at all, days it seemed as if she must be in the psych ward at Columbia Hospital suffering from the delusion that she and all her fellow inmates were park rangers.

Tired of the insanity *du jour*, Anna had escaped into the library and returned the call from Tim Dayton at the Roswell lab. He was on vacation but his assistant, an eager and efficient woman, found the blood-test results. The sample Anna had sent was not human. As far as the woman knew there was no test to determine what kind of an animal. And, no, Tim hadn't left any information regarding the other samples she'd sent. Duty done: the blood found in Karl's truck wasn't human. The other samples didn't matter much.

Anna leaned back against Christina's pillows. A delicate

floral scent floated up from the shams. She closed her eyes. Molly was right: she needed to get away for a while.

A timid tap at the bedroom door brought her head up. The door opened a crack and Christina peeked in. "If you're done with your call, supper is ready," she whispered. Then she pushed open the door all the way, flipped on the light and smiled. "If you're not done, supper is still ready."

"I'm done," Anna replied, trying unsuccessfully to restore the kitten to his former resting place without waking him. "I was just enjoying being in a real house, in a real room, where real people live."

Supper was "grown-up supper" as Christina called it. It was after eight o'clock. Alison had eaten her grilled-cheese and green beans and been tucked in bed. Christina and Anna sat on the screened-in porch drinking a chilled California blush wine and eating overpriced artichokes. The light was velvety gray, casting no shadows. To the west it deepened to a bruised purple. Stars shone; diamonds to a distant radio tower's insistent ruby light. Though the sun had gone it was still near eighty degrees. Silence settled like dust over the desert. No crickets, no coyotes, not even the sound of trucks hauling natural gas to Juárez.

"Marta told me you were sick last week," Anna said. "Nothing serious, I hope."

Heavy quiet prevailed for a minute and Anna wished she'd let well enough alone, enjoyed the evening, the wine, the company.

"The day you fell? The day I said I heard it on the office radio? Still your prime suspect, am I?" Christina said lightly, but Anna thought she could hear an underlying edge to her voice. "If you prove I'm a liar, will that prove I'm a killer, too?"

"No murder: no suspects," Anna returned.

"You are supposed to let go of all this. The autopsy; you promised Paul," Christina said.

Anna wanted to see her face but it had grown too dark. She reached instead for the wine. Christina's fingers closed over hers, imprisoning her hand and her glass in a gentle grip. She lifted the bottle, refilled Anna's half-empty glass.

"Why can't you let go? I have, and Sheila was my friend. She was my lover."

"I don't know," Anna answered honestly. Then, stringing the thoughts together, she spoke: "I guess because things just aren't right. They don't fit. Puzzle pieces from a half a dozen puzzles and they—Paul, Corinne—are pretending they all go together, make a whole picture. They just don't. The autopsy said lion kill. But the neck wasn't snapped, the body not eviscerated."

"Maybe Craig's space aliens did it," Christina teased. "Like those mysterious cow slayings in Nebraska a few years ago."

Anna ignored the interruption. "The killer lion has apparently no hind feet. Sheila hiked in, high on acid, no water, no cuts or scratches. She must've been one hell of an acid freak to negotiate the climb out of Dog Canyon two thousand feet, no trail, full pack, then eight miles down the roughest country in the park into a saw grass swamp, stoned out of her mind, and not sustain a single scratch."

"Acid?" Christina said. "They say Sheila was taking acid?"

"The autopsy showed it. Why?"

"I didn't know is all." Christina sounded sad.

"She didn't do drugs?"

"I really don't know. She used to."

"We all used to." Anna's voice sharpened with interest. "Did she still?"

"Anna." Christina said the name in a maternal tone designed to dampen growing excitement in children. "I honestly don't know. She smoked a little dope sometimes. She believed drugs could expand your consciousness. She wasn't an old hippy—she had missed all that. But she 'dabbled,' if that's the word."

Anna was dampened but not quenched.

Christina cleaned the artichoke heart, split it carefully in two and pushed half to Anna's side of the plate.

"Pieces. Ill-fitting, motherfucking pieces," Anna grumbled. "Have you ever watched somebody talk—somebody with something wrong with them? A toupee coming unglued, a bit of mustard in their mustache? You don't hear a word they say. All you can see is that silly bit of something askew.

"That's all I'm seeing, Chris. That wrong bit of something. I'm too tired to let go. Like one of those bulldogs who lock their jaws, hang on even after they're dead."

Christina sipped her wine.

"Were you?" Anna asked, cursing herself as she did. "Sick, I mean?"

"No," Christina replied pleasantly. "I was up on that mountain, lurking behind an agave, hoping to push you over the precipice. I wish I'd pushed harder now."

"Sorry. I don't mean that," Anna said. "Nobody pushed me. Nobody was near me. It's just. I don't know . . . Maybe I'm just tired of stories with holes in them. Fill all the holes: understand the story." She took all of her half of the heart, dipped it in mayonnaise, and ate it in one bite. "Were you?"

The other woman laughed. It sounded genuine if exasperated. "No. Alison's sitter was. I couldn't find anyone else."

"Why did you say you heard my accident reported on the radio?"

Darkness had come, had filled the porch with warm anonymity. Anna heard a sigh, then a tiny galloping horse: soft fingertips drumming on the chair arm.

"It was easier," Christina said at last. "You're like a hawk sometimes, Anna. Waiting to swoop down on any suspicious little act that dares to creep out of some hole. I just didn't want to deal with it. I lied. So sue me."

Anna's shoulder was beginning to ache. Her head had been aching for half an hour. "Craig's launching another search for his Martians," she said, trying for a lighter mood. "Soon as the moon is full again."

"I wouldn't be surprised if he found something," Christina returned shortly. "Craig may be crazy but he's no fool."

Anna was not forgiven.

The silence stretched, grew less strained, mellowed into the night.

"Christina?" Anna asked of the shadow in the chair next to hers.

"Yes?"

"I don't think you killed anybody. I'm just tired, thinking out loud. Not very considerate of other people's feelings."

"Thank you, Anna."

"And if you did, I would drop it."

"Even if the ranchers kept pushing to kill the mountain lions in the park?"

"Sure," she said. It rang hollow.

Christina laughed, touched Anna's arm in the dark. "It's okay. Your lions need you. Alison and I don't. So. You'll go away for a while?" Christina harked back to their conversation before Anna had telephoned her sister.

"I guess," Anna said, feeling lost.

"I'll feed Piedmont."

"Ah-ah."

"I'll lift down the sack and Alison will feed Piedmont," Christina corrected herself.

Anna laughed but it hurt, pulled sore muscles in her chest and shoulder. "I'd appreciate it." Somewhere a cow lowed. The porch roof creaked with cooling. Soon Anna should go. She wished she could stay, sleep over like in junior high.

Grown-up suppers were nice but grown-up nights were long.

# CHAPTER 15

South of Ajo, Arizona, fifteen miles south of the Mexican/American border, Anna sat in the shade of a ramada built from the weathered branches of an ironwood. It was attached to the three-room adobe and wood house Rogelio called home. There was hand-pumped water in the kitchen and an outdoor shower rigged from a wooden barrel raised up on stilts. A pit toilet made of cedar stood twenty yards out back.

Rogelio, it seemed, had talents Anna'd never taken the time to notice. The rustic comforts were ingeniously crafted. The house was clean and well kept. Inside the thick cooling walls, cheap Mexican blankets, beautiful and raw and smelling of wool, brightened the bed. Rugs were scattered over the whitewashed floors. Straw matting woven in intricate patterns was rolled above the windows. Bits of bleached animal skeletons—desert sculptures Rogelio called them—intermixed with brightly painted wooden fishes and birds decorated the rough wooden tables. Coarse handwoven cottons in brilliant hues of red and orange, the kind Anna had seen glowing in a dozen street markets in border towns, hung over the doorways.

It was a home. Anna'd never pictured Rogelio with a home. Since Zachary, she'd never given any thought to making a home for herself, let alone for anyone else. Rogelio had made a home, he said, for her.

Desert rolled away in four directions. Small mountains, sharp and scattered like broken teeth, bit into the blue horizon. Everywhere the mysterious and, to Anna, miraculous life of the Sonoran Desert made itself felt.

Under an unrelenting sun, temperatures one hundred and ten to one hundred and fifteen during the heat of the day, the landscape was still: a green and gray graveyard with fantastically shaped tombstones stretching away over the desert pavement—the flat rocky, lifeless soil. But in the cool of the evening and under night skies, life crept out from beneath every stone, from the boles of trees and cacti.

In this harsh and fertile cradle Anna slept and healed, drank beer and made love, worked on her Spanish and wondered if she could live in this gentle rendition of "Margaritaville."

She'd been there ten days when Rogelio asked if she would marry him and she knew it was time to leave.

He leaned on the door of her Rambler. In the light of the setting sun he was impossibly beautiful. The wide-set hazel eyes reflecting the afternoon sun were nearly amber, his cheekbones high, hollowed by shadows.

"Can I come back?" Anna asked. "Drink your beer, make love with you in the desert?"

"I want to be more to you than that, Anna. More than just a good time." He smiled, teeth white in the dark-skinned face. "I'm not that kind of boy. You can't save me for later. I want to share my desert, my life, with a woman. With you if I can.

With someone else if I can't. Two choices, Anna; take me or leave me." He laughed, a mix of self-mockery and hope.

"Can I come back?" Anna asked again. Rogelio thought so long she began to be afraid.

"You can come back," he said finally. "But I don't know for how long. Or how many times."

Through the cool of the night, she drove. The roads were nearly empty and the desert glowed with a moon two days past full. By the time the sun began to heat up the day she was out of the hottest part of the country, heading into the tangle of freeways that cut the heart out of El Paso. Her mind had churned the night away mixing Zachary and Rogelio, Harland and Murder, Christina and Lions into a great aching lump of thought that, by sunrise, had settled at the base of her skull.

More than once since she'd fled New York, Anna had feared for her sanity. Often she saw things others did not. Maybe because she was more clear-sighted than most. Or had less to lose by seeing the truth. Maybe because those things were not there.

Had there been a murder? Had mysterious clues appeared? There was such a thing as coincidence. Once Anna's car had broken down outside Wichita, Kansas. She'd stuck out her thumb. The woman who stopped to give her a lift was her old third-grade teacher from Janesville, California. Everyone had stories like that. The lion, the acid, the ranger, no water: it could be coincidence. Even the paw prints. Some freakish nature of the mud—soft in one place, hard and dry two feet away. There could be some explanation: underground seeps, shadows.

Why did she see such evil when no one else could? Sheila was dead. No one had cared desperately about her. Not even

Christina. People wanted to go on with their lives and jobs and plans. To see a murder would interfere. Anna understood that. And the lions that might yet die in reaction? Even people who cared about animals thought of them basically as things: things to eat or wear, own, take pictures of. Things for people to use and enjoy. Sad to lose one, certainly, but nothing to lose sleep over. That was the attitude that prevailed and Anna had learned to live with it.

People wanted the "disruption" to be over.

As Anna drove across the broad salt flats to the west of the Guadalupe Mountains, the bold gray prow of El Capitan cutting into the morning, she knew that she, too, wanted it to be over, wanted to let sleeping dogs lie, wanted to get on with her life. Maybe to find again some of the peace she'd felt in Rogelio's Mexico.

Just before ten o'clock, she pulled the Rambler into the employee parking lot behind the Administration building. There was only one slot left. Every vehicle in the park was jammed into the usually half-empty lot. Sensing bad news, she tried to rub the grit of nine hundred miles out of her eyes. It crossed her mind to go home, face whatever it was after a bath and some sleep. But she was already here. And she wanted her mail. Taking comfort in the fact that if it were a wildland fire—and the Southwest was ablaze from the drought and dry lightning—her collarbone would prevent Paul from sending her out with one of the crews to fight it, she climbed stiffly from the car.

Christina was not at her desk. Marta looked up when Anna walked into the office. She was dressed up, almost as if for a special occasion, and she'd had her hair done. A carefully arranged look of tragedy composed her features. Anna guessed she was dying to tell the bad news. Fear dragged her quickly back into the hall. Whatever it was she didn't want to hear it from Marta Freeman.

"You've got a phone message," Marta called after her. Anna went in, took it, shoved it in her pocket without reading it, and scurried out again without apology.

Head bent over a sheaf of papers, Christina Walters walked out of the copy room almost into Anna's arms. Relief rocked Anna back on her heels, and she realized she'd been afraid for her friend. "Chris," she croaked.

Christina looked up. She looked strained, tired around the eyes, but her smile was warm and welcoming.

"What's happened?" Anna was whispering. Two doors down was the conference room. The door was shut. Most of the staff was probably closeted behind it. "What is going on?"

"Come on," Christina whispered back. She walked down the carpeted hall. Anna followed into the small employee lunchroom and closed the door.

"Welcome home," Christina said.

Anna sat down at the white Formica table and waited while the other woman poured two cups of coffee, gave her one, and sat down in the chair opposite. "Big safety meeting," Christina said. "There's been another accident, they think"

"Who?"

"Maybe Craig."

Equal parts relief and guilt washed over Anna.

"What happened?"

"Remember that space alien hunt he was going to go on?"

Anna nodded.

"Well, he went. The moon had to be full for these creatures to visit or something. He went five days ago—took all his snake stuff with him. He was going to kill two birds with one stone, I guess. Anyway, he never came back. Nobody even knew he was missing till today. Yesterday and the day before were his lieu days. What with the two accidents, Corinne's afraid Region's going to land on her with both feet so she's called a safety meeting. From what Marta and I've been hearing through her office door, we're going to have to wear full body armor to type up purchase orders from now on. Everything's going to be safety first. If something's happened to Craig it'll be the third accident. Three is too many."

"Three? Who else?"

"You."

"Oh. Yeah." Anna drank the coffee Christina had poured. There was already so much caffeine in her system, she doubted it would keep her awake, just add to her indigestion.

Christina eyed her narrowly. "What? You don't think he's lost? Hurt by accident?"

Anna said nothing. Tomorrow, when she'd had some sleep, she'd think about it. The search for Craig wouldn't begin for another twenty-four hours, the usual time allotted for adults to wander back of their own accord.

"My ex is here," Christina said suddenly. "Erik came five days after you left. He's staying two weeks. *Two.* Lord!"

Anna closed her eyes, the light made them hurt. She felt a gentle touch: fingertips on the back of her wrist.

"I'm so glad you're home."

For the first time since she'd driven in, Anna was too.

She let herself out the fire exit. If she tried the front again, she might be seen and roped into the meeting. Corinne Mathers's meetings weren't known for their brevity. With the Regional Office breathing down her neck they could become interminable. Corinne had wanted to keep the Drury case low-key, uncontroversial. Since Craig's disappearance had set the alarm bells off, Anna was willing to bet she'd change tactics, make a noisy show of taking command of the situation. For a while the name of the game at Guadalupe Mountains would be Cover Your Ass.

Home in her tiny apartment, spread catty-corner on the

Murphy bed, Anna relaxed into the waiting darkness of unconsciousness. Piedmont, too warm to sleep on her, was stretched out nearby, his head on the pillow. As she drifted, Anna marveled at how much better she rested when she slept with a cat than when she slept with a man. Cats' purring was a powerful soporific.

Four hours' sleep and a shower put her back on her feet with a clear head. The afternoon would be spent nesting, settling in. So abruptly had she fled Guadalupe, dishes were still in the sink and garbage in the pail. She'd not even bothered to unpack the cardboard box of ripped and bloody clothes the hospital had sent home with her.

The hiking shorts were salvageable. The shirt was not. Her name tag was gone. Anna rescued the badge and dropped the rest into the trash. Socks went into the laundry. The boots were scraped nearly white but after a polish would be good as ever. They were tossed in the general direction of the closet.

A stone from the sole of one of the boots clung to the palm of her hand. Alison's magic rock, Anna thought. Then she remembered the little girl carefully sticking her rock to the footboard of the hospital bed. It was doubtful the Carlsbad Hospital was so meticulous about patients' belongings that they'd restuck a bit of gravel to her boot sole.

Anna plucked the stone from her palm and looked it over. It was an ordinary pebble, the kind the heavy lug of her boots picked up on most trails in the park. But this one had a whitish mark on one side. Alison had said her magic rock tasted like something. Not blessed with a four-year-old's fearless culinary tastes, Anna licked the stone gingerly.

Library paste.

Some things are never forgotten: the smell of Jade East, the feel of a man, the sound of ambulance sirens, the taste of library paste.

Anna pulled the boots out into the light, dug every particle of rock and sand and thorn out of the soles and uppers. Nothing else was out of the ordinary. Just the two magic rocks.

Cross-legged on the carpet, Anna tried to recall her fall. She had been walking down the McKittrick Ridge Trail alone. There had been nothing unusual: no sound, no smell, no movement. Suddenly, she'd stepped into mid-air, overbalanced because of her pack, and fallen. She'd managed to break her slide till a stone, dislodged by her fall, had struck her.

Dislodged by her fall.

A minute, maybe more, had passed before the rock hit her.

Stepped into mid-air. Magic rocks. Library paste. Laboriously, Anna fitted the oddments together as she pulled on the boots, threw some cheese and bread and water into a daypack, kissed an ungrateful cat, and left the apartment in as much of a mess as she had found it.

At Pratt Cabin she liberated a climbing harness and rope from the small Search and Rescue cache kept there. By late afternoon she was above Turtle Rock. Finding where she fell was more difficult than she thought it would be. In memory every foot of rock she'd crawled up was clearly etched. When she'd finally climbed free, she'd evidently relaxed, shut down. The top of the trail was a blur.

When she did find it, there was not a doubt in her mind that she was at the right place. Training binoculars on the stone below she found traces of blood marring the limestone, the iron deposit that had saved her life, and the crack-chimney she had shinnied up.

Walking uphill a hundred yards or so, Anna retraced her steps down the trail to where she'd gone over the edge. The path was rocky, but level. Lining up the tree she had been planning to throw a line to just before the rock had hit her, Anna was able to locate exactly where she'd stepped into nothing.

The trail was flat, well-maintained. Having divested herself of pack and rope, Anna began to dig. Gravel came away easily at first, then she hit a stone. When she'd cleared away all the dirt, she could see a rock about the size of a basketball set in a trough on the trail. Along with smaller rubble, it plugged a ditch a couple feet wide and half the trail deep. Anna worked it loose and rolled it down the cut and over the cliff. It followed the path she had taken on the way down.

She swept away the sand. Smooth bites of a shovel and the sharp scoring of a pick marked the sides of the hole. A trough a foot deep and canted steeply toward the cliff had been carved out of the trail. Crawling on hands and knees, Anna examined the path for fifteen feet in either direction but found nothing more of interest.

She buckled on the climbing harness and, using upslope juniper as anchor and belay, began rappelling slowly down the cliff face searching every ledge and crevice, every tuft of grass that clung to the stone. Against the trunk of a stunted madrone she found what she was looking for: four tangled sticks. Anna tied them carefully in a kerchief, knotted it to her belt, and began the slow and painful task of pulling herself back up to the trail.

By the time she stood again on level ground she was certain she had unraveled every stitch her collarbone had knit in the two weeks since the accident. For several minutes she rested, drank in the air. Then she examined her find.

Four sticks, three broken but one over a foot long. Gravel was stuck to the sticks in several places, affixed by the same white paste Anna found on the magic rock. The sticks were woven in and out of one another as if someone had started a basket.

She laid the longest stick across the trough cut in the trail. It just reached. Someone had built a tiger trap and she had fallen into it. They had dug a ditch on the outside of the trail wide enough it wouldn't be stepped over. A mat of sticks had been woven to cover the hole and pebbles glued to the mat to make it look like the rest of the trail's surface.

Anna's radioed itinerary had been heard by the entire park. All anyone had to do was put the camouflage mat over the hole and wait. There was a good view of the trail below and above. If another hiker happened along, all they need do was remove the stone-covered mat. The hiker would see the hole, step over, and continue on.

That meant someone had watched as she fell. The same someone had rolled a rock down on her when it looked as if she would save herself. Her second slide had taken her so far down they must've trusted to luck—their good and her bad—that she would fall to her death. They wouldn't have wished to remain in the vicinity any longer than necessary. The sticks could've been picked up in minutes, the trail repaired almost as quickly and what few sticks tumbled down would be washed free of library paste with the first good rain. They had planned it well.

"Not they," Anna said to herself. "The murderer." Someone had tried to kill her. The thought frightened her. And it pissed her off.

Anna spent the night annoying Piedmont and fretting out lists in her head. Paul, Marta, Christina, Corinne, Harland, Karl, Manny, Craig, and Cheryl all worked with radios. All of them could've heard her radio in her backcountry itinerary. Christina had called in sick: she was free to lay traps. Harland had mentioned he was in Carlsbad buying lumber. Cheryl was in McKittrick Canyon on day patrol. It was she the tourist had reported the accident to. Karl, Paul, and Corinne were unaccounted for. Marta was off the hook. She never left her desk.

Too many personal calls to make, Anna thought uncharitably. Lord knew where Mrs. Drury—Sheila's mother—was. And Erik Walters was in the park.

Since sleep was proving elusive, Anna got up and switched on the desk lamp. On a bit of scratch paper she made another list. Craig Eastern was at the top of this one. He knew the policies of the park as well as anyone. The aliens, the back-country jaunt, lieu days, the grace period: if he were running away it provided a very convenient five-day lead.

# CHAPTER 16

At ten till eight the following morning Anna's disability leave came to an end. She was back in uniform. Along with Paul, Corinne, and Cheryl, she sat in the conference room in the Administration building. At the head of the long, well-polished oak table, Corinne blinked benignly from behind aviator-style spectacles. It was a habit Anna had learned not to be comforted by. The sleepy, rabbit-eyed winks meant nothing. It was just a facial gesture the Chief Ranger adopted when she was waiting; a disarming, feminine version of the poker face.

Harland Roberts came in and the waiting was over. Corinne looked pointedly at the wall clock but the minute hand still held at two minutes till eight. He was not late. Inspired by the assumption of guilt, he apologized anyway and Corinne accepted it.

"I don't want this dragging on," Ranger Mathers began the meeting without preamble. "What've you got, Paul?"

Paul Decker, head of Search and Rescue for the Guadalupes, quickly adopted her manner: clipped, no frills. "Every search is an emergency," he began. "But we don't know yet whether we've got a search. Craig went into the backcountry on the West Side on July fifteenth—five days ago. From what I understand, mostly from conversations he had with Manny, he'd planned staying two days and two nights. The next two days, the seventeenth and eighteenth, were his lieu days. He didn't report to work yesterday and he didn't return to the housing area.

"We've no way of knowing whether he's still in the backcountry or if he came out when he told Manny he would and went someplace for the weekend and got hurt or delayed there.

"Yesterday I called the University in El Paso and followed up on a few leads they gave me. No one has seen him. I doubt there's any cause for panic but, by the same token, there's no excuse for delay.

"All we know is he was collecting on the West Side but not precisely what or where. He had gathering permits for the entire park and left no itinerary. We need to locate his vehicle and narrow the area of the search. I'll go into Williams's ranch house near the escarpment. Anna will drive around the far western boundary to PX Well and a couple of other places where he may have parked and walked in. Cheryl is going to hold the fort down here. You'll be the only law enforcement within hailing distance so keep in touch with the Visitors Center," Paul said to Cheryl and she nodded. "Harland will head over to Dog Canyon and drive around to Marcus to see if Craig left his Volvo outside the fence on that old access road. It's unlikely Craig would walk in over Cut Off Mountain but who knows what he was looking for. Anybody?"

Corinne looked at each of them expectantly, almost a nonverbal demand.

Maintaining, as always, a low political profile, Cheryl Light stared at her finger-ends.

"Martians," Harland said gently when the Chief Ranger's gaze raked across him. The sadness of his smile disarmed the remark's cruelty.

When Corinne came to her, Anna just shook her head. She had been interested in the reptiles Craig was collecting but wasn't informed enough about his project to know any particular animal or habitat he might've been studying this trip.

Paul started to speak again but before he could, Harland raised his hand a few inches. A habit very few people shake regardless of how many years have elapsed since they were in third grade. Paul waited.

"He might not have been delayed or injured," Harland said slowly. "He may have just taken off. Craig is . . ." He caught Anna's eye and she looked back without expression, curious to see if he would give away Craig's secret to the staff. ". . . spontaneous," Roberts finished and Anna was relieved. Not so much because Craig Eastern had been protected but because Harland hadn't proved a cad.

"That's a possibility," Paul conceded. "Let's hope that's the case. Then nothing is lost but a little time and sleep. Still, we've got to search."

"Of course," Harland agreed.

Before the meeting broke up the search plan had been established. If the car was found they would begin at that point. Meanwhile, Christina Walters would be detailed to conduct a phone search of the usual places: police, hospitals, Border Patrol, family, friends, etc.

Anna fell into step beside Harland as he walked out the back door to the employee parking lot. Remembering the sad "Martian" smile, she stopped at his truck, rested her elbows on the tailgate.

One hand on the door handle, he waited politely for her to speak.

"Have you got any particular reason to think Craig just ran off?" she asked. For a moment she thought he wasn't going to answer. Behind his gray eyes, she could see a small struggle taking place. When he finally did speak, she felt he was choosing his way carefully, censoring his thoughts before they became words.

"Nothing I can prove in a court of law," he said with a feeble attempt at lightness. Even that tiny spark vanished with the next sentence. "Not even something I'd want bantered around, run though the gossip mill."

Anna did gossip, loved a good gossip, but seldom with anyone in the park. Her reputation for being able to keep her mouth shut was better than it deserved to be. Evidently it was about to pay off. Harland continued.

"It crossed my mind that Craig might be running away from something. It would be true to form. He's not a psychopath. When he commits . . . when he does something maybe he shouldn't, he's aware of it. He has a conscience. It hurts him. If he'd done something he felt pretty bad about, I don't think he could deal with his feelings, or with being found out. I think he'd run away. Like a little kid."

"What do you think he might have done?" Anna prodded but Harland was done confiding.

"Could've been anything," he replied easily. "Something we might even think was silly. It only needed to be important in Craig's mind." With that, he opened the door of his pickup and Anna took it correctly as a dismissal.

On the long drive around the western boundary of the park to PX Well, Anna pondered the crimes Craig could be running from: guilt at slandering Drury, maybe even Sheila's death, the attempt on her own life.

Craig was passionate, dedicated. And insane. It didn't take

a great stretch of the imagination to picture him killing to keep the developers out of the park, the bulldozers and concrete mixers out of Dog Canyon. Not only would he be fighting against the destruction of the fragile canyon when the RV sites were put in, but against the ongoing degradation of the area as the great roaring, gas-guzzling beasts rolled in with their baggage of humanity. People who had no intention of meeting Nature on her own terms but who must travel to the wilderness in a motorized hotel room replete with TVs, VCRs, showers, toilets, and growling generators.

Then would come the demands that inevitably followed RV invasions: sewage dumps, water and electric hookups, and, finally, the cry of "Why can't we drive *through* the park? How are people supposed to *see* it?"

Anna could envision Craig committing murder to save the Guadalupe Mountains from such defilement. With very little effort, she could picture herself helping him.

And then trying to kill her because she wouldn't leave Drury's demise well enough alone? Eastern couldn't have known she'd reached enough dead ends, was shaken enough from her fall to drop the investigation. Maybe he thought when she came back from Mexico she'd begin to dig again, with twice the energy now her life, too, had been threatened.

So he ran.

He'd left his pet snakes behind. Paul had noticed when he checked Craig's apartment. Snakes, though, could live for weeks without food. Anna couldn't imagine they would suffer undue psychological trauma from the loss of Craig's companionship.

According to Paul, he'd not taken any clothes or books or anything, either. But then Craig was crazy. Maybe he'd run from everything—murder, snakes, laundry, phone bills.

Anna sighed and switched on the radio. Trying to second-guess lunatics, drunks, or the Office of Personnel Management was an exercise in frustration. Their logic totally eluded her.

Jarring bones and rattling teeth drowned out any thought for a while as she forced the truck over the broken rock of the rutted road. So bad was the surface, even ten miles an hour was too fast to maintain control. Anna doubted Craig's old Volvo could make it over such rugged terrain, but she'd seen cars in stranger places.

The heat grew oppressive. The plastic steering wheel burned her hands. Her feet, in their regulation boots, felt as if her socks had been dipped in kerosene and set on fire.

Mentally excusing herself to Rogelio's environmental purism, she rolled up the window and cranked up the air conditioner.

Eastern's Volvo was not at PX Well. While she was there, Anna checked the rain gauge. Dry, as she'd expected. Not a trace of rain had fallen on the West Side since February and very little more than that in the entire Southwest. The region was in its fourth year of drought. Fires burned out of control in Arizona, Nevada, and all over New Mexico. Every morning in the ranger report was news of another fifteen-, twenty-, thirty-thousand acres burned. Even Yosemite was on fire.

Close to four-thirty Anna arrived back at Park Headquarters. Harland's Roads and Trails truck wasn't in the lot but Paul's one-ton was there between the jeep Cheryl was driving and the Chief Ranger's van.

Climbing out of the air-conditioned cab, Anna was hit by the heat. For a few seconds it felt delicious. Then the caress grew heavy, gluing her clothes to her body. Escaping up the cement steps, she let herself in the rear door of the building.

The others were already gathered around the conference table. Christina Walters had joined them. She smiled faintly when Anna caught her eye and Anna walked around the table and took the chair next to hers. The glower of the Chief

Ranger, shorn of its amiable sheep's clothing, filled the room with a silence too active to allow for conversation.

Paul sat across the table poring through a sheaf of forms. Looking busy, Anna speculated. Corinne's silences clamored too loudly to allow for reading.

Cheryl was lost again in her finger-ends.

Shifting her revolver and radio so they didn't bite into her ribs quite so hard, Anna settled in to await Corinne's signal that the meeting could begin.

Through the door connecting the conference room with the offices came an irregular tattoo of muffled thumps and slaps, as though in the adjoining room a confession were being beaten out of some uncooperative suspect. Marta, huffing through books and manuals, telegraphed sullen disapproval that Christina was asked to the meeting and she was not.

A pointed look from Corinne Mathers sent Christina to close the door.

As she resumed her seat, Harland Roberts came in from the hall. His dark hair was ruffled like a boy's, one lock falling over his forehead as if he had driven with his window rolled down.

Corinne glanced at the wall clock: 4:34. He was late. This time he didn't apologize. Apparently, the actuality of his guilt satisfied the Chief Ranger. Her face relaxed and she smiled; the meeting could begin.

No trace had been found of Craig's vehicle: no tracks, nothing. There were six gates in the fence around the boundary, most were the dead ends of rutted gravel roads leading into old wells and stock tanks left over from when the Guadalupes had been used for sheep and cattle grazing. The Volvo hadn't been found at any of them.

Next, Christina gave her report. There had been no official recognition of Eastern in the past seven days: no traffic violations, accidents, hospitalizations, arrests, or parking tickets concerning a Craig Eastern anywhere in a one-hundred-and-fifteen-mile radius of the park. Nor had any of the names and numbers she'd followed up from the University of Texas at El Paso proved fruitful.

Anna wondered whether or not Harland had given her the phone number of the mental institution in Austin. As if her thought cued Roberts's voice, he said: "Austin?"

"I followed up on the number you suggested, Harland," Christina replied carefully. Anna was not surprised at her natural sensitivity. She'd come to expect it. "The information had to be pried out of them, but I finally found a nurse who would talk with me. They've not seen Craig for two years."

"Nurse?" Corinne pounced on the word. "Does Craig have a physical problem?"

Christina looked uncomfortable. This was not her secret to tell. In truth, it wasn't Harland's either, but somehow it seemed he'd earned a right to it.

"Not a physical problem, Corinne," he replied.

The Chief Ranger waited, both of her small capable hands palm-down on the blond wood of the table.

Anna was put in mind of Piedmont: alert, casually deadly, waiting for a mouse to run out from behind the stove.

Sure as death, the mouse panicked.

"It's a personal matter, Corinne," Harland said when the pressure got to him. "Not something I feel I can discuss without Craig's permission."

"I understand your reticence to tell something you might have learned in confidence," Corinne said reasonably. "But any information we get could save Craig's life. It will not leave this room." She didn't look at any of them for compliance. She didn't have to. The implied threat was clear in her tone. If the story worked its way back to her in any form there would be hell to pay.

Harland caved in. Anna didn't blame him. The information was relevant. And Corinne demanded it.

"I'm in a position to know that Craig has, in the past, suffered from a mental illness severe enough to get him institutionalized on more than one occasion."

A silence as deep as the one Corinne imposed before meetings developed on the conference table in front of them. To Anna it felt as if it were comprised of one part guilt and nine parts embarrassment. Mental illness was still taboo. They felt guilty because they'd thought Craig was crazy. Now they were embarrassed because they knew he was. If he came back to work, the first few days they'd all tiptoe around glad-handing him as if he were the most regular Joe they'd ever met.

"Hunting Martians," Corinne muttered and shook her head. "Christina, after the meeting get me that clinic on the phone. They'll talk to me." To Harland, she said only: "I should have been informed."

Paul screwed himself around in his chair like a drill-bit emerging straight and true out of soft pine. "We don't know where Craig is, but we can infer from what information we do have that he may be in trouble. I'd like some air coverage. If we could borrow a helicopter from the Forest Service we could try and locate his camp. See if he left the backcountry."

"Craig's tent is desert camo," Harland said. "He was bragging about it to me the other day. It'll be a bitch to find in broken country."

Corinne jerked her chin at Christina. With a certain awe of Chris's telepathic powers, Anna watched her quietly leave the conference room.

Several minutes later she returned in the midst of a discussion of Craig Eastern's probable itineraries. Corinne looked at her and everyone stopped talking.

"Due to the fires, all helicopters in the Southwest region

are in use. Highest priority. It will be a week or ten days before they can guarantee us one for this search."

"Paulsen's got one," Anna said, remembering suddenly.

"Jerimiah D.? That's right," Harland added. "He has."

Christina went without the nod, and returned to report that Paulsen's helicopter was undergoing repairs. The rotor was in Sante Fe being worked on. As soon as it was running, he'd be glad to lend it to the National Park Service.

The meeting adjourned at five after six. Search dogs had been promised by the El Paso Police Department in two days' time. At present all their dogs were in use searching for a ten-year-old boy lost in the Gila National Forest.

Tomorrow Anna and Paul would begin a manhunt, starting with the most likely points of entry: Williams Ranch and PX Well. Anna would ride Gideon; Paul, Pesky. Harland was to coordinate transportation for the rangers and the livestock.

It was, Paul pointed out, better than sitting on their hands.

Christina would continue her search by phone.

Harland was waiting at PX Well when Anna and Gideon rode out the next evening. She was late, nearly two hours. Always, as she rode, was the nagging sense that just a little farther, just over the next ragged, rocky hill, she would find something. She'd blown her shrill plastic search whistle till her ears were buzzing and Gideon had begun to flinch as if she laid a lash to him. Between the two of them they'd consumed forty pounds of water—five gallons—and would've consumed another gallon if they'd had it.

The sight of the waiting horse trailer gave the old horse back his youth. Then he saw Roberts and began to flag. Gideon stumbled half a dozen times in the last quarter-mile. He was putting on a show for Harland.

A long drink of water was waiting for the horse and a cold

Milwaukee Black Label for Anna, courtesy of Harland Roberts. She was popping the top as she said: "I'm in uniform, I really shouldn't."

Harland opened a can for himself, sipping to her gulps. More of a promise never to tell on her than a serious drinking of beer. Anna slid to the ground in the shade of the horse trailer, her back against the fender.

"Not a damn thing," she said to his questioning look. "Davy Crockett couldn't track a tank over this kind of country. Yours Truly was totally baffled. We played it by ear. Followed the obvious animal trails, sought out the snakiest-looking country. Not so much as a gum wrapper. Maybe the Martians did beam him up." She leaned her head back against the warm metal of the trailer and poured another quarter of a can of beer down her throat. It was the finest beverage she'd ever tasted. Heaven was just Hell in the shade with a cold beer.

"Maybe tomorrow," Harland said.

"Maybe tomorrow."

Tomorrow brought the dog from El Paso and the policewoman who worked with her. The dog's name was Natasha Osirus. Her handler, Betsy McLeod, called her Nosy. Nosy was an eleven-year-old golden retriever trained to search. Serious, almost grave, she was terribly dedicated until Betsy produced a well-chewed Raggedy Ann doll, then she was the silliest of puppies. Like Nosy, Betsy was blond, though Anna suspected it was due more to Lady Clairol than the desert sun. Both had a loose-jointed unkempt look that put Anna at ease immediately. They also shared a warmth and a brown-eyed sincerity that gave one faith.

Noon found Paul, Anna, Betsy, and the dog on the porch of the Williams ranch house. A plain wooden building, it had been constructed at the turn of the century for a new bride who took one look at the desert stretching barbarous miles out from her very doorstep and fled back to civilization.

The next woman had loved the place, the land, the house. Anna'd never read any official documentation to that fact; she simply felt it. Love was there in the choice of wallpaper in the entry hall, in the careful border prints along the ceilings, and the neatly nailed tin gliders on the threshholds.

Now the paper hung in colorless ribbons. Collared lizards peeked unfathomable eyes up through gaps between the floorboards. Black-throated sparrows nested under the elevated porch. Some days, on West Side patrol, Anna would take her lunch onto the porch and, in her mind, redecorate and inhabit this graceful little home on the skirttails of the Guadalupes with all the deserts of Texas rolling away.

Nosy, her snout full of Craig's scent—socks, a shirt, the EARTH FIRST! cap Paul had taken from Eastern's apartment—made short work of the house and, on Betsy's command, began to circle farther afield. At every other step the poor creature got sand burrs or mesquite barbs in her paws. Betsy, walking with her, pulled out the stickers and murmured comfort. The dog was too well trained to quit working, but it was easy to see her concentration was affected.

No trail was found. With the heat, the stickers, the varied smells of visitors who'd come to see the Williams ranch house, Paul was not confident Nosy could sort out one six-day-old track.

Betsy was sure. Nosy was loaded back into the jeep and Anna began the seven-mile, forty-five-minute drive out the guttered road. Betsy sat in back with the dog, fashioning little canvas booties from an old piece of tarp that had been covering the jack.

At four o'clock they reached PX Well. Nosy was more comfortable with her paws tied up in canvas, and the well had been so long in disuse that there were few human scents to sort through, but the end result was the same: no sign of Craig Eastern.

After supper that night, Anna went over to Christina's to visit. Erik—who Anna had assiduously avoided meeting—had taken Alison into Carlsbad to see *The Little Mermaid*. The two women talked little. Christina seemed to need the quiet and Anna found it soothing. They sat out in the garden, enjoying the heady scent of Chris's carefully tended exotics and sipping tiny crystal glasses of ice-cold peppermint schnapps.

The phone search, Christina said, had become so general as to be absurd. Craig had few friends and was a virtual stranger to his one living relative—a sister in Brownsville. Christina was down to calling his grammar school teachers and the night security guards at the University lab where he worked. No one had seen or heard from him.

The following day, at the Marcus entrance to the park, Betsy and Nosy sniffed out a tarantula, a great granddaddy of a western diamondback rattler, and two Texas horned lizards. The three remaining entrance gates didn't produce even that much in the way of results. Come sundown, Betsy loaded Nosy back into her Camaro and headed for El Paso.

The next morning's Incident Command Meeting was glum. Nothing to report. The Forest Service, pressured by Corinne, promised a helicopter in three days. No one fooled themselves that, if Craig were indeed on the West Side, he was still alive. There were no springs. No one could carry in water enough for seven days.

Corinne had worked her way around to the all-important chore of placing the blame—or at least shrugging herself free of any taint of it—when the call came in.

Frank Kanavel, the rancher owning the property along the boundary between the gate to the Williams ranch road and PX Well, had let some "snake guy" from the park leave his car on his property for two days. More than a week later he comes back from his sister's wedding in Lubbock to find the damn thing's there again. Did the park think they had an open invitation to walk over his land any time they wanted, trample down his fences, upset his cows?

Mr. Kanavel must've been shocked at the genuine joy with which his rambling grievance was met. The joy was short-lived. If Craig's vehicle was there, then Craig was lost or injured in the Patterson Hills. That meant Craig Eastern was dead. They had failed him.

Anna consoled herself with the thought that he was undoubtedly dead before they'd even known he was missing.

Paul put in a call to the El Paso Police Department and Betsy McLeod was dispatched back to Guadalupe. Paul gave the phone to Christina to provide the police with exact directions to Frank Kanavel's ranch. The rangers would meet her at the missing man's vehicle.

As they left the Administration building, Anna marveled at how language altered subtly as tragedy closed in. Words grew longer, more impersonal, forming a wall around the mind, holding out the less tolerable images. Craig's Volvo had become "the missing man's vehicle."

While Anna put their Search and Rescue packs in the back of the truck, Paul radioed Harland for horse backup.

Kanavel met them at the gate to his ranch. He'd been filled in on the particulars and his growling complaints had been replaced with genuine concern. In the deserts of Texas, to survive, one saved one's fellow man, then questioned him and hanged him later if the answers were wrong.

Craig's car was parked along the boundary fence. Looking at the Pattersons a couple of miles distant, it was easy to guess the direction he had probably taken.

Across the flats, to where the desert began to wrinkle back on itself, mesquite and ocotillo etched the arid soil with dusty green. Low cacti, invisible at that distance, replaced the greenery as the hills folded into sharp ridges and ravines. The Pattersons were scattered in a pattern clear only to geologists and the gods. To anyone else they formed a hell of a maze.

One wash cut deep enough to erode a valley into the flank of a tall hill. Eastern would've walked up that wash, Anna guessed.

Paul radioed the base station. "Seven-two-five," Christina's voice replied. A moment's checking discovered Betsy and Nosy less than half an hour from Kanavel's.

They waited.

The policewoman and Harland, with the horses, arrived at the same time.

Betsy chose to walk. Paul climbed on Pesky, Anna on Gideon. Harland rode Jack, one of the mules. Jack was the strongest, smartest animal in the park but he was a treacherous mount. Under Harland's hand he was the soul of decorum. Jill, the smaller mule, followed on a lead.

Nosy never hesitated. So great was her dedication, even in canvas booties, her tongue and ears flopping, she didn't appear ridiculous. Betsy followed behind the dog. Six or seven yards back, so they wouldn't interfere, rode Anna and the two men.

The golden retriever led them across the flatlands toward the wash. Under Betsy's direction, the dog was made to stop and drink every five or ten minutes.

The sun was merciless. Anna half believed she could see the life of the desert floating upward like the ghost from a slain body, but she knew it was only distortions in the air caused by the heat. Despite hat and sunblock, she could feel her flesh burn. At thirty-nine she had age spots at her temples and on the backs of her hands.

The horses plodded on with the fatalism of all slave races.

The dry wash provided no relief: no breeze, no shade, only

the hard light of the sun reflected back from three sides. Anna drank constantly. So much moisture was sucked up by heat and wind that it was almost impossible to keep hydrated. In the Pattersons there were days a human could not carry enough water to survive, regardless of personal strength.

The policewoman, though game, was unused to the rigors of backcountry desert travel. Paul was the first to notice she was flagging. Under flushed cheekbones, her skin was slightly pale. In her concern for the dog, she wasn't drinking enough or pacing herself.

At the District Ranger's insistence, she climbed onto Jill's back and directed Nosy from there.

A mile and a half in, the canyon petered out. A hill of cactus and scree rose up at a forty-five or fifty-degree angle above them. They dismounted and hobbled the stock. Betsy leashed Nosy so she wouldn't go over the crest and out of sight. Fanning out, they each found their way up as best they could. Anna wished she'd had the sense to bring her leather work gloves. The only way to make the ascent was on hands and feet. Rocks were hot to the touch and small barrel cacti poked their round heads up where they were least expected.

Topping the hill first, Anna stood catching her breath, sucking the air in through her nostrils in the hope they still had some power to moisten it.

The hill was round on top and sloped steeply away on all sides like the hump of a camel. Opposite from where she stood, about a quarter of the way down, a web of desert joined this hump to the next hump over. The bridge of land flattened out along the spine, then dropped off on either side into deep ravines.

Anna hoped Craig had hiked across that land bridge. Scrambling up these hills would get old very quickly.

Paul puffed up beside her, stood a moment, then looked back down. Watching out for other people seemed second nature to him. Anna followed his example. Betsy McLeod and Nosy were about three-quarters of the way up. Harland was with them. Betsy was drinking from his canteen. In the excitement of the chase she'd forgotten or lost hers. Harland waved and smiled. Betsy looked beat; a good candidate for heat exhaustion.

Anna turned back to her fruitless study of the terrain.

"There," Paul said.

Anna's eyes followed his finger where it pointed to the crown of the little hill on which they stood. She saw nothing. "Where?"

"There," he said again.

Feeling a fool, Anna stared. Into the nothing a shape began to form. A mottled sand- and gray-colored canvas tarp was stretched tightly between two poles and pegged down close to the ground on both sides. Hidden in its shade was a two-man tent with a top of open mosquito netting. "Desert camo works," she remarked.

"At least we know for sure he was here," Paul said. From the camp they would follow scent trails out. At the end of one of them Nosy would find a corpse.

"Craig!" Paul called. Neither of them expected an answer.

The District Ranger started toward the tent and Anna followed. Craig's pack materialized. He'd covered it with sand-colored burlap. Ever the minimum impact camper, Anna thought. She made a mental note to buy all fluorescent orange gear. If she were injured in the Pattersons, she wanted to be found. Being dead had its attractions. Dying did not.

"Craig!" Paul called again, but Anna suspected he was just cheering himself, making a noise because he was alive. At Craig's pack he stopped and folded back the burlap carefully. Anna was reminded this, like all deaths—assuming it was a death—that did not take place under a physician's care, was considered a potential crime scene.

Alert for anything that was not as it should be, she walked over to the tent and reached for the zipper on the flap. As her thumb and finger pinched the hot metal of the pull, she heard the tiniest of sounds; a mere whispered rustling. It froze her in her tracks.

"What?" Paul demanded.

Afraid even to shake her head, Anna listened.

"What is it?" he asked again and, when she didn't answer, he too fell into a listening attitude. Gravel crunched: Betsy and Harland topping the hill. The desert creaked faintly in the heat. Nosy's tongue slopped over her paw. Then Anna heard it again; a faint rattling almost at her feet. Fear older than the Bible caught at her stomach.

Seeing a rattlesnake was one thing. Hearing one and not knowing where it was, was another altogether.

Keeping absolutely still, holding her now slightly comic stoop, she searched the area around her feet. The rattling subsided but she was not relieved. The sound had not crept away on a slither of sand and scale, it had stopped. The snake was still there. Anna's eyes moved up, over the tent. Bent close as she was she could see through the netting. Before, the shadow of the tarp had rendered it virtually opaque.

"Whoa . . ." She breathed. The rattling began again. Inside the tent lay a bloated, monstrous figure. Not human, though humanlike. Its head and neck were swollen and black. The features of the face had been destroyed by puffed and stretching flesh. The left arm was four times the size of a human being's arm. Big and glossy as waxed cucumbers, the fingers had burst open on the ends. The rest of the creature was pathetically human: pale legs, shrunken genitalia, flat white belly and hairless chest.

And all around, on the sleeping bag, like the ancient Greeks lounging on couches at a feast, were rattlesnakes.

Slowly Anna straightened, backed away.

"What is it?" Paul asked softly. Training or good instincts had kept them all quiet till Anna was clear of the tent.

"It looks like the snakes have collected Craig," she managed. Paul started to come forward and she held up a hand. "Somehow they got loose. His collecting buckets are overturned. There's half a dozen snakes in there with him, maybe more."

"Dead?" Paul asked.

"Not the snakes."

The tarp was easily dismantled leaving only the snake-filled tent. It was supported by two flexible poles forming a large arch for the head and a smaller one for the foot. Plexiglas rods were pushed through sleeves in the fabric and hooked into rings to keep their shape. Guy lines pegged down in opposite directions pulled the arches upright, stretching the nylon between them.

Using pocketknives affixed with surgical tape to long sticks, Anna and Paul cut the nylon down the center and sides like opening the foil around a baked potato. When the cuts were complete, they peeled the nylon back, keeping the distance of the sticks.

There were seven rattlesnakes: three blacktails and four western diamondbacks. Eventually the snakes would have departed of their own volition. It was much too hot for them to survive long without shade. But no one cared to sit and watch the macabre tableau longer than they had to. Under the gentle urging of tossed pebbles, the snakes were induced to slither away. When the last tail had vanished into a crevice between some stones, Anna, Harland, and Paul approached the body. Paul gave Anna a camera and, while she snapped pictures, Harland sketched the layout of the camp and the corpse.

The aridity of the West Side had desiccated the body. What had appeared black and monstrous through the filtering gauze of mosquito netting was actually discolored and prune-like, the swelling only half what it had originally seemed. Craig had been virtually mummified within the convection oven his tent had become, the moisture in his body sucked out, escaping through the netting. That accounted for the lack of a warning odor of decay.

Craig had died of snakebite, that much was obvious. The characteristic double puncture wound of the pit viper was unmistakable. He'd been bitten seven times: twice in the face and twice in the neck, with three bites on his left arm, one directly into the artery at the wrist.

From the disarray, it appeared he had kicked over the two specimen buckets as he slept, knocking the lids off. The snakes, frightened, confused, had begun to strike. Craig's thrashing attempts to escape had only excited them to further attacks.

That was the picture Paul pieced together from what little evidence they had.

As a matter of course, they searched the area and made notes of condition and location of all items found. Then Harland and Paul folded Craig Eastern's mortal remains into the ruined nylon tent and, slipping, smothering irreverent curses, carried the body down the slope.

Anna shouldered Craig's backpack and followed Betsy McLeod and Nosy down to where the stock waited.

Like an old-time cowboy slain on the range, Craig was tied across Jill's saddle. Betsy, her dog in her arms, rode pillion behind Harland.

Seven bites, Anna thought as Gideon plodded, head down through the curtains of super-heated air. Pesky, too worn out even to bite the mules' butts, slogged ahead.

"Death: accidental by snakebite."

Seven. And why was Craig sleeping with his collection buckets inside the tent? A bizarre form of suicide? No. Had Craig chosen to die by snakebite, he would have freed the reptiles after they had performed the chore. He loved them; he would not have left them imprisoned in the tent to die. If not suicide, how hard must he have thrashed in his sleep to overset both buckets with such violence the lids popped off?

A lot of questions.

Only one answer: Craig hadn't killed Sheila Drury. His "accident," like hers, had been carefully orchestrated by the same hand.

The hand that had sent Anna reeling off McKittrick Ridge.

# CHAPTER 17

The coroner's report was brief. Time of death: between midnight and six a.m. on July 16. Cause of death: accidental, by snakebite.

Drury's read: "Death: accidental, by lion kill." Anna would have been "Death: accidental, by falling." Too many accidents. Just as on Eastern there were too many bites. Unlike sharks, rattlers, even dumped out of bed in the middle of the night, did not go into feeding frenzies.

Anna was sitting at her desk in the Frijole Ranger Station going over the 343 Case Incident Report on the Eastern snakebite incident. It looked like hell. The entire thing needed to be retyped. For the moment, she shoved it into her briefcase and pulled out the list she'd made the night before the search began.

Craig's name was still on the top of it. Neatly, Anna drew a single line through the letters. The next names were "Christina/Erik" and "Karl." Christina: a friend, a confidante, a shoulder to cry on; Anna repressed a sigh and looked farther down. The names remaining were of people she had come to think of more as "extras" than suspects. First she would rid her mind—and her list—of them.

She dialed Minnegasco in St. Paul, Minnesota. Some pleading and much fabrication led to the information that, but for one trip to Texas when her daughter died, Sheila Drury's mother had not missed a day's work in twenty-three years and was not due to take her vacation until December 11. On the day Anna fell and the day Eastern died, Mrs. Drury had been at her desk on the second floor above St. Peter Street in St. Paul.

Almost in Heaven, Anna thought wryly, glad to have the troublesome and troubled woman off of her lists and out of her thoughts for good. On impulse, and because she wanted to hear a kindly voice, Anna called her mother-in-law in White Plains, New York. Usually she called only on the first Sunday of every month—Edith led a regulated life and Anna couldn't bear to talk of Zachary more often than that. This time Anna kept the conversation general. Edith didn't even flinch at the mention of grapefruit spoons. Anna thought of calling Rogelio, though she knew intimately where he had been the day Eastern died. But he would ask questions she did not want to answer.

She drove the mile to the Visitors Center and, with Manny's help, went back through the backcountry permits issued for July 2, the night before she fell; June 17, the night Drury was killed; and July 16, the night Craig died.

Both Sheila and Craig had been found miles from any of the designated camping areas in the park and there had been no special permits issued. It was unlikely the killer would fill out a permit for any area that was not regularly patrolled—the odds of getting caught would not outweigh the exposure of getting a permit. July 2 had a possible: an E. Wheelan driving a white Toyota with California plates had been permitted to camp at the McKittrick Ridge campground.

Anna would talk with the Walterses. She no longer believed Christina would kill—at least not her. But if she knew something about the accidents, Anna wasn't sure whether she would have the courage to report it. Especially if she were afraid of the perpetrator.

Erik Walters's Toyota was burgundy with black upholstery. The plate number didn't match that of E. Wheelan. Otherwise Christina's ex-husband was, to Anna's mind, everything a murderer should be. He was suave and self-assured. He dressed too well for his surroundings. His teeth were too white, too straight. Cat hair didn't adhere to his trousers and the wind didn't ruffle his hair. He looked the type able to strangle his CEO at the eleventh hole and still come in under par.

Christina, though clearly uncomfortable around him, fetched and carried, hovered and scraped like a Total Woman. Anna picked at the dinner she'd invited herself over to eat and wondered what she would ask Mr. Walters when she got the chance. Wilderness murder didn't seem to fit with his ultra-urban demeanor. Neither did profitless murder. Revenge wouldn't go to the bank. And why Craig? Trying to fit Erik into the picture created more questions than answers.

Anna looked at him over the candles Christina had lit. Glossy head bowed, he was listening attentively to a long plotless story Alison had been relating for several minutes. Christina, her face drawn up like a spaniel hoping for approval, appeared to be suspended two inches above the seat of her chair, ready to spring up to do her master's bidding.

Sit! Anna wanted to order in her best Woodward School voice. But she kept silent. She would ask Erik about Christina, she decided. She would hit every nerve she could. He'd been dumped, left with his "weak specimen" in his hand, while his wife ran off with another woman. Anna was betting, given the chance, poison would leak through that polished facade like manure through the tines of a pitchfork.

Nine o'clock: an hour past Alison's bedtime. Finally Christina left the table to tuck her daughter in. Alison's pajamas were laid out on Christina's bed. Erik's one suitcase was in the child's room. All of the dolls, moved to the dresser, stared glassy-eyed at the bed the intruder had deprived them of. Anna knew this because she'd checked on her way to the bathroom before dinner. The arrangement suited her. Did it suit Erik?

"Chrissy tells me you're a ranger," Erik said in his pleasant educated voice.

"Law Enforcement," Anna said, unsure of what she was trying to prove. The "Chrissy" had irritated her.

"Is your husband a ranger as well?"

"I'm a widow," Anna said.

"I'm sorry."

Some repressed emotion had shown in his light-colored eyes just before he lowered them to his coffee cup. Disappointment? Anna wondered if he were fishing, hoping to catch some whiff of indiscretion, something he could use to drag Christina into another custody battle.

"What brings you to this part of the country?" she asked.

"Business. Brown and Coldwell has a prospective client in El Paso—Gunnison Oil. And I wanted to see my little girl."

"Do you have any other children?" Anna was pleased to see his mouth harden at the corners.

"I plan to," he said a little too determinedly.

"I know adoption is all the rage," Anna said. "But I think I'd want my own. I'd want to see myself, my mother, my dad—reflections, anyway. These days with drugs and AIDS and whatever, if it wasn't really yours, you'd never know." She laughed. It was genuine. She was enjoying herself. "You know what they say: If you want something done right, you've got to do it yourself."

"Do you have children?" The question was abrupt, aggressive. Erik was beginning to twitch under her lash.

"No," Anna replied. She let his look of self-satisfaction settle for a couple seconds. Then she added. "I wish I did now Zach is gone. He wanted to wait. We were so broke. Both times I got pregnant—well, abortion seemed the right choice at the time."

"Abortion!"

Anna had him. "We used birth control but . . ." She allowed herself a small secret-sad smile. "Zach was exceedingly virile . . . Anyway, I doubt I'll have kids now. But maybe I'll be an honorary aunt. I know Christina plans to have another child." Anna sipped her coffee, hoping she hadn't laid it on too thick. Maybe he'd clam up, leave the room or something.

"That'd be a shame," he said quietly after nearly a minute had elapsed.

Anna waited, egging him on with silence.

"Criminals ought to be sterilized," he said with sudden vehemence. "Thieves and perverts breed thieves and perverts."

Perverts held no interest for Anna. It was clear to her which of the two had perverted love to their own ends and it wasn't Christina. "Thieves?"

Erik laughed. "I see Chrissy didn't tell you. Good old Mommy is a crook. She wrote nearly ten thousand dollars in bad checks signed in my name. That phony Madonna-and-Child act she does so well is all that kept her out of jail. Linda—" He made the name sound like an adjective describing something vile. "Linda, it seems, required recompense for her services."

Christina walked into the ensuing silence. The apologetic

half-smile that she wore constantly in Erik's company flickered unsteadily at the hostility in the room.

"Is the coffee okay, Erik?" she asked anxiously.

"It's fine, Chrissy," he said. His tone implied: "for the best effort of a fool."

Christina took his cup away.

Anna wished Chris had written a hundred thousand dollars worth of bad checks.

"Ally asked if you would read her a bedtime story," Christina said while she busied herself at the sink. "Could you?"

Without a word, Erik got up and walked into the dark hallway toward the bedrooms.

There was a sharp crack, the sound of broken glass falling. Christina had smashed his coffee cup against the side of the stainless-steel sink.

"Walk me home?" Anna said.

Clouds obscured the stars to the west and lightning flickered formlessly, too distant to be more than a vague and sudden glow. Christina sucked air noisily into her lungs. "God! Erik seems to take up all the oxygen in a room, doesn't he?"

"I can see why you left him. He sucks the life out of you."

"I suppose he told you about the checks?" Christina said.

It saddened Anna to hear herself addressed in the same anxious apologetic tone Christina used with Erik. "He told me."

"He did try to get Ally on the lesbian angle, too. I just left out the forgery part. I didn't mean to lie to you."

"I know," Anna replied. "It was easier."

As they approached Anna's door both women slowed. Neither had much reason to go home and the night was warm, the stars deep overhead. In common unspoken agreement they sat side by side on the curb fifteen feet from Anna's apartment.

"What happened to Zach?" Christina asked. Then quickly added: "You needn't tell me, if you don't want to."

"I don't mind," Anna said. "We were having a special supper, celebrating the fact that it was Thursday and there were no other holidays declared to infringe on ours. Zach was broiling steak on a little hibachi out on the fire escape. I wanted A-1 sauce. He was sprinting across Ninth Avenue to Goodman's to get it. A cab hit him. The cabby drove off. Nobody got the license number. Zach died. That's about it."

Christina was quiet for a while but she shifted closer and Anna felt comforted by the warmth of her shoulder in the darkness. "Such a sad thing," she said. "Is that why you are a vegetarian?"

"No. Maybe it's why I drink."

"A little wine is good for the soul."

"A lot is better."

# CHAPTER 18

At ten past nine in the morning pacific daylight time, Anna called the California DMV. They reaffirmed what she'd already guessed: E. Wheelan was legitimate; an Ernest Wheelan from San Anselmo, California. She then called Brown and Coldwell in San Francisco. Dianne, Mr. Walters's secretary, was glad to check a date for a Gunnison Oil secretary. No, no trouble. She'd loused up a few times in her career. Secretaries had to stick together. No need for the boss to know every little glitch.

Mr. Walters had been in a board meeting from three p.m. till nearly eight on July 2. Yes, she was certain. She'd been kept running the whole time fetching coffee and sandwiches and Xerox copies, then had to take the bus home at eight-thirty at night because Brown and Coldwell wouldn't spring for cab fare.

Anna hung up, leaned her head on her hands and stared out the dirty attic window of the Frijole ranger station. The attic was hot and fly-specked but it housed the only phone in the park where one could be relatively assured of privacy. The escarpment showed nearly white in the early sun, evergreens at the top fine and black as a fringe of silk. Anna found it difficult to believe there was more than one murderer stalking the backcountry of Guadalupe Mountains National Park. If that were true, then alibis for the time of her or Craig's attacks would imply innocence in the Drury Lion Kill. Unless one of the "accidents" were really an accident. Unlikely but far from impossible.

For the moment she would put Erik and Christina into the "Innocent" category. She looked down at her list.

Karl Johnson was next.

In front of her on the desk was a yellow slip of paper: the phone message Marta had pressed on her when she'd first returned from Mexico. Anna had forgotten it. Then at five p.m. the previous evening, when she'd finally gotten around to doing her laundry, she'd found it crushed in the pocket of her Levi's. It was from Tim Dayton at the Roswell lab where she had sent the samples from Karl's truck. The note said only that he called and to call back. Nothing urgent.

She dialed the number. Tim was in. From the faint swallowing sounds that came through the wire as she waited, Anna guessed the man who answered had laid the receiver down by a Bunsen burner with something boiling on it. She preferred it to Muzak.

After several minutes, Tim came on the line.

"Thanks for the blood test," Anna said. "Your assistant told me the samples were animal blood."

"Yes," Tim replied. He was older than Anna but, to his eternal annoyance, he sounded like a little kid over the phone. "Tessie said. Since you didn't call back, I figured it was no big deal, but I wanted to check with you before I threw out that hypo you sent—the one with the ketamine."

"Ketamine?"

"Yeah. It's pretty common. Vets use it to anesthetize animals. It puts them under more safely than the depressants they used to use."

Anna knew Roads and Trails sometimes sedated a problem animal so the Resource Management team could relocate it. It seemed odd that the stuff was in Karl's truck, but no one had been anesthetized. Not yet, anyhow. "Thanks, Tim. Go ahead and toss it."

"Sure you don't want it back?" His voice took on a teasing edge. "Used on people, the stuff is one hell of a hallucinogen. One more time for auld lang syne?"

"LSD!" Anna exclaimed, remembering Drury's autopsy. "My God."

"Not exactly, but it'll get you there."

"Tim, hang on to it a while for me, would you?"

"Sure."

"How about the dirt I sent?" This time Anna was leaving no loose ends, no unchecked facts.

"Looked like dirt to me," Dayton replied.

Anna thanked him, promised a sordid recital of all the facts one day soon over a six-pack, and hung up. She drove home, made herself a pot of coffee, settled Piedmont across her knees, and went through her calendar, marking the days Karl's vehicle was seen in McKittrick after the canyon was closed. Both were Fridays, Karl's day off. The truck had been there all night. Even Karl wouldn't dare camp in McKittrick Canyon. The area was closed to camping. If he were caught, he would be fired, asked to leave the Guadalupe Mountains. For Karl that would be tantamount to being exiled from the Garden of Eden.

According to the backcountry permits she'd gone over with Manny the day before, he hadn't camped on McKittrick Ridge or at the Permian Ridge campground either. When off duty, park employees had to obtain permits to use the backcountry just as visitors did. Again, Anna doubted Karl would risk his job to flout a simple rule then leave his truck in plain sight.

The only alternatives were hiking up North McKittrick Canyon or the Permian Reef Trail and camping beyond the park's boundary in the Lincoln National Forest. No permits were needed there. The Permian Reef Trail was more likely. North McKittrick was rough going and it was a long way before one reached good campsites.

Leaning back, Anna stroked Piedmont's melted form spread across her knees. There was no way she could follow Karl, undetected, up the Permian Reef trail. It was too exposed: four miles of switchbacks up a rocky mountainside. She looked back to the calendar. Today was Thursday. She would hike up and camp, wait for him up in the trees where there was cover.

After packing her gear, Anna drove to the Administration building. She told Christina what she intended and asked if she would drop her off at McKittrick Canyon on her lunch hour. Looking pleased that Anna trusted her with her plans, she said she would.

Anna stopped briefly at the McKittrick Visitors Center and checked the closing log. Karl's truck was logged in the canyon half a dozen times over the past few months, always on a Friday. By two-thirty Anna had hiked up the mountain. The top of the ridge bridged McKittrick Canyon to the west and Big Canyon to the east. Big Canyon was over the line in the Lincoln. A trail joined the two tracts of public land, crossing through a revolving gate in the boundary fence separating them. A couple miles of forested land blanketed the ridge where it flattened out between the two canyons. It was a part of the relict forest that made the high country in Guadalupe so magical. Sotol and yucca held the desert's place on the edges of the escarpment.

If Karl followed his pattern he would hike up Friday. Still, Anna ate Thursday's supper at the edge of the reef where she could look down two thousand feet to the Visitors Center. Through binoculars, she watched the last visitors straggling out of the canyon, the cars drive away, then, just after six, the white one-ton pickup drive in. A tiny figure, probably Manny, checked the doors and windows of the building then got back into the truck and drove away. The canyon had been put to bed.

Anna watched the sun set and the stars come out, the half moon rise. Near ten-thirty she unrolled her sleeping bag in the hollow trough of the trail and slept. Around midnight a deer, confused but not alarmed by this obstacle, woke her with questioning snorts and irritated scufflings. Otherwise the night was restful. Morning put her back on the cliff's edge, binoculars in one hand, a mug of tea in the other, watching the miles of trail zigzagging below.

At nine-thirty a blue truck pulled into the parking lot. A man that could only be Karl Johnson—even at a distance he looked big—got out. He shouldered a red backpack and started up the trail toward the Permian Reef.

Anna put a bottle of water and her .357 on her belt, then stashed her pack deep in a rock crevice a good hundred feet off the trail. Satisfied it couldn't be seen, she continued her vigil.

It took Karl only ninety minutes to climb the four miles and two thousand feet. Following him would require more than stealth, it would take stamina. He was still below her on the exposed switchbacks. Soon she would need a new hiding place, one close to the trail where it ran through the trees on the ridgetop. From there she would fall into place behind him when he passed.

As soon as he disappeared from sight around the last bend

in the trail before it leveled out in the trees on high ground, Anna left the edge of the escarpment.

Situated behind a dense stand of gray-leaf oak near a bend in the trail, she began again to wait. By holding down a branch, she could see almost to where the trail broke through the boulders on the edge of the escarpment. A quarter of a mile of trail was hidden from view. Unless Karl took off cross-country at that point, she would have him in sight again within minutes.

Scarcely had she finished her thought when he appeared. Even half a mile away, he looked enormous. The battered, lumpy face was set, the wiry ogre head held low. He charged up the trail like a bull. For the first time since she'd started this pursuit, Anna felt afraid. Intent on planning, on hiding, reality had been pushed from her mind: she was stalking a man she believed might have murdered two people and tried, most brutally, to murder her. Despite the revolver she felt unpleasantly small and fragile, wrists and neck breakable as toothpicks.

Karl's long legs, swinging like tree trunks, ate up the trail. Stones crunched under his heavy boots. Feeling exposed, she held her breath as he approached, looked down as if the force of her eyes upon him would bring his gaze up and she would be discovered.

Without any change in rhythm, the footfalls passed. Anna opened her eyes. This small success calmed her. So might a lion sit atop a boulder, unseen, and watch its prey go by. This was natural, not supernatural. Karl would not feel her eyes. If she kept her wits about her she would be okay.

Sacrificing time for silence, she worked out of the scrub oak, then ran lightly down the trail. Having chosen tennis shoes over hiking boots, she made very little noise. Glimpses of Karl's red pack showed through the trees when she got close or when the trail curved back on itself sharply.

Three-quarters of a mile from the boundary between the park and the Lincoln, the trail broke free of the forest and followed a stony spine through low-growing shrubs and succulents.

As she hit the open stretch, Karl was less than fifty yards in front of her. Anna dropped down behind a rock and followed him with her ears. When she could no longer hear his grinding steps she peeked out. His wiry orange hair was just disappearing over the hogback and down a gentle slope.

He would be approaching the boundary fence. The forest began again there, thicker and denser in the moist hollow between the ridges of the two canyons.

Anna trotted slowly down the trail, aware that if Karl stopped to pee or take a drink or look at the view, she could come upon him more suddenly than she intended. She had a lie ready for such an event but she hoped not to have to use it. If Karl was the killer he probably wouldn't buy it. If he wasn't, she probably wouldn't need it.

Slowing, she came over the rise. Below her was the barbed-wire fence and the rusting revolving gate. Beyond she could see about a mile of trail winding up a steep slope in the Lincoln. To the left North McKittrick Canyon dropped off in a sheer stone cliff. To the right, beyond the gate, the forest crowded up to the trail.

Karl was gone.

It crossed Anna's mind that he'd seen her, was waiting behind rock or tree and would reach out one great hairy arm like the ogre he so resembled. She stopped a moment, reassured herself he'd not seen her, and ran on. If he'd gone off trail anywhere before the fence she'd most likely be able to see him still. A hundred or so feet of scrub lay between the trail and the more heavily wooded area.

At the revolving gate she slowed to a creep, her eyes on the ground. The trail was bone dry and packed hard. A bad surface for tracking. It was also seldom used and Karl was a heavy man. A toe print, the familiar star and waffle horseshoe pattern of NPS boots, was imprinted in the dust. Four feet or so away, a scuffed mark: whitish sand and stone scraped away exposing the darker soil beneath. Anna measured off another yard and a third and looked. In the normal course of events, a foot must have fallen there.

If there was a sign of Karl's passing, she could not find it. Another four feet were marked off. Nothing. She went back to where she'd found the scuff and studied the side of the trail. A line, very faint, probably an animal track, led off into the trees. Several feet down it a pinecone had been crushed absolutely flat. Not clipped or partially broken as by a hoof, but flattened entirely.

Anna ran down the faint track. Indians, she'd read time and again, had run through the forest silently. Not the Lincoln, she decided. Careful as she was, her soft-soled sneakers made a distinct rustling in the dry grass and needles. Even the tiniest of snakes would be heard slithering through this high desert woodland.

Red, a fragment no bigger than a songbird, flickered ahead. Karl was in front of her. She could see his right shoulder and arm through the trees and underbrush. He stopped. A long second later Anna's command to her feet took effect and she, too, was still.

Karl's arm made no move. He didn't pull off his pack or reach for his water bottle. He hadn't stopped for a rest or a drink.

Karl was listening.

Anna was afraid to breathe and afraid to hold her breath. She'd run so far she knew if she tried, her lungs would rebel and she'd gasp aloud. The pounding of her heart, resounding through the woods like a jungle drum, seemed enough to give her away.

The shoulder moved. Karl was turning. If she could see a scrap of red, what would he see? Blessing her foresight in wearing olive trousers and a khaki shirt, she slowly put her hands behind her, lowered her head till her face was pointing toward the ground, and willed herself utterly still. Her heartbeat slowed, she felt or imagined her energy slowing. Playing a mind-game with herself, Anna rooted, became as a tree.

Rustling, the crack of a twig: Karl was moving on. If he had seen her, he had chosen to lead her deeper into the woods.

Anna gambled he had not. Placing each foot with care, she followed. Trailing through the forest was easier than on the trail in the sense that she had ample cover. But walking quietly was proving difficult. Matching him step for step, she hoped the sound of his own passage would mask hers.

The animal track faded out. Karl walked on like a man sure of his way. Down a dry ravine, the narrow bottom littered with stones, Anna followed. It emptied out into a slightly wider drainage. Downstream it would end in a fall down into Big Canyon. Karl turned upstream.

Trees had been scoured out by boulders rolled on summer floods. Rocks twenty feet high and that many across were jumbled together forming caves and hallways. From boulder to boulder Anna crept, trusting more to the fact that there wasn't any direction to go but up the creekbed than to sight or sound in keeping on Karl's trail. To have kept him in view would've been impossible without the risk of being seen.

Sun reflected off rock and the heat in the airless confines of the wash became intense. Having soaked her handkerchief in water, Anna tied it around her head. It was one-fifteen. She had been following Karl for over two hours. Never once had he let up on the pace he had set down on the groomed trail leading across the canyon from the McKittrick Visitors Center. Anna breathed deeply, filling her lungs to aching. There would be time to rest when Karl did. If he did.

The perfect murder, she thought. He will keep going till I drop dead from exhaustion.

Karl had been nowhere in sight for nearly twenty minutes when Anna came to the end of the ravine. The drainage was a small box canyon, its head a hallway of stone ending in a rock wall fifty feet high. Karl was not there.

The ogre theory seemed more and more plausible and images of hidden doors, caves under spells of invisibility, stones that rotated to reveal underground passages flickered through Anna's head. She sat down in the shade of a courageous little pine tree that clung to a crevice and took a pull at her canteen.

The ravine rose steeply on three sides. No trail, not even places to scramble up, presented themselves. All was sheer stone wall or crumbling rock embedded with catclaw and lechugilla. The dead end of the box was scarcely five feet wide and in deep shadow. Wary of falling stones and tiger traps, Anna made her way into the slot.

No magic doors. No invisible caves. A prosaic solution in use since the Anasazi had built cliff dwellings: hand and toe holds had been chipped into the rock. From the distance they were apart, Anna guessed Karl had made them to fit his own long reach. She had to stretch precariously to reach from one to another. Twenty feet up she remembered reading that the Anasazi had often planned their stone "ladders" so an enemy, starting out on the wrong foot, would find himself halfway up without a grip, unable to ascend or descend.

She hoped Karl hadn't read that far.

The muscles in her arms and legs were quivering by the time she pulled herself over the top. There wasn't any way she could do it safely or discreetly but merely hauled herself over the lip of stone and sprawled gasping on a natural landing fifteen or twenty feet wide.

Her shoulder throbbed. Cracks took nearly as long to heal as breaks. Climbing fifty feet probably wasn't included under the prescription of "taking it easy." Breath and caution recovered, she sat up.

The climb had landed her at the mouth of a small hanging valley not more than half a mile deep and about that wide. Met by an unyielding horseshoe-shaped escarpment of hard stone, the rains had carved, instead of the usual steep-sided ravine, a shallow flat-bottomed canyon. Soil, washed down the many tiny runoffs from the high country, had filled the little valley with rich fertile earth.

Hidden from above by steep tree-covered slopes and from below by the ragged ravine-cut land dropping into Big Canyon, the valley had a mysterious quality. Like all magical lands, it was protected by a cloak of invisibility.

Anna got to her feet and walked quietly across the stone landing and stepped into the trees. Delicate music reached her and she paused mid-step. Whistling, faint and clear: "Never Never Land." Karl was in the valley. Anna hadn't doubted that; the whistling reassured her that he believed himself alone. Unless she had severely underestimated him and it was part of a well-laid trap.

A path formed beneath her feet. More than just a narrow animal track, this trail had been trod by heavy boots many times. She guessed Karl approached his little kingdom from a number of different routes to avoid leaving a trail others might be tempted to follow. Here he felt safe enough to take the easiest way.

Karl's whistle kept him placed in Anna's ear as she moved quickly up the trail. With the sweet scent of pine, the towering walls, soft dirt instead of unforgiving stone underfoot, it was hard to retain the adrenaline level that had given her strength on the forced march Karl had led.

A tearing sound in the trees to her left brought her back to nervous reality. Two does tore placidly at the dry grass less than fifteen feet from the trail. Both looked at her with mild interest then went back to their lunch. One of them had an eight-inch scar on the left side of her neck. The other was missing her right rear hoof. The leg ended just below the ankle. Both showed a complete lack of fear.

Curiouser and curiouser, Anna thought.

The whistling stopped and she proceeded with more caution. Twenty feet beyond the grazing animals, she came to a small clearing. What looked at first glance to be a child's fort was built against a venerable old ponderosa growing between two boulders.

The shack was at most eight feet square and not quite that high. Walls and roof were made of sticks and small branches held together with nails, twine, and baling wire. Tar paper served as weatherproofing. A blackened length of stovepipe held up by wire affixed to the pine tree poked up from the roof. A faded horse blanket curtained off the doorway.

Keeping to the cover of the trees, Anna skirted the clearing till she stood under the pine next to the stick and paper hut. There she listened until she could hear the blood rushing in her ears. Nothing moved within. From up the valley came again the notes of a whistled song.

She slipped around the cabin and pulled the horse blanket aside. The room was uninhabited. Stepping inside she then steadied the blanket lest its movement give her away.

After the glare of the afternoon it took her eyes a minute to adjust to the gloom. Light trickled in from gaps around the stovepipe and tears in the tar paper. Karl's red backpack lay on the earthen floor as if he'd thought better of leaning its considerable weight against the walls. A stove, fashioned from half of a fifty-gallon drum, took up most of one wall. Evidently unused in summer, the stove was all but hidden by eight five-gallon plastic cubitainers the park used to haul and store water. Six were full. There were no shelves. Rude benches crafted of stones and branches lined two of the walls. Both were littered with bottles and cans, boxes and tools.

A short search disclosed several lengths of rope, some chain, two scalpels, surgical tape, syringes, needles, a bottle of chloroform, cotton wool, a ten-pound bag of Purina Dog Chow, and a bottle of ketamine partially empty.

Sunlight flashed as the blanket covering the door was jerked aside.

# CHAPTER 19

Nails cried from the wood and the blanket was torn free of the tacks holding it in place. Karl and Anna screamed at the same time. Standing in the sun, the horse blanket trailing from one great fist, a shovel held like a toy in the other, he looked the giant he was. Anna felt like a small furry animal cornered in its den.

"Anna!" he said, and for an instant she thought he looked pleased to see her. The moment passed. His heavy features settled into stony disapproval. "You can't be telling about this," he said deliberately, seeming to use his words to carve out his thoughts. "You can't be telling." The blanket fell to the ground and Anna saw his left hand tense up on the shovel's handle.

Feeling oddly melodramatic, she pulled her revolver and leveled it at him. It was the first time she had ever drawn it outside a firing range. The sensation of pointing it at another living creature was disquieting. As was the sudden knowledge that she would not hesitate to use it.

Karl raised the shovel an inch or two. Though his eyes were locked on hers, Anna found his face as unreadable as she always had.

"Put the shovel down, Karl," she said gently. "Just let it fall there beside you."

"You can't be telling," he said stubbornly and his thick fingers rippled on the wooden handle as if he assured himself of his grip.

Shifting her weight, Anna eased back from the square of sunlight shining in through the doorway. In the shadows her movements, her plans would be less easily read. "Let it go, Karl. It'll be easy. Nobody will be hurt."

To her surprise, tears, big and bright as crystals, rolled down either side of his bulbous nose. "Everybody depends on me," he said.

The sense of unreality she had felt since entering the valley deepened. "Who depends on you?"

He waved the shovel vaguely and every muscle in Anna's body quivered. She was strung tight. Consciously, she relaxed, letting the air pull deeper into her lungs. "Everybody," Karl said again.

"Karl," Anna said, careful to keep her voice even, nonthreatening. "I want you to do something for me. I want you to set down your shovel. You holding it like that is frightening me. You're kind of a scary man with that shovel. After I stop being scared for a while, maybe I can put away this gun and we can talk better. Will you do that for me? Will you put down that shovel?"

Karl put the shovel down. His big shoulders sagged. It was almost as if he were shrinking before her eyes. She lowered the pistol but kept it ready at her side.

"Will you show me who everybody is?" A fleeting image out of the horror movies she'd seen as a teenager sickened her: bodies strung up with baling wire and twine presided over by a psychotic killer.

Without protest, Karl turned and walked toward the trees up the valley from the hut. Keeping a good fifteen feet between them, her side arm still unholstered, Anna followed.

Things were clarified in Anna's eye to the point of appearing almost surreal. Each movement of Karl's shoulders, every shift of his weight as he plodded heavily along in front of her was noted, judged, rated nonaggressive and dismissed. All in a second, in a footfall. The world surrounding that thick back and shoulders receded from vision. Consequently it took her a moment to refocus when he stopped.

To his left was a natural overhang in the stone that formed the narrow valley's walls. A grotto fifteen or twenty feet deep and fifty feet long had been formed over the centuries as the tiny seeps in the stone had melted away the soft lime. At its mouth the grotto was half again as tall as Karl. Within this shelter were several cages made from sticks and wire and a pen about ten feet square.

"Everybody," Karl said. From the warmth and pride in his voice, one might've thought he was introducing his family. Edging closer, Anna peered into the thick shadow under the overhang. The pen held a mule deer—a fawn still in spots. White bandages, wrapped as carefully as if a trained nurse had done the binding, striped its forelegs. When it saw Karl it trotted over to the fence, thrusting its rubbery little nose through the sticks. "I was getting her some lunch," Karl said accusingly. "The little guys get so hungry."

Anna looked beyond, to the cages. The rust-colored back of a ring-tail cat showed against the chicken wire of one. The cage beyond began to rattle.

"Looky," Karl said, his eyes glowing. He had apparently forgotten the gun. Anna slipped it back into its holster and, snapping the keeper in place, followed him down the mouth of the grotto. The little fawn kept pace as long as it could then reared up like a dog, putting its tiny hooves against the fence.

Karl knelt. The rough slow voice was as gentle as a nursemaid's. "Are my girls bored?" he asked. As he reached to lift the door of the cage, a tawny paw met his brown one and he laughed. For the moment Anna had been forgotten. The door slid open and out bounded a fat cougar kitten with enormous paws. It stopped at the sight of Anna, its hind quarters piling up on its front quarters, landing it on its nose.

"It's okay," Karl said, folding the twenty-five-pound kitten into his arms. Held in his massive grip, it looked no bigger than a house cat.

"That's my shy baby," Karl said fondly and Anna followed his look back to the cage. A single round ear and dark blue eye peeked around the door.

"The orphaned kittens. You found them," Anna said. She dropped to her knees and held her hands out palm-up like a supplicant. The baby cougar crept out, smelled her hands, then batted at one experimentally.

"They're hungry girls," Karl said in the same doting voice. Without having to be told, Anna picked up the second kitten and followed Karl back to the hut. He filled two baby bottles with powdered milk using water from the cubitainers.

Outside, in the shade of the spreading pine branches, their backs against a boulder, he and Anna bottle-fed the little lions.

Anna was transfixed. Karl's valley was indeed a magical place. "Was that you I heard whistling the day I rode Gideon up after their mother was shot?" she asked.

Karl nodded. He kissed the nursing kitten between its ears.

"Were you whistling 'Tender Shepherd'?"

"I knew it was you'd come for the babies. I wanted to tell you they were okay. But you couldn't know." He looked around his valley.

"No," Anna said. Karl's hospital was most illegally built

and operated on Forest Service land. And the official park policy was to let injured animals fend for themselves or, if seen to be suffering, or if dangerous or offensive to visitors, to be dispatched. "Let nature take its course," Anna quoted.

"I'm nature, too," Karl replied. "This is my course."

Anna didn't argue. "The ketamine is for the animals?"

"Sometimes I have to put them out for a while so I can help them."

"How do you get them up here? This valley is like a fortress."

"I carry them," Karl said simply.

Anna was reminded of Father Flanagan's boys: "He ain't heavy, he's my brother."

"I can carry as much as three hundred pounds sometimes."

Anna believed him. He'd carried, on his back, everything the animals needed. And he'd carried them. "The deer?" Anna asked. "I saw them as I came in."

"Chris and Al. They got to stay here always now," he answered sadly. "Chris is lame and the littler one is blind. Outside, the cats and coyotes would get them. Maybe they'll come here and eat them but maybe not."

"Chris and Al?"

Karl said only: "The eyes." Anna understood. The does' eyes, so dark and trusting, were very like Christina Walters's.

"What are the kittens called?" she asked as he refilled the bottles.

Karl looked shy. On so big a man the expression was almost laughable but Anna didn't laugh. "Annabelle and Annalee."

"Anna."

"You came for them when they were left," he said. "They can play here," Karl added as the kittens, finally full, tumbled off their laps.

The kitten Anna held caught its claw in her shirt and began

to struggle. Karl expertly squeezed the paw's pad and detached the claw from the fabric. "They're so little, they're not good at retracting their claws yet," he said. The gesture triggered something in Anna's mind. A connection she should be making and wasn't.

Karl gathered up both kittens.

"You must feed them more than once a week," Anna said as she followed him back toward the enclosure under the rock.

"While they're little I'll come every day. I don't like people seeing my truck all the time in McKittrick so they might guess. I drive up back of the Lincoln and come in there most times."

Anna drew a quick map in her head. A two-and-a-half-hour drive and a two-hour hike every day after work to feed his kittens. "When do you sleep?" she asked with a laugh.

"When they're bigger," he replied.

"Karl—" Something in her voice made him stop, turn, and look at her. "Your secret is safe with me. I won't tell anybody. Ever." Driven by the remarkable innocence in his face, Anna crossed her heart.

"I know that you wouldn't, so I put down the shovel," he said. It didn't seem odd to Anna. A man might be willing to face a gun armed only with a shovel to keep his family safe.

Karl let Anna feed the fawn. He had named her Yolanda after Manny's fawn-skinned wife. "Is this the fawn Manny radioed was caught in the fence?" Anna asked, remembering. "The one they couldn't find?"

"I got there first." He sounded triumphant.

A triumph deserved, Anna thought. Harland would've dispatched the little animal. It had been injured and it was too young to live on its own. Karl had worked it free of the wire and spirited it away. Anna guessed the blood she had sent to the Roswell lab had come from the body of the creature she held in her arms.

A low growl set Yolanda to struggling. The hairs on the back of Anna's neck prickled.

Karl gathered the little mule deer protectively to his chest as Anna turned and squinted into the recesses of the last and largest of the sheltered cages. A grown cougar lay in the shadows, his unwinking yellow eyes upon her. "My God," Anna breathed.

Karl nuzzled the fawn, started it nursing again. "He was shot in the hind end. I wouldn't've found him except I was looking after Manny's dog when they were gone and Dinky went with me to the West Side and set to barking. He's going to heal up soon."

"You found him on the West Side?"

"Out in the Patterson Hills by PX Well, way over there. I was checking the rain gauge."

"What will you do with him?"

"I'll put him to sleep, then I'll take him up onto the ridge where the babies' momma was killed and look after him till he wakes up good."

"What's his name?" Anna asked.

"Fluffy," Karl replied. Anna looked at him over her shoulder and he smiled broadly. "It's a joke we have," he explained.

Fluffy stretched, rose gracefully to his feet. Behind him, near where the stone wall met the grotto floor, there was a gleam of green, the color of a glowworm, but close to a foot long.

"What's that?" Anna asked, pointing.

"I cut it off Fluff's neck when I took off the radio collar. It's one of those things you shake up and then they light. Kids play with them in the towns."

"Ah . . . Fluffy . . . was one of our radio-collared lions?"

"I cut it off him and busted it so nobody'd come following the signal to see why he'd stayed in one spot so long. You can have it back," Karl offered.

Anna smiled and shook her head. Anything Karl busted was apt to stay busted. "This is where you were the night Sheila was killed, wasn't it?"

"I came up special. I thought what with that first lightning and the Forest Service flying all over looking for strikes, it would scare Ally. She was just little and blind."

"Lightning. Of course," Anna said. The pieces of all the puzzles were beginning to fit together into a single picture. "Karl, do you remember what day it was that you shoed Gabe, Sheila's horse, over in Dog Canyon?"

Karl began a long and laborious thought process. The fawn wriggled free and stood bandy-legged next to him sucking his fingers. "I got everybody new shoes in June. Mules first as they have such a lot of hard work. Then our guys. It'd've been after the fourteenth because they hadn't their good shoes on for the Van Horn parade."

Anna waited but that was as far as Karl could take that line of thought by himself. "Was it done before the first lightning storm when you came up here to be with Ally?"

Again Karl thought. "Yes," he said with certainty.

"So the fifteenth or the sixteenth," Anna said. Karl looked impressed with her reasoning.

Annabelle and Annalee skirmished for their attention then, and Anna watched Karl play with them, keeping the injured fawn safe from the fray.

Anna's mother-in-law, just turned eighty-one, said when she was a young woman she valued intelligence over all other human attributes. Now that she was older she valued kindness.

Anna was learning.

# CHAPTER 20

Two days later, driving down Dark Canyon, the image of Karl's hanging valley floated pleasantly into Anna's mind. One mystery at least had been solved: she knew now what the inside of Karl's brain looked like. Not an attic full of well-cared-for toys, but a garden full of well-cared-for creatures.

She doubted her next stop would have such a pastoral outcome.

On Queens Highway she turned left, up through the Lincoln. She'd timed it so she would arrive at Paulsen's ranch just after lunch. Anna hoped to catch him at his house. Chasing over twenty-five thousand acres of lonely desert in search of the man didn't appeal to her in the least.

As she drove, she went over the links in the chain that was pulling her toward Paulsen's. Karl had shod Gabe on the fifteenth or the sixteenth of June; there had been pictures of him in Sheila's camera. The pictures after that on the same roll of film had been of lightning taken up behind Dog Canyon on

Jerry Paulsen's ranch. They could only be photos of the storm that hit the north side of the park the night Sheila had been killed. Anna had been camped on the ridge above Dog Canyon that night. She'd watched the storm build. The lightning had started a couple of hours before sundown.

Sheila had been alive and pursuing her hobby around six p.m. Less than nine hours later she was dead in Middle McKittrick, miles across the park's ruggedest country. In her stomach were the remains of a meal the other half of which Anna had found in her daypack with the camera. In her neck a puncture wound half an inch deeper than it should've been. Sheila had not gone to McKittrick under her own power and she had not been killed there.

The Rambler rolled out of the hills and onto the long straight road hemmed close on both sides by Paulsen's new barbed-wire fence. Ahead was a gate made of welded lengths of pipe under an arch of weathered tree trunks bearing the JP brand.

Anna pulled the car into the dirt lane and sat for a moment behind the wheel wondering just how she would handle the next couple of hours. She wished she were not tackling Paulsen alone. Of all the strong-arm people in her life—Karl and Rogelio and Paul—it was Christina whom Anna wished for; Christina with her dark eyes and credible lies and good sense.

Before leaving Guadalupe, Anna had put a note in Chris's mailbox. She'd tried to avoid the dramatic cliché, but her note conveyed the same basic idea: If I'm not back by dark, call the police.

Reminding herself that she'd not come to Paulsen's like the Earps to the O.K. Corral, that she had come to look, to talk, mostly to listen, Anna was comforted. No lights and sirens, no accusations; there had been, after all, no official crime—simply a string of freak accidents. At best she would find a few more answers. At worst, Paulsen would.

"Quit stalling," Anna said and levered herself out of the car to open the gate. It was the first in a series and she began to wish she'd brought Christina along for reasons other than company and courage. Passengers traditionally opened and closed all the gates.

A grove of ponderosa pine and fine old cottonwoods let her know she was nearing the end of her journey. Nestled in the vee of two skirting foothills, near the main spring, the dependable water source that guaranteed life to his ranch, would be Jerry Paulsen's home.

The rutted dirt road Anna had been following for four miles through cow pastures didn't prepare her for the imposing formality of the Paulsen homestead. Built of white-painted clapboard, it rose two stories over lawns that had once been groomed to east-coast standards but had since succumbed to drought and pine needles. Traditional green ornamental shutters framed the windows. A deep portico with antebellum-style pillars protected wide double doors.

There were no flowers of any kind. Window boxes were empty, the planters lining the short front walk were bare. To Anna it indicated that there was no Mrs. Paulsen and that either there once had been or Mr. Paulsen had once hoped there would be.

The old Rambler couldn't face the snobbery of the portico. Anna parked off the gravel in the shade of a cottonwood and walked the twenty yards to the front door. The knocker, two horseshoes hinged together, was jarring in the context of the house's architecture. In front of the formal doors lay a worn mat reading WELCOME Y'ALL. Beside it was a rudely welded boot-scraper.

Anna lifted the knocker and let it drop. Against the thick oak it made a pathetic "plink." Using more vigor, she banged it again. From inside she heard a voice. The words were unintelligible but the singsong rhythm clearly telegraphed: "Just a minute."

The door was opened by a Mexican woman in jeans and a T-shirt with the *America's Funniest Home Videos* logo on the front. She was probably near Anna's age but an extra thirty pounds and a bad perm made her seem older. Cold air poured from inside the house.

"You better come in," the woman said. "We don't wanna air-condition alla New Mexico." A cheeky smile wrinkled up to her eyes and made Anna smile back. "You looking for Jerry or Jonah?"

Vaguely, Anna remembered Mr. Paulsen had a son of that name. "Jerry," she said.

"Good, 'cause Jonah's away at college." The woman laughed then as at a favorite joke, one that never palled no matter how many times she played it. "Jerry's out back havin' his cigarette. I'm Lydia." Lydia led the way back into the refrigerated house. They passed through a formal parlor with wing-backed chairs, which Anna surmised were never touched by anything but a dust cloth from one year to the next. Down a long hall lined with animal prints and through a smaller room that had been a butler's pantry, Anna followed. Abruptly, Lydia stopped. The old pantry opened directly into the den. Clearly this was the house's heart; where people did their living.

Anna found it oppressively masculine. The walls were done in dark wood and adorned with the severed heads of animals. Mostly indigenous—or once indigenous—to the United States: grizzly bear, big-horned sheep, bobcat, mountain lion, moose, elk, pronghorn, wolf, and the pathetic little joke of the Southwest: the jackalope—a bunny's head with the horns of a young antelope glued on.

The severed parts; Karl unhooking the kitten's claw. Two

more pieces clicked in. Suddenly Anna knew when a lion wasn't a lion: when it's dead. And she knew how Sheila Drury had been killed. Tearing her gaze from the dismembered creatures lest the knowledge could be read in her eyes, she surveyed the rest of the room.

Guns finished the decor. The collection was impressive. German dueling pistols from near the turn of the century, a pearl-handled revolver, several long rifles, an ornate iron tube that could only be a custom-made silencer.

The owner and sole inhabitant of this lair was seated in a bentwood rocker looking out over a flagstone patio to the brown hills beyond. He held a cigarette between his thumb and index finger, smoking with careful pleasure. Though surely he had heard their clattering entrance a second or two before, he turned with evident surprise.

"Mr. Paulsen, this is . . ." Lydia turned to let Anna finish the introduction.

"Miss Anna Pigeon of Guadalupe," Jerry Paulsen filled in. "We've met before."

They had. Twice that Anna could remember. Both times fleetingly, both times she was merely "another ranger" hovering impatiently at Corinne or Paul's elbow while short insincere exchanges were made at gate and cattleguard. Not really enough to spark this instant recognition unless Mr. Paulsen had a phenomenal memory. Or someone had been talking about her; and recently.

He rose and took Anna's proffered hand. In lieu of shaking it, he clasped it between his own, patting it in an avuncular fashion. He had the look of a kindly old uncle as well as the manner: He was not tall but of good size—five-foot-ten or -eleven with the boots—broad shouldered with a bit of a belly hanging over his silver-dollar belt buckle. The deep leathery tan of the Southwest looked good over a ruddy complexion. White mustache and thick white hair with its natural wave coaxed to perfection set off very keen blue eyes.

A Good Old Boy, Anna thought as he played the host, beaming her into a chair, sending Lydia to the kitchen to make coffee. Anna wondered what he knew. More than she did, probably.

"You're looking fit," he remarked when his duties had been done and he sat again in the bentwood opposite her. His eyes took all of her in from stem to stern. Or withers to rump. He had the look of a man admiring a bit of horseflesh.

"I heard you'd taken a tumble above Turtle Rock."

"Stepped into nothing," Anna said and accepted the coffee Lydia brought. The usual cowboy-sized mugs were missing. The coffee was served in white fluted china cups bordered with gold. She took a sip: instant. Anna added a generous dollop from the cream pitcher and the mess turned bluish gray: skim milk.

Paulsen drank his steaming hot and black. "Bad luck. Y'all have had a rash of bad luck from what I hear. Some old boy just got himself snakebit? Hate those damn things. I know you folks over at the park coddle 'em like new calves but by God I still stomp every one that slithers across my path. Hating snakes is the natural state of man."

Anna looked at him over the rim of her cup. The only thing the blue eyes gave away was a pleasant twinkle. Jerimiah D. was enjoying himself, Anna realized. He'd sparred with the National Park Service for twenty years. It was probably his favorite sport next to hunting.

Jerimiah D. Bells rang in Anna's head.

"What's the 'D' for?" she asked suddenly. "Jerimiah D. Paulsen."

"Well, now, where did you hear that?" he drawled and the twinkle in his eyes grew, if anything, brighter. Anna'd stumbled onto something but she had no idea what and, as he seemed to enjoy it, she suspected it was of no value.

Unable to remember where she'd heard it, Anna just smiled.

Paulsen rocked back, crossed his legs, resting his ankle on his knee, and grinned hugely. "Since you been so nice as to come all the way over here to pay me a visit, I'll tell you."

Now she knew it was of no value. Or he was going to tell her a lie.

"Dalrimple. My momma's maiden name. Daddy built this house for her. Jerimiah D. Paulsen. My old friends call me Jerimiah D."

With a start, Anna remembered then where she'd heard it. The information wasn't nearly so useless as he'd thought. Maybe she didn't have what she wanted, but she had enough.

Sheila had seen something—probably stumbled on it by accident while patrolling the park perimeter for lightning strikes. They, in turn, had stumbled on her. Whatever the specifics were, Anna did not doubt Paulsen knew. She also knew this was not the way to outfox the bluff and hearty Mr. Paulsen. He'd been at it too many years, enjoyed the game too much.

Time had come to leave.

"You've an impressive collection," Anna said, looking at a Sako hung above a wide mantel made of native rock. The barrel was polished with love and long use. The stock was intricately carved dark wood.

Paulsen, following her gaze, stood and walked over to the fireplace. He lifted the weapon down with the reverence of a pilgrim handling a piece of the true cross.

"This is my baby." He sounded as if it were the literal truth. "Finest weapon ever made. Bar none."

Anna put down her coffee and joined him by the cold grate. "May I?" she asked holding out her hands for the rifle.

He all but snatched it away, holding it possessively to his chest, then chuckling at his own reaction. "Sorry, honey. Nobody touches her but Jerimiah D. Nobody. A man's got to have something that's all his own." Reverently he replaced the rifle on its stone pegs.

"Now," he said turning to Anna. "What's on your mind? Much as it flatters an old man, you didn't drive all this way to have a cup of coffee with me."

"I've been nosing around about the Dog Canyon ranger's death," Anna told him. He would already know that much. "There's talk of local ranchers wanting to wipe out the lion population in retaliation."

Paulsen laughed, a series of voiceless gusts that came out his nose. "Hell, we've been trying to do that for years. Y'all breed 'em up there in that damned park. It's a wonder there's a cow left west of the Pecos."

Anna let that pass. She wanted to get on with her lie and get home. "I was hoping I could convince you to speak out against it. You're one of the most influential ranchers on the New Mexico side."

Paulsen was used to the ineffectual flattery and pleas of environmentalists. Anna hoped hers was commonplace enough to be believed.

He draped an arm around her shoulders. "It ain't gonna happen. You got a lot to learn about ranchers. We defend what's ours. From varmints and the goddam Park Service."

Anna shrugged off the heavy weight. "Thanks for the coffee," she said. "I'll show myself out."

The snorty chuckle followed her as far as the butler's pantry.

# CHAPTER 21

"Dr. Pigeon is in session . . . ah . . . Just a moment. Hold please."

Anna sat in the semi-darkness of the Cholla Chateau's laundry room listening to Cheryl's laundry squeak around and around in the dryer.

The voice returned. "May I say who's calling?" Molly had had the same receptionist for eleven years, an efficient woman who steadfastly refused to recognize Anna's voice.

"Her sister," Anna said. The Open Sesame.

"One moment please." There was a click, then strains of Handel's *Water Music* filled the earpiece. Molly soothing the savage beasts.

"Hallelujah!" Molly came on the line.

Anna glanced at her watch: five-thirty in Texas, seven-thirty in New York. "You ran late with your last client."

"Silly bugger wouldn't stop crying. I couldn't get a profound sentence in edgewise. And I was feeling particularly insightful today. What's up? You don't usually call this early in the week."

The sucking sound: toxic, killing smoke going deep into her sister's lungs. Anna repressed a comment. It crossed her mind that, were she gone, there would be no one left to nag Molly, get her to quit before it was too late. "Not much. Another 'accident.' A herpetologist bit the dust. Death by snakebite this time."

"Jesus!" Molly laughed with the career New Yorker's reliance on black humor. "Lions and tigers and snakes, oh my! You're on hold . . . can I pour you a drink?"

"Got one," Anna replied and clinked her wine glass against the plastic mouthpiece.

"It figures," Molly said. Handel flooded in. Anna was sorry she'd refrained from comment on the cigarette.

"Cheers." A glass containing one careful shot of scotch clinked down the two thousand miles of wire from Manhattan.

"To old friends and better days," Anna said and they drank in silence. "I'm coming to New York," she announced, deciding it in that instant. "I'm going to camp on you and make end runs up to Westchester County to see Edith."

"When? When are you coming?" Molly didn't sound as pleased as Anna had anticipated.

"I don't know . . ." Anna faltered. The plan was too new for dates. "I've got a ton of annual leave coming to me. I thought I'd come in September if—"

"Ha!" Molly exploded. "IF. What in the hell are you up to, Anna? What's going on? You're doing some silly damn thing with that snake and lion business."

"What makes—"

"Hmph!" Molly cut her off. As children they'd both practiced doing *hmph* like it was spelled in books. Molly had become very good at it. "Psychiatrists aren't omniscient for nothing," she said. "The snake and lion business, Anna. Out with it. I hate suspense. Always read the last page first. Adjust expectations."

Anna sighed. "I've done 'How,'" she admitted.

"And?" Molly demanded.

There were times Anna wished her sister had gone into interior decorating, labor relations, anything but what she had. But the obvious had never held any interest for Molly. EFFECT left her cold. It was CAUSE she was fascinated with.

"And I've got some final checking to do," Anna equivocated. "Then I'll know everything."

"Everything? Like who is going to win the World Series? Whether God can make a stone so big He cannot lift it? What Scotsmen wear under their kilts? Or just enough to get shoved under whatever passes for a trolley there in Timbuktu?"

"Do you know what Scotsmen wear under their kilts?" Anna countered.

"I'm a psychiatrist," Molly returned. "Not a sociologist. I know what they *want* to wear under their kilts."

Anna laughed despite the acid drippings from the New York exchange into her West Texas ear. "I'll know everything," Anna said. "Then I'll come hang my shingle out next to yours: 'Psychiatry: 5 cents.'"

"It'll never sell on Park Avenue," Molly told her. "We're like physicians of old but instead of bleeding the patient, we bleed the bank account. Take the Root of Evil onto our own broad shoulders."

"A modern-day sin-eater," Anna said.

"You got it. Now what the bloody hell are you up to? Back to the snakes and lions, Anna."

Anna did not intend to tell Molly anything, not until she had a story with a beginning and a middle and an end. She'd called because she needed to hear her sister's voice once more. "Some checking. I'll call you Saturday and tell you what I found."

"It's Tuesday. Four days of checking?"

"No. Thursday and maybe Friday of checking."

"You're going to creep about like the Lone Ranger stalking the forces of evil clad in Virtue and Right, is that the deal? A miniature, middle-aged John Wayne."

"They're dead," Anna snapped. "Pathetic as it is, I'm it. Nobody else gives a damn. Bureaucrats—monkeys who hear no evil and see no evil—are first in line for promotion."

A long silence paralyzed the phone lines. Not even the sighing of cigarette smoke broke the darkness.

"You there?" Anna asked hesitantly.

"I'm here," Molly said. Then, very deliberately: "If you get yourself killed, I will kill you. Is that clear? I will donate all of your things to the Pentecostal Church. I will have you embalmed and put on display in the Smithsonian as the World's Biggest Horse's Ass. Call me Saturday."

"I will," Anna promised.

"Before noon. At noon, Eastern time, I call out the National Guard."

"Molly, I—"

"Gotta go. I'm reviewing *Suicide As a Solution* for the *Washington Post*."

The click. The dead line.

What the hell, Anna thought. She knows I love her.

Thursday night the moon rose full and round at nine-twelve p.m. Anna was waiting for it. The light came first, a faint silvery glow on the bottom of the few ragged clouds left from the afternoon's fruitless thunderheads. Then a dome, slightly flattened, pushing up into the saddle between El Capitan and Guadalupe Peak. Fainthearted stars faded from sight. Cool, colorless light poured down the park's western escarpment, rolled out like liquid silver across the ravine-torn desert to pool black under the spreading brambles of the mesquite and shine in the cholla needles.

Sand sparkled as if lit from beneath, the white salt flats glowed with reflected glory. Shadows became fathomless. The moon, as if held to a regal creep by a suddenly broken string, popped clear of the Guadalupe Mountains. Its light bathed the Patterson Hills. Desert hills: rugged and stony and cut deep with washes. No roads, no trails intruded on this outlying stretch of land. No people hiked or camped there. Not in July when daytime temperatures rose above a hundred and ten degrees and there was no water for miles in any direction.

It was there Anna waited for the moon. The tent she would use for its meager shade if she had to sleep away the next day's heat was stuffed into its nylon sack. The gray Ensolite sleeping pad she'd folded in half to use as a seat cushion. Cross-legged, hands loosely clasped in her lap, she sat in the pose of a classic desert pilgrim.

A boulder, flaked into miniscule staircases by heat and cold, threw its inky cloak of shadow over her. Sand was strewn over her tent and pack. To creatures dependent on sight and sound for their prey, she was invisible. She sipped at one of the jugs of water she had carried in. In the Pattersons, in July, she would sweat all night, losing water to the desert even in darkness. Since six p.m., when she'd begun the hike in, she had consumed almost a gallon. Two more gallons were cached close by.

Once above the escarpment the moon dwindled rapidly in size but its light flowed unabated through the dry clean air, caught the iridescent shells in the ancient reef-become-mountains and the salt crystals of the long dead sea. Anna could see each spine on the small barrel cactus growing at the edge of the shadow that hid her. Each petal of its glorious bloom was perfectly illuminated but robbed of all color. The papery flower showed blood-black.

Soon, night hunters would be coming out: the scorpion, the rattlesnake, the tarantula.

And me, Anna thought. Despite her feeling at one with the night, she was aware of a certain creepiness, a feeling of hairy-legged beasties tickling up her arms and legs.

The moon shrank to the size of a dime, passed overhead, slipped down after the stars. Shadows moved in their prescribed arcs. Anna's joints stiffened, her ears ached from listening for the alien footsteps that had heralded Craig's death the night of the last full moon. Sleep swirled around her, catching her head dropping, her dreams encroaching.

Anna rubbed her face hard, twisted her spine, hearing the settled bones cracking back into line. She took a sip of the lukewarm water. What she wanted was wine: a drink for her brain, not her body. It crossed her mind to take the pledge, go on the wagon, but she couldn't decide which was worse: pending alcoholism, or remorseless unrelenting sobriety of the rest of her days.

Taking another pull of the water, she let the sky draw her eyes into its perfect depths. No fear, nothing so petty as murder: it soothed her, overwhelmed her as it always did with a comforting sense of her own littleness; the reassuring knowledge that she was but a single note in the desert's song, a minute singing in the concert of the earth. She thought of Molly, of her office full of clients.

In the city the lights blinded the night sky, robbed it of stars. Only the moon could compete, a pale contender against the roving searchlights of mall openings, the unwinking concern of security lights. No one was given an opportunity to feel deliciously small, magnificently unimportant. Everyone was forced, always, to take their dying littles as truth.

Slowly, Anna breathed in through her nostrils, inhaling the

desert, knowing this wisdom would pass, knowing she would flounder in nets of her own devising a thousand times before her dust blew across the mountain ridges. But as long as the desert remained, as long as the night sky's darkness was preserved, she could read again her salvation there.

The jagged teeth of the Cornudas Mountains to the west devoured the moon just after four a.m.

Craig Eastern's Martians were not coming. The Smithsonian was not getting its exhibit of the World's Biggest Horse's Ass. Not tonight.

Anna brushed the sand from her pack and put up the one-man tent on the west side of her boulder where the morning sun wouldn't find her. She unfolded the pad and lay down, enjoying the freedom to stretch. Luxuriating in the knowledge that snakes and spiders and scorpions were zipped outside in their own world, Anna slept.

The sun turned her nylon home into a Dutch oven an hour before noon. Unable to sleep any longer, she read and ate and dreamed the afternoon away moving as little as possible. There was no sound but the audible sear of sun on stone. Creatures of the Patterson Hills were hidden away waiting, like Anna, for the night.

At sunset, she folded her tent and ate her supper. The second gallon of water and half the third were gone. In the cooler evening air, she began her inspection of the area. She'd arrived too near dark the night before to do any searching. Pulling out her binoculars, she examined the hills for three-hundred-and-sixty degrees around. Nothing moved but air shimmering with heat.

Anna's boulder was near the top of a rugged hill three-quarters of a mile south of where Craig Eastern had camped, across the narrow talus saddle from where they had found his corpse in a bed of rattlesnakes. Between her and Eastern's camp the saddle flattened out, made a table of broken slate.

Anna studied it through the glasses. It was the only possible place in a three-mile radius of the ridge where Craig had camped. In the shadowless light she could see a game trail along the spine of the ridge she camped on and down to the land bridge between the two hills.

Again she searched land and sky full circle. For the moment she was alone but for a jet in the northeast quadrant of the sky. Leaving the binoculars behind, she trotted down the ridge, following the faint animal track. Lechugilla spines curved like daggers shin-high. Low, rugged barrel cacti, aptly named "Horse Crippler," pushed up through the rocky soil. No trees, no shrubs more than twenty or thirty inches tall grew on the hills, and the cacti were a foot or more apart, rationing the meager rainfall.

On the land bridge connecting her hill with Eastern's at the head of a long L-shaped ravine, she stopped. Gridding the saddle in her mind, Anna began a foot-by-foot search. The hard ground held no prints, but near the center of the ridge she found what she was looking for: a broken piece of slate, a stone with a scratch on it, and a crushed cactus. Eight feet away, running parallel, was another short line of destruction. Satisfied, she trotted back to her comfortless bivouac.

As the first pinprick stars dared the blue above the mountains, she camouflaged her pack with sand and pebbles and took up her vigil on the dark side of the terraced stone.

Ten-fifteen brought the moon's silver bulge, pushing up the sky above El Capitan. The desert hills began to itch and skitter with small close life.

Anna began to wait.

Waiting changed from the passive to the active, became a burden to bear, a weight to lift with each breath. Time seemed to change direction, flow backward.

I don't do well at this, she thought. Good or bad she ached to make something happen, take action. She pulled out her watch. 11:17. Fourteen minutes had elapsed since she had last checked the time. How many more to go? Thirty? An hour? Never? Irrationally she wondered if she could survive another vigil at the next full moon; if she could survive the next half hour of this one. Surely her nerves, taut an hour and two minutes after moonrise, would begin snapping soon. She'd hear tiny cracks, like rubber bands breaking under pressure, and bit by bit her body would begin to grow numb.

Another waiting, as intense, as desperate, flashed into her mind and she almost laughed aloud. She'd been fifteen, waiting for Dan Woolrick to call. Sylvia had said he'd told Donny he was going to ask her to the Tennis Court dance. All one Saturday she'd waited for the phone to ring, afraid even to go to the toilet lest she miss it.

A small comfort: waiting for death was easier than waiting for a boy to call.

Somewhere after midnight consciousness crept away, dreams took the place of thoughts. Into this unstable world came the sound of alien footsteps. Craig's aliens walked the desert with faint pounding footfalls and glowing halos of green. The air throbbed with their advance, the regular rhythm beating into Anna's lungs till she couldn't draw breath.

Nightmare jerked too hard and she woke, still sitting tailor fashion in her shadow. The Martians vanished.

The pulsing footsteps did not.

Anna cupped both hands behind her ears. "Make moose ears," she remembered absurdly from some naturalist's program. Swiveling her head like a radar dish, she picked up the sound more clearly. The pounding steps plodded methodically down from the northeast, marching up the long L-shaped wrinkle between her camp and Eastern's.

Pulling on her sneakers, Anna laced them tightly then belted her .357 to her waist and took a last, long drink of water. The thumping grew louder and she pulled herself carefully within the moonless shadow.

The helicopter, flying low, passed so close she had to close her eyes against the sand blasted from beneath the propeller blades. It swung up, cleared the ridge by what seemed only inches. For a second it hovered there, silhouetted against the distant pale cliffs of Guadalupe's high country, then settled onto the flat saddle.

Anna pressed her binoculars to her eyes, cupping her hands around the end lest some stray gleam of light catch the glass and give her away.

No lights were struck, no navigation lights marked the helicopter. The only illumination was the eerie glow of the pilot's instrument panel through the bubble of Plexiglas on the front of the fuselage.

Two men jumped from the helicopter. One's hair shone like a white flame in the cold light. The other was dark—another shadow in the night. Between them they dragged a crate six feet long and three feet square from the back of the helicopter. Moving quickly, with practiced motions, they lifted two more boxes, one from each of the wire-mesh baskets suspended above the runners to either side of the aircraft, and set them on the ground. If they spoke, the sound of the rotors drowned out their voices.

The white-haired man climbed back into the helicopter. Shadowman waved once and the aircraft lifted up, slipped over the ridge and dropped again from sight down the long ravine.

"Cheeky bastards," Anna whispered. Flashes sparked in the periphery of her vision. She was pressing the binoculars too hard into her eye sockets. Easing back, she forced herself to breathe slowly. Then she let herself look again. The shadow man had disappeared. Focusing her glasses on the largest of the three crates, Anna studied it. Through the slats she could just discern a faint green light, the color of a glowworm.

Anna had expected it, waited for it, considered it when she was planning this night venture. This time she was to watch and wait, make notes and remember. She'd promised herself and, in her mind if not via AT&T, promised Molly. There'd be no Lone Ranger, no John Wayne, no Rambolina, no misguided tragic heroines. Just the watching and the waiting and the gathering of evidence. Then channels: proper channels and legal gymnastics. And faith.

"One whole hell of a lot of faith," Anna muttered. Staring hard at the dying green light inside the crate, she wondered where she'd thought she would find that faith, the strength to sit and watch the slaughter, the belief that this one must die to get the system rolling. A system that didn't give a damn, a system that counted non-human lives as "resources."

"Fuck that," she said aloud, frightening herself with the noise. For a second she froze, a palm clamped across her mouth, in horror of her outburst. But Shadowman did not reappear.

Where was he?

Anna cursed silently.

Slipped off for a pee? Why hide? To his knowledge none but spiders and snakes looked on. Anna forced every spark of her concentration into her hearing until it felt as if her ears waved around her head on stalks.

Faint, scrabbling: a tiny avalanche scraped loose in the ravine between the hills, down from the saddle. Shadowman had made a misstep. Anna knew where he was and, from where he was, he couldn't see the crates. That decided her.

Rising in one fluid motion, she moved to the far edge of the ridge where she, too, would be out of sight from the inhabited darkness of the ravine, and ran lightly down the animal track she'd followed that afternoon. In the glareless light of the moon with its hard contrasts of shadow and light, Anna could see the faint trail clearly. Stones gouged her feet through the soft rubber of her running shoes. Cactus spines would easily penetrate the thin leather. But she moved with scarcely a sound.

Within minutes she reached the flattened saddle where the helicopter had landed. There she dropped to a crouch and, willing heart and lungs to be quiet, again pushed her ears out over the desert. From the ravine came the sound of feet crunching on gravel, rustling. A man unself-consciously moving about, comfortable in the knowledge that he was alone. A metallic ringing: the top of a canister pried loose.

Shadowman had climbed down to a cache hidden somewhere in the rocks on the side of the ravine. This rendezvous point had all the amenities neatly arranged right on National Park lands. Bastards! Anna repeated, this time without sound.

Staying low, she trotted over to the large crate. A lechugilla spine, sharp as a dagger, cut across her shin above her sneaker top. Anna hardly felt it. She knelt by the box. Snoring, deep and labored, came from inside. Pale fur pressed through the flat metal slats that formed the sides of the cage. Stripes of moonlight painted the panther within. A ghostly midnight tiger with a glowing green necklace and a black radio collar.

Anna squeezed a hand between the slats, touched the fur. Gently, she worked her fingers under the collar, feeling for a pulse. The animal was still deeply under the effects of the ketamine.

The latch on the cage was simple, made to withstand paws, not fingers. Anna tripped it and eased the end of the cage open. The lion's head lolled out, the mouth open, tongue protruding black and deathlike in the colorless light.

Anna unsnapped the glow-ring and dragged it from the cat's neck. The radio collar would not be so easy. Radio collars were riveted on. It would take more time than she had to saw through the heavy leather with her pocketknife. Somewhere there would be a rivet punch.

Great White Hunters don't like their trophies cluttered up with proof of cowardice, Anna thought bitterly. One ear on the ravine, she crept to the crates that had been unloaded from the helicopter's side panniers. Dreading the squeak of metal hinges, she lifted the lid of the first. Noiseless. Oiled. Everything bespoke well-planned, often executed night operations. How often? Anna did the simple arithmetic in her head: twenty radio-collared lions; three left. One lay in the crate. Karl tended one in his animal Shangri-la. One still roamed free. This was the nineteenth time. Nineteen full moons had spotlighted this murder-that-was-not-murder.

"Goddamned sons of bitches," Anna whispered. In the crate she had opened rifle barrels gleamed. Cold polished metal catching the moon. The top rifle, resting on a cloth of felt, was ornately carved. Anna dragged it out where she could see the stock clearly: the Sako, Paulsen's baby. Beneath were four more rifles, a cleaning kit, four custom-made silencers and several hundred rounds of ammunition.

Anna moved to the second crate and opened it. A radio receiving device set, no doubt, to the stolen frequency; the frequency emitted by the collars on the lions. What better way to locate one's prey in this technological age? In a canvas pouch affixed to the crate's inside edge she found the rivet punch.

The panther's breathing seemed slightly less stenorous. Again Anna felt for a pulse. Slightly stronger, perhaps. "It's okay, sweetie," she whispered as she pushed her hands beneath the lion and dragged it partially out of the crate where she would have room to work. Near a hundred pounds: the lion was fully grown, probably male.

The rivet punch was less straightforward than Anna had hoped. Wrestling with the leather and the inert lion, trying to thread the jaws of the punch through the proper holes, the light of the moon was suddenly inadequate. A final wrench and the collar fell free.

Anna smoothed down the fur of the lion's neck where it had been worn ragged beneath the collar. Feeling blessed, she stroked the darker ears, the fine muscled shoulders. Wake up, Anna thought, run away. Then I can, too.

A scraping, stone on stone, jerked her attention from the panther. Shadowman. Just below the ridge. She had stayed way too long. He was so close she could hear his puffing breaths. She didn't bother to look around. There was no place to hide.

Unsnapping the keeper with her thumb, she drew the .357 from its holster and steadied her arms on the top of the lion's crate. Without moving, she waited until the man had climbed clear of the ravine, taken a few steps onto the flat. His arms were full of goods retrieved from the cache: a canvas tarp meant to shroud the lion's corpse, flares so the helicopter could find the hunters at the end of the hunt.

"Stop where you are, Harland," Anna ordered.

Harland Roberts stopped. If he was surprised, Anna couldn't see it. The moon was at his back.

"Anna!" he said in the tone of a man with his mistress on his arm, meeting his wife unexpectedly. "I'll be damned."

"That's the plan," she returned. "Drop what you are holding. Open your arms slowly and place them on top of your head. Do it now."

He did as he was told.

Anna stood, the .357 held shoulder-point. She began moving slowly around, sure of each step, getting the moon behind her. He echoed her movements and she let him. He was too far from the rifle crate to frighten her. When the moon was behind her left shoulder and Harland stood several feet from the unconscious panther, she said: "That's far enough."

"You liked me, Anna." Harland sounded genuinely hurt. The moon was shining in his face but all Anna could read there was disappointment.

"I liked you," she said. "But you keep killing my friends."

He smiled a boyish smile. "Anna, you wouldn't shoot me." Slowly he began to move his hands down from his head.

"Yes. I would," Anna said evenly. "It isn't a problem."

His hands stopped moving.

"I'm going to tell you what to do," she stated. "You won't move until I tell you. Is this clear?"

Harland nodded. For the first time Anna read something other than fine acting in his face. Not fear: an alertness, an aliveness, a moving of mental gears. It scared her. She wanted to shoot him and be done with cat and mouse, hunter and hunted. But training took over.

"Kneel down. Do it now."

Harland knelt.

"When I tell you, take your hands from your head, walk them out in front of you. Lay facedown. Do it now."

Carefully, Harland moved his hands from the top of his head. "Anna, I don't want you to shoot me. I haven't got a gun or a weapon of any kind. Listen to me. This is important." The hands were moving slowly down, held well away from his body, every movement clear, innocent. He ducked his head, bending at the waist, arms out to the side as if he would let himself fall facedown onto stone and cactus rather than risk alarming her into pulling the trigger by moving too quickly.

One hand vanished behind the prone lion's head. "Listen, Anna. The lion is choking." The animal's breathing had changed, was more rasping than before. "The ketamine can cause them to swallow their tongues. When you moved it to cut the collar you didn't put its head back in a position where it could breathe."

Anna's eyes flicked to the lion. She knew there was nothing Harland could use as a weapon near or inside the crate. Not even the heavy radio collar. She'd thrown it a couple of yards off. "Move his head," she said.

Harland brought his other arm slowly around, careful to keep it always in her sight. Both hands buried in the thick fur around the lion's throat, he began lifting the big beast gently. With a liquid motion, so smooth as not to seem sudden or even startling, he yanked the lion onto his lap, held its torso against his chest, his face almost hidden behind the lolling head.

"You would shoot me, Anna. You might even enjoy it. Will you shoot your kitty cat? I'm betting not." Harland stood up, holding the hundred-pound lion down the length of his body. The cat's belly, white and fuzzy, covered him from shoulders to knees. Its legs and tail dangled in front of his.

Anna felt sick. She moved her sights to Harland's head but it was ducked peek-a-boo fashion behind the lion's. Shoot the damn cat, Anna said to herself. Maybe the hollow point shells she carried would penetrate the lion's body, kill Harland Roberts. The white tummy, looking so soft, so vulnerable stretched before her. A perfect target. Shoot the goddam cat, Anna's mind screamed to her soul. But her finger would not move on the trigger.

Harland began to sidle toward the boxes, toward the hunting rifles. Anna followed, the sight of her Smith & Wesson searching for a target, a three-by-three-inch square of Roberts left exposed.

The man was careful. Dancing his macabre dance, his partner a demon lover in lion form, Harland waltzed over the stony ground. He reached the crate. One hand slid out, ran along the carved stock of Paulsen's hunting rifle. Not once did a square big enough to fill with .357 cartridge show clear of the inert, living, lion-skin armor.

Anna squeezed off a shot. Not at Roberts, but at Paulsen's

Sako. In the shadow of the crate lid, the rifle was little more than a narrow line a shade lighter than midnight. She missed.

Harland snatched up the Sako, held it shoulder high. Turning slightly, he pointed it at her. The shining barrel caught the night's silver sheen. Its tiny, deadly, black eye met Anna's.

"The cat is waking up, Harland," she tried and saw a spark of what might have been fear—or excitement—bloom and as quickly fade in his eyes. He didn't spare even a glance for the unconscious lion.

"Don't you fancy hand-to-hand combat anymore?" Anna asked. "Like the good old days 'wrassling 'gators' at the Deadly Poison Snakes show? Is that where you learned to milk snakes so you could pump Craig full of venom?"

He just smiled, slow and easy. Anna sensed more than saw it. His head was still shielded by the lions. Harland was not going to be lulled or baited into exposing enough of himself to kill.

"You never know when a liberal education is going to come in handy," he said and: "Put down the gun, Anna."

"Fuck you," she replied, the .357 unwavering.

The glinting rifle barrel dropped, swung in an arc, ending beneath the lion's left ear. "Do it now," Harland mocked her.

Anna's brain screamed to her fingers: shoot the cat, please God damn it, shoot. But her hand opened and the revolver dropped to the ground.

Harland let go of the lion. Dead weight, the animal fell to the stones. The bones of its jaw or skull cracked audibly against the rock. Anna winced. "You son of a bitch," she whispered.

Harland laughed. "It's not nice to call an armed man a son of a bitch," he said.

"Fuck you."

"Anna, Anna, Anna, your vocabulary is disintegrating under pressure. Obscenity is the last resort of the ignorant.

Didn't you learn that in Sunday school? I expected better from a woman willing to lay down her life that a lion might live a couple hours longer." Harland kicked the lion with an indifference more cruel than hatred. "That's what you've done, you know."

Anna had thought that one's mind would race at a time like this, that it would whirl and spin, dart at solutions probable and improbable. It didn't. It was as clear as the desert night, as still. "Well?" she said and smiled. She was not afraid. It wasn't that she was ready to die there among the Texas stars; she merely felt invulnerable, out of the normal realities of flesh that could rip, bones that could break.

Fleetingly, she wondered if she were going into shock. Or overdrive. How long would this detachment last before terrible fear, deep enough to be a bone sickness, would flood through her and she would understand that now, tonight, she was to die?

"Well? Are you going to shoot me or not?"

"Oh, I'm going to shoot you all right. Bury you here in the Pattersons under enough rock the coyotes won't drag you out at an embarrassing moment." Harland stepped over the lion and moved several steps closer. Not close enough she could grab the rifle; close enough he could see her face. "And damn you for making it necessary, Anna. You're more fun than I've had in years."

"More fun than big-game hunting?" Anna jerked her chin toward the crated rifles.

He didn't look away from her for an instant. "I told you, I don't hunt anymore. No challenge. I like my prey to have an IQ higher than your average two-year-old. Most of the elk these hotshots pay Paulsen to shoot I could club to death with a baseball bat."

"Park elk," Anna said flatly.

"Some of them. I'm an equal-opportunity employer."

"You stole the radio frequency from the Resource Management office, used it to pinpoint the location of the lions we collared, didn't you? Big game to order."

"You're playing for time, Anna," Harland said, clearly amused. "Okay. Play. But the game will have to be short. You can live just until I hear Jerimiah D.'s helicopter coming back with the hunters. Can't have the clients upset either by your presence or your corpse. The silly SOBs get dressed up in camo and carry big guns but the poor bastards just can't get it up if the quarry can fight back."

Till the helicopter returned with its second load. Ten minutes—maybe fifteen—for something to happen, to even the odds. "What do they pay you for a kill?" Anna asked. Harland didn't reply. He seemed to be thinking better of letting the game go on. "If I've got to die," she said, "don't make me die curious."

He laughed then. She could feel him relax. "Seventy-five hundred dollars. For that they get dinner at Paulsen's, the hunt, a guaranteed kill, the lion's head, and—the best part—they get the story. The 'battle of wills,' the 'ultimate challenge,' 'man against the elements.' Trophies. Cheap at twice the price."

"Trophies. You used them to make Drury's death look like a lion kill, didn't you? Severed her spinal cord with an icepick or something, then bit her with dead jaws, raked her with severed claws."

"Ah, Anna." Harland sighed. "We could've been beautiful lovers, you know that? Our minds work alike. Our bodies would be a concert. If we must spend your last minutes on this earth playing 'you show me yours and I'll show you mine,' you must take your turn. How did you guess?"

"I didn't guess," Anna retorted. "You fucked up. One of the neck punctures, the fatal one, was too deep; deeper than any living lion's tooth." Anna hoped he would become annoyed. Maybe, if she was lucky, tempted to close the distance between them to strike her.

Harland laughed, seemingly delighted with her cleverness. "And what made you think of me? Or do you often think of me?"

She ignored the second question. If his face was the last sight she was to see on earth, she didn't want to read satisfaction there. "Everything. You had access to the radio frequency, you use ketamine in your work, you'd worked with reptiles, led hunts, had too much money for a government employee, and you called Paulsen 'Jerimiah D.' Only his old friends call him that.

"You made a lot of mistakes, Harland. You lowered the body into the canyon from the helicopter. Right into a saw grass swamp. But you forgot to scratch the body up, forgot to put any water in the pack. Not very clever."

"Clever enough to stay alive, my dear. Clever enough to stay alive." He smiled, the rifle he held never wavering so much as a fraction of an inch from her heart. He was, she realized, truly enjoying himself. A hunter who'd lost his taste for the easy kill, finding in murder, in the covert and illegal taking of game, in the fleecing of fools, a spark of the old feeling.

"Why the ketamine?" she asked.

"Didn't want to kill her till the last minute. Time of death and all. Didn't want marks of a struggle on the body. There's not a problem with needle marks using ketamine: the stuff is so strong you can administer it in eyedrops."

"Eyedrops. Fitting. She had seen something. What?"

"Just what you're seeing tonight, but on the other end. Our brave hunters dividing up the spoils," Harland said. "And with the same unfortunate—and rather fatal—results."

Behind Harland, Anna saw a faint flicker of movement pale against the stones. The lion had flicked its tail.

"Kitty is waking up," she said.

Harland looked merely annoyed. "That didn't work the first time, Anna."

"The first time it wasn't true."

As if responding to a stage cue, the lion growled, a low threatening cascade of gravelly notes.

Harland turned—not far, maybe half a turn—toward the cat. The barrel of the rifle moved eight inches to the left of Anna's heart and she sprang. It was utterly without thought. Mind at one with muscle, as countless animals had sprung at their prey since there had been a difference between the quick and the dead.

Her hands hit the rifle; both hands, hard, like a gymnast on the uneven parallel bars. Harland's considerable strength went into holding on to the gun and it stayed rigid in his grasp. Rigid enough Anna used it for leverage. Pulling against Roberts, she let her center of gravity sink to her butt and with all of the muscles of thigh and fanny, she drove her knee into Harland's groin.

Harland, protective instincts born of years of painstaking care of "the family jewels," pivoted and her knee struck the inside of his thigh. Pain forced a grunt from him but he did not collapse and Anna knew, with her first rational thought since the lion's tail had moved, that the fight was not over.

Banking on the surprise of sudden reversal, she let all pressure off the rifle, turned her energy with his, and he helped her to shove the gun hard against his chest.

A round fired into the air. The powerful recoil jerked them both off-balance. Stumbling back, Harland tripped over the goods he'd dropped at her first command. Anna felt herself falling with him. Neither dared relinquish their hold on the weapon to break the fall. The rifle butt struck first and another round ripped down the barrel just as Anna's shoulder pounded into the hard earth.

The report was muffled. Flesh and bone had silenced the bullet. Anna didn't know whether it was she or Harland who had been hit.

"Oh no . . ." she heard him whisper.

There is a God, she thought. And She is on my side. With renewed energy, she pulled herself to her knees, her fingers still locked tight around the weapon.

"Give it up! You're dying!" she screamed, willing him to believe, to die. "You've been hit. You're bleeding to death. Give it up. You'll die."

With a suddenness that caught her off-guard, Harland wrenched the rifle from her grasp. Anna lunged across him, slamming her weight into the arm that held the Sako and heard the rifle skitter downslope into the black ravine.

Harland closed her in a deadly embrace. "I'm not dead yet." The words were harsh and hot in her ear, more air than sound. "But I'm the last lover you'll ever know." His arms began to clamp down, crushing her.

Anna's legs were tangled in his, held tight, but her arms were free. She dragged at his hair, pounded his skull, but the grip never loosened. He'd tucked his face tight into her neck, his throat, his eyes were protected by her flesh. She sank her teeth into his shoulder and felt an answering bite on her neck, an animal bite tearing down through skin toward tendon and vein.

Like a jackal, he was ripping her throat out with his teeth. Terror gripped her, paralyzed her. Unrelentingly he was bending her spine. Soon it must snap. She could not breathe. The soft flesh of her throat was being eaten away.

Like the blind things they were, Anna's hands scrabbled over the stony ground above Harland's head. A long smooth stick came under her fingers. A flare. Hope sparked thought; hope made life possible. Hope blanked the fear and the pain that froze her mind. With every ounce of concentration she had, Anna forced her hands to uncap the flare, strike its tip against the safety cap.

Searing pain in her right wrist and hard pink light burning beyond her closed eyelids let her know she had been successful. Yelling, Anna drove the flare down inside Harland's shirt, pushed the spurting, chemical-driven torch into the back of his neck.

A scream pulled his teeth from her throat. Convulsively, his arms released her and he began clawing at the dragon consuming him from behind.

Crawling free, Anna struggled to her feet. The .357 was lost in the shadows. Snatching up a second flare, she struck it to life. In its hot light, she watched Roberts, mad with pain, ripping at his shirt. The flare fell free, tumbled downslope.

Crying, Harland sat up. Blood seeped from a hole in his left shoulder. His back, Anna knew, would have a gaping wound where the bullet had exploded from his body. The smell of burnt flesh polluted the night.

The lion was gone.

Silently, her breath coming in gasps, Anna was crying, too. Ready to push it into his eyes, she held the gout of flame from the flare toward Harland. Roberts's face was ragged, wild with more than pain: with unacceptable defeat. Drawing on reserves Anna would marvel at later, he pushed himself upright, stood swaying in the wavering light. Like an angry bull, his head dropped and he glared at her from beneath straight dark brows.

Rage had taken the place of cunning. With a roar, he charged. Anna stepped aside and he stumbled over the lip of the ravine, crashing down the talus slope into the darkness. One final cry broke up through the shadows. Then silence.

Anna hung back. Harland's fall had taken the same path as Paulsen's hunting rifle. Using her flare, she found the .357. The moon had moved scarcely at all since she'd cut the lion free of its lighted collar. Minutes only had passed. Soon Paulsen would be returning with the "clients."

Shoving the burning end into the earth, she stubbed out the flare like a gigantic cigarette. Cool white light returned and she saw the trails of black on her hands: blood. It seeped down from her throat, dripped to the ground. Anna chose not to worry about it. Had an artery been severed, she'd be dead by now. Next time she was in town she could get her rabies booster.

Free of the chemical glare of the fire, her eyes began to adjust again to the semi-darkness. The garish ghosts receded from her peripheral vision. Making her breathing as even and soundless as she could, Anna watched and listened. From beyond the lip of the ravine came a pink glow and the insistent hissing of the first flare. Other than that, no sound. Even the skritching and slithering natural to the desert night was hushed.

She ran quickly twenty yards to her right, approached the edge of the ravine from an unexpected—she hoped—direction. Leading with the revolver, she looked down. The inky shadows were given unholy life by the guttering flare. First Anna sought the dark and bright wood and metal of Paulsen's hunting rifle. It had lodged fifteen or twenty feet down, butt wedged between a small rainbow cactus and a rock. Below, perhaps twenty yards, crumpled at the edge of the uncertain light, was Harland Roberts. He did not move.

Crablike, Anna scuttled down the loose stone of the ravine's side. Partway down she stopped and picked up the hunting rifle. For a moment she watched Roberts. He seemed not even to breathe and it crossed her mind that he'd broken his neck in the fall. Or he was playing possum.

She slung Paulsen's Sako across her back on its strap. Her shoulder was aching. The collarbone, incompletely knit, had cracked again. Once more she started her slow descent. A dozen feet from Harland she stopped. The moonlight didn't penetrate this far and the flare, burning its way out in the arid soil, made little of Harland but a shadow darker than the rest.

"I'm not coming any closer, Harland," Anna said. "Maybe you're dead and maybe you're not. Either way, I win."

The lump never moved. Anna turned and started up the slope. She was past the raided cache when his voice brought her to a halt.

"You can't win, Anna." Though he tried to keep it out of his voice, she could hear the pain. He was shot. He was burned. Maybe he'd broken something in the fall. Still Anna didn't trust his helplessness.

She turned back but went no lower.

"You can't ever win, Anna. Your system is against you. Maybe I'll get fired. Maybe not. They won't put me out of business, though. One good hunt will pay off any fines for poaching. Nobody cares, Anna. They're just animals. In Texas they may even give me a medal."

"Craig, Sheila—even in Texas that will be considered murder," Anna said.

"No murders. Just the ravings of a crazy lady ranger. Your word against mine."

The dull chopping of a helicopter engine sounded as it marched down the northern sky, toward the ravine.

"Jerimiah and I and every scrap of evidence will be gone in thirty minutes. Your word against mine. And you may not live long enough to talk too much. You don't win."

The helicopter was in the ravine, flying up from where the hills opened onto the salt flats to the west.

"He's coming, Anna, Jerimiah D. and three men. Maybe if you run we won't find you. We won't find you tonight," he amended and laughed. The laughter was cut short. Anna hoped it was from pain.

She unslung the hunting rifle, put it to her shoulder, and

braced for the recoil. As the helicopter flew over, she fired four rounds. One sang off metal. There was a light tinkling sound as fragments of Plexiglas rained down onto the rocks.

The helicopter climbed abruptly, was silhouetted against the moon. A spotlight beneath the fuselage switched on and a white finger of light began probing back down the narrow canyon. Anna fired again. The light shattered.

The helicopter spun on its axis and flew north, straight over the hills, not even attempting to seek cover from prying eyes. The pounding noise of the blades receded.

"You can bring the law down on me, Anna. But you won't win," Harland said. He was only a voice from the shadows. The flare had died, and the helicopter's light had robbed Anna of her night vision.

"You can beat the law," Anna said. "But you can't beat the desert." She started up the slope.

"You can't leave me here," he called after her and there was fear in his voice for the first time.

"Fence crew will find you in a couple of months," she returned without stopping. "What's left of you."

"I'll die of thirst. Anna, I broke my ankle. Swear to Christ."

Anna said nothing. She didn't much care.

"Paulsen'll be back in the morning. He'll get me," Roberts cried.

Anna doubted that. For all Paulsen knew this was a trap and the place was crawling with Feds. He'd steer clear of the West Side for a long time to come.

Reaching the flat of the saddle, she unslung Paulsen's fancy rifle. Using the tail of her shirt, she smudged her prints from the stock and barrel but didn't wipe the stock clean. Half New Mexico knew Paulsen's gun, knew he never let anyone touch it. And it was the gun that shot Harland Roberts. Anna set it on the ground.

"What're you doing, Anna?" Harland called up the hill.

"Leaving."

"I'll die of thirst," he cried.

Anna walked over to the ravine, looked into the depths. She couldn't see Roberts. "You never know," she said. "You might not live long enough. That lion could still be around. Here kitty, kitty, kitty," she called.

"Don't!" Harland screamed.

Anna walked across the flat toward the ridge where her camp was. The moon had moved partway down the sky. A silver trail led down the ridges: the path she would follow home. She began to run.

"Please!" she heard Harland yelling.

Maybe she'd saddle up Gideon, ride out tomorrow with water and bring Harland in. Then again, Gideon's hoof wasn't healing like she'd hoped.

Maybe she'd give him the day off.

**Turn the page for a sneak preview of Nevada Barr's Anna Pigeon mystery**

# FLASHBACK

**Available now**

Until she ran out of oxygen, Anna was willing to believe she was taking part in a PBS special. The water was so clear sunlight shone through as if the sea were but mountain air. Cloud shadows, stealthy and faintly magical at four fathoms, moved lazily across patches of sand that showed startlingly white against the dark, ragged coral. Fishes colored so brightly it seemed it must be a trick of the eye or the tail end of an altered state flitted, nibbled, explored, and slept. Without moving, Anna could see a school of silverfish, tiny anchovies, synchronized, moving like polished chain mail in a glittering curtain. Four Blue Tangs, so blue her eyes ached with the joy of them, nosed along the edge of a screamingly purple sea fan bigger than a coffee table. A jewfish, six feet long and easily three hundred pounds, his blotchy hide mimicking the sun-dappled rock, pouting lower lip thick as Anna's wrist, lay without moving beneath an overhang of a coral-covered rock less than half his size, his wee fish brain assuring him he was hidden. Countless other fish, big and small, bright and dull, ever more delightful to Anna because she'd not named them and so robbed them of a modicum of their mystery, moved around her on their fishy business.

Air, and with it time, was running out. If she wished to live, she needed to breathe. Her lungs ached with that peculiar sensation of being full to bursting. Familiar desperation licked at the edges of her mind. One more kick, greetings to a spiny lobster (a creature whose body design was only possible in a weightless world), and, with a strong sense of being hounded from paradise, she swam for the surface, drove a foot or more into the air and breathed.

The sky was as blue as the eye-watering fishes and every bit as merciless as the sea. The ocean was calm. Even with her chin barely above the surface she could see for miles. There was remarkably little to soothe the eye between the unrelenting glare of sea and sky. To the north was Garden Key, a scrap of sand no more than thirteen acres in total and, at its highest point, a few meters above sea level. Covering the key, two of its sides spilling out into the water, was the most bizarre duty station at which she had served.

Fort Jefferson, a massive brick fortress, had been built on this last lick of America, the Dry Tortugas, seventy miles off Key West in the Gulf of Mexico. At the time construction started in 1846, it was the cutting edge of national defense. Made of brick and mortar with five bastions jutting out from the corners of a pentagon, it had been built as the first line of defense for the southern states, guarding an immense natural—and invisible—harbor; it was the only place for sixty miles where ships could sit out the hurricanes that menaced the Gulf and the southeastern seaboard or come under the protection of the fort's guns in time of war. Though real, the harbor was invisible because its breakwaters, a great broken ring of coral, were submerged.

Jefferson never fired a single shot in defense of its country. Time and substrata conspired against it. Before the third tier of the fort could be completed, the engineers noticed the weight of the massive structure was causing it to sink and stopped construction. Even unfinished it might have seen honorable—if not glamorous—duty, but the rifled cannon was invented, and the seven-to-fifteen-foot-thick brick-and-mortar walls were designed only to withstand old-style cannons. Under siege by these new weapons of war, the fort would not stand. Though destined for glorious battle, Jefferson sat out the Civil War as a union prison.

Till Anna had been assigned temporary duty at the Dry Tortugas, she'd not even heard of it. Now it was home.

For a moment she merely treaded water, head thrown back to let the sun seek out any epithelial cell it hadn't already destroyed over the last ten years. Just breathing—when the practice had recently been denied—was heaven. Somewhere she'd read that a meager seventeen percent of air pulled in by the lungs was actually used. Idly, she wondered if she could train her body to salvage the other eighty-three percent so she could remain underwater ten minutes at a stretch rather than two. Scuba gave one the time but, with the required gear, not the freedom. Anna preferred free diving. Three times she breathed deep, on the third she held it, upended and kicked again for bliss of the bottom.

Flashing in the sun, she was as colorful as any fish. Her mask and fins were iridescent lime green, her dive skin startling blue. Though the water was a welcoming eighty-eight degrees in late June, that was still eight point six degrees below where she functioned best. For prolonged stays in this captivating netherworld she wore a skin, a lightweight body-hugging suit with a close-fitting hood and matching socks. Not only did it conserve body heat, but it also protected her from the sometimes vicious bite of the coral. Like all divers who weren't vandals, Anna assiduously avoided touching—

and so harming—living coral, but when they occasionally did collide, human skin was usually as damaged as the coral.

Again she stayed with and played with the fish until her lungs felt close to bursting. Though it would be hotly debated by a good percentage of Dry Tortugas National Park's visitors, as far as she was concerned the "paradise" part of this subtropical paradise was hidden beneath the waves.

Anna had never understood how people could go to the beach and lie in the sand to relax. The shore was a far harsher environment than the mountains. Air was hot and heavy and clung to the skin. Wind scoured. Sand itched. Salt sucked moisture from flesh. The sun, in the sky and again off the surface of the sea, seared and blinded. For a couple of hours each day it was heaven. After that it began to wear one down as the ocean wears away rock and bone.

Two dive sites, twenty dives—the deepest over forty feet—and Anna finally tired herself out. Legs reduced to jelly from pushing through an alien universe, she couldn't kick hard enough to rise above the surface and pull herself over the gunwale. Glad there were no witnesses, she wriggled and flopped over the transom beside the outboard motor to spill on deck, splattering like a bushel of sardines. Her Sunday was over. She'd managed to spend yet one more weekend in Davy Jones's locker. There wasn't really any place else to go.

The *Reef Ranger*, one of the park's patrol boats, a twenty-five-foot inboard/outboard Boston Whaler, the bridge consisting of a high bench and a Plexiglas windscreen, fired up at a touch. Anna upped anchor, then turned the bow toward the bastinadoed fortress that was to be her home for another eight to twelve weeks. Seen from the level of the surrounding ocean, Fort Jefferson presented a bleak and surreal picture: an overwhelming geometric tonnage floating, apparently unsupported, on the surface of the sea.

Enjoying the feel of a boat beneath her after so many years

in landlocked parks, Anna headed for the fort. The mariners' rhyme used to help those new to the water remember which markers to follow when entering heavy traffic areas rattled meaninglessly through her mind: *red on right returning*. Shrunken by salt and sun, her skin felt two sizes too small for her bones, and even with dark glasses and the sun at her back, it was hard to keep her eyes open against the glare.

The opportunity to serve as interim supervisory ranger for the hundred square miles of park, scarcely one of which was above water, came in May. Word trickled down from the southeastern region that the Dry Tortugas's supervisory ranger had to take a leave of absence for personal reasons and a replacement was needed until he returned or, failing that, a permanent replacement was found.

Dry Tortugas National Park was managed jointly with southern Florida's Everglades National Park. The brass all worked out of Homestead, near Everglades. Marooned as it was, seventy miles into the Gulf, day-to-day operations of the Dry Tortugas were run by a supervisory ranger, who managed one law enforcement ranger, two interpreters, and an office administrator. Additional law enforcement had been budgeted and two rangers hired. They were new to the service and, at present, being trained at the Federal Law Enforcement Training Center in Georgia.

"Supervisory Ranger" was a title that bridged a gray area in the NPS hierarchy. For reasons to which Anna was not privy, the head office chose not to upgrade the position to Chief Ranger but left it as a subsidiary position to the Chief Ranger at Everglades. Still, it was a step above Anna's current District Ranger level on the Natchez Trace. To serve as "Acting Supervisory Ranger" was a good career move.

That wasn't entirely why she'd chosen to abandon home and hound for three months to accept the position. Anna was in no hurry to rush out of the field and into a desk job. There'd be time enough for that when her knees gave out or her tolerance for the elements—both natural and criminal—wore thin.

She had taken the Dry Tortugas assignment for personal reasons. When she was in a good frame of mind, she told herself she'd needed to retreat to a less populated and mechanized post to find the solitude and unmarred horizons wherein to renew herself, to seek answers. When cranky or down, she felt it was the craven running away of a yellow-bellied deserter.

Paul Davidson, his divorce finalized, had asked her to marry him.

Two days later, a car, a boat and a plane ride behind her—not to mention two thousand miles of real estate, a goodly chunk of it submerged—she was settling into her quarters at Fort Jefferson.

"Coincidence?" her sister Molly had asked sarcastically. "You be the judge."

The fort had only one phone, which worked sporadically, and mail was delivered once a week. Two weeks had passed in sandy exile, and she was no more ready to think about marriage than she had been the day she left. But, given the paucity of entertainments—even a devotee could only commune with fish for so long—she was rapidly getting to the point where there was nothing else to think about.

Under these pressing circumstances, she'd done the only sensible thing: she stuck her nose in somebody else's business. Daniel Barrons, a maintenance man-of-all-trades and the closest thing Anna'd made to a friend at the fort, had a weakness for gossip that she shamelessly exploited.

He was a block of a man, with what her father would have referred to as a "peasant build," one designed for carrying sick calves into the barn. Perhaps in his late forties, Daniel covered his blunt face with a brown-black beard. On his left arm, seldom seen as the man wasn't given to tank tops, was a tattoo so classic Anna smiled whenever she glimpsed its bottom edge: a naked girl reclining on elbows and fanny under a cartoon palm tree.

Given this rough and manly exterior, tradition would have had him strong and silent. Every time he snuggled down in his favorite position to dish the dirt, elbows on workbench, hindquarters stuck out and usually bristling with tools shoved in his pockets, furry chin in scarred hands, Anna was charmed and tickled.

With only a small nudge, Daniel had assumed the position and filled her in on why she'd been given the opportunity to explore this oddly harsh, boring, beautiful, magical bit of the earth. Her predecessor, Lanny Wilcox, hadn't taken an extended leave willingly. It had been forced upon him when he'd begun to come unglued.

"His girlfriend, a little Cuban number as cute as a basket full of kittens, ran out on him," Daniel had told her, his voice low and gentle as usual. He consistently spoke as if a baby slept in the next room and he was loath to wake it.

"Lanny was a terrific guy, but he was getting up there, fifty-one this last birthday. At his peak he couldn't a been much to look at. Hey, I like Lanny just fine, but, well, even he knew he was about as good-looking as the south end of a northbound spiny lobster. Five, six months ago he hooked up with Theresa. She's not yet thirty, smart, funny and a nice addition to a bathing suit. Next thing you know, she's living out here. When she cut out, Lanny just sort of lost it."

From what Anna had gathered, the old Supervisory Ranger's "losing it" consisted of increasingly bizarre behavior that revolved around the seeing and hearing of things that no one else saw or heard. "Ghosts," murmured a couple of the more melodramatic inhabitants of the fort. "Hallucinations," said the practical ones, and Lanny was bundled up and shipped off to play with his imaginary friends out of sight of the tax-paying public.

On first arriving, struck by the beauty of the sky and sea, the fishes and the masonry, Anna couldn't understand what stresses could possibly chase even a heartbroken man around the bend. Piloting the *Reef Ranger* into the harbor, the glow of her swimming with the fishes burned and blown away, she realized that after a mere couple weeks of isolation, wet heat, and scouring winds, she was tempted to dream up companions of her own. She needed a sense of connection to something, somebody to keep her on an even keel.

She laughed. The sound whipped away on the liquid wind over the bow. Soon she was going to have to relinquish her self-image as a hermit. Paul—or perhaps just the passage of years—had socialized her to some extent. Molly would be pleased. Anna made a mental note to tell her sister when next she phoned. It could be a while. Not only was the fort's only phone in much demand, but it also had a one-to-two-second delay, like a phone call from Mars, that made communication an exercise in frustration.

Red on right.

Anna slowed the *Ranger* to a sedate and wakeless speed as she entered the small jewel of a harbor on the east side of Garden Key. Eleven pleasure boats were anchored, two she recognized from the weekend before, *Moonshadow* and *Key to My Heart*, both expensive, both exquisitely kept. They were owned by two well-to-do couples out of Miami who seemed joined at the hip as their boats were joined at the gunwale, one rafting off the other. Anna waved as she passed.

At the end of the harbor away from the tourists, as if there were an invisible set of tracks running from Bush Key—Garden's near neighbor—to the harbor mouth and they had been condemned to live on the wrong side of them, two commercial shrimpers cuddled up to one another.

Commercial fishing and, much to the shriek and lament of the locals, sport fishing was banned in the park, but right outside the boundaries was good shrimping. The boats stalked the perimeters, the honest—or the cautious—keeping outside the imaginary line established by NPS buoys. Perhaps a few sought to poach, but there were plenty of shrimp outside. Most came for the same reasons ships had been coming for two hundred years, the reason the fort had been built in the middle of the ocean: the natural safe zone of flat water the coral reefs provided.

Shrimp boats, their side nets looking like tattered wings falling from a complex skeleton of wood and metal, were a complication Anna'd not foreseen. They sailed from many ports, most in the south and southeast, following the shrimp: four weeks in Texas, then through the Gulf to the Keys. Some boats were family owned, most were not. All were manned and kept in a way unique to an idiosyncratic and inbred culture. Daniel called them "bikers of the sea." Having spent an unspecified and largely undiscussed number of years in the land version of that violent fraternity before, as he put it, "breaking my back and seeing the light," he would know.

The shrimpers were a scabrous lot, not just the boats, which reeked of dead fish, cigarette smoke and old grease—part cooking, part engine—but the sailors themselves. The family boats were crewed by men and women, three or four to a boat. The others were all male, but for the occasional unfortunate who, like a biker chick out of favor, was passed from boat to boat, usually fueled for her duties with drugs and alcohol.

Anna had yet to see a shrimper with all his or her teeth. The violence of the culture coupled with months at sea away from modern dentistry marked their faces. A lot of them went to sea to kick drugs and found more onboard. A startling percentage had felony records.

This borderline lifestyle would not have affected Anna had not a symbiotic relationship sprung up between them and the tourists and park employees at the fort. Fresh gulf shrimp were delicious. The shrimpers were glad to trade a few for the culinary delight of those in the park. The problem was that the currency was alcohol—mostly cheap beer, but enough whiskey to make things interesting. Drunk, the shrimpers lived up to Daniel's name for them. They came ashore; they yelled, disrupted tours, urinated in public, knocked one another's few remaining teeth out, beat their women and occasionally knifed one another.

Her third day at Fort Jefferson Anna had been made painfully aware of a few administrational oddities of Dry Tortugas National Park: there was no place to hold prisoners and, though they were legally allowed to make arrests, it was highly discouraged by headquarters in Homestead. Two law-enforcement rangers keeping drunken violent shrimpers under guard in the open air for hours till the Coast Guard arrived wasn't a great idea. Transporting them three hours one way to Key West and so leaving the park without law enforcement or EMTs for a day didn't work either.

The best they could do was separate the combatants, bind the ugliest wounds and shoo the lot of them back onboard their boats.

The two shrimpers anchored in the harbor as Anna motored in were family owned. They'd never caused problems, and the lady on one of the boats had a terrific little dog she let Anna pet. Tonight should be quiet. Anna didn't know if she was grateful or not. With only one other ranger—Bob Shaw—in house, neither ever truly had a day off but slept with a radio ready to serve as backup for the person on duty. Quiet promised uninterrupted sleep. Anna supposed that was a good thing. Still, she would have welcomed something to do.

As she backed the *Reef Ranger* neatly into the employee

dock, Bob Shaw walked down the weathered planking. Opposite where Anna tied up, on the far side of the park pier with its public bathrooms and commercial loading area that the ferries from Key West used, the NPS supply boat, the *Activa*, was moored. Like Christmas every Tuesday, but better, the *Activa* arrived with supplies, groceries, mail and Cliff and Linda. Cliff was the captain, Linda the first mate. New blood was as exciting to the inhabitants of Fort Jefferson as fresh food. The crew of the *Activa* could be counted on to bring the latest news and gossip along with other treats and necessities.

"Teddy took your stuff up to your quarters for you and stuck the perishables in the refrigerator," Bob said as Anna cut the engine. She tossed him the stern line and he tied it neatly to the cleat on the starboard side. Wind was more or less a constant on DRTO, and the NPS boats were tied to both sides of their slips to keep them from banging into the sides of the dock. Fenders could only do so much when the winds flirted with hurricane force.

"I'll be sure and thank her. Is Teddy in the office?" Anna asked. Teddy, short for Theodora, was Bob's wife.

"Till five, like always." He stood stiffly to one side as Anna heaved towel, fins, snorkel, and water bottle onto the dock.

Bob was a strange fit with the park. He'd been there for eleven years and clearly loved the place. He said, and Anna believed him, that he never wanted to work anywhere else and intended to serve out his remaining six years till retirement at the fort.

Anna suspected his desire to remain in this isolated post was due only partly to his love for the resource. A good chunk of it, she theorized, was because nowhere else could he live such a rich and rewarding fantasy life without coming head-to-head with the cynicism of his fellows.

Fortunately for her, Bob's particular brand of psychosis made him a great ranger.

Swearing he was five-six, though Anna, at five-four, could look him in the eye in flat shoes, he seemed bent on being the poster boy for a benign version of the Napoleon complex. Now, as he readied to go on his evening rounds—showing the flag, boarding boats he deemed suspicious, handing out brochures to newcomers and checking the boundaries because they were there—he wore full gear: sidearm, baton, pepper spray, cuffs, and a Kevlar bulletproof vest. If the man hadn't been such a strong swimmer, Anna's greatest worry would have been that he'd fall overboard and his defensive equipment would sink him like a stone. The only concession he made to the cloying heat was to wear shorts.

Though Anna would never have dreamed of telling him so, they tended to spoil the effect. Not only was he no taller than Anna, but he couldn't have exceeded her one hundred twenty pounds by much either. Like a lot of men who take to the water, most of that was in his chest and shoulders. Chickens would have been insulted to hear his legs compared to theirs.

"Anything up for tonight?" she asked as they made lines fast. Mostly she asked for the fun of hearing Bob's answer. His fantasy, as luck would have it, was that he was the sole protector (she didn't count for reasons of gender, and Lanny hadn't counted for reasons Bob clearly had but was too honorable to speak of) of this jewel in the ocean. Like all other great and honorable lawmen of history, Bob was constantly in danger from the forces of evil. Each and every boat could be smuggling cocaine from Panama, heroin from the east, guns from pretty much anywhere. All shrimpers were ready, willing and able to knife him in the back.

Given that he apparently genuinely believed this despite eleven years in a sleepy port, Anna couldn't help but admire his stalwart courage in facing each day, never late, never shirking. Having been exposed to this criminal-under-every-bush, Marshal Dillon under siege mentality the day she arrived, Anna was pleasantly surprised the first time she'd patrolled with him. Part of honor and duty—and natural inclination probably, though his tough-guy image would never let him admit it even to himself—required he be gracious, polite, and, when he thought no one was looking, overtly kind. Seeing that, Anna had been quite taken with the man and made it a point to resist the temptation to tease him about the boogeymen that lived under his boat. She didn't even resent his sexism. Respect for a superior overrode it, and it wasn't personal. There were no women patrolling the streets of Dodge City, flying fighters over Nazi Germany, or walking shoulder-to-shoulder with Clint Eastwood through the saloon's swinging doors.

Sans petticoat and fan, Anna simply didn't fit into Bob's worldview.

"Did you see the boats on the south side, anchored out a ways, not in the harbor?" Bob asked. He smoothed his sandy-red and handsome mustache with one hand and pointed with the other.

Vaguely Anna remembered passing them, but had paid them little mind.

"I saw them."

"They've been here two and a half days. Never come into the harbor. Never visit the fort. Something's up with them."

Anna'd not noticed those things. And they were pertinent. Most folks, if they bothered to come to Garden Key, made use of the harbor and at least paid a curiosity visit to the fort.

"Good eye," Anna said and meant it. "I'll keep close to the radio."

Bob jumped lightly into the second of DRTO's five patrol boats. Only four were working. The fifth was beached behind the dock up on blocks. Bob took the *Bay Ranger*, a twenty-foot aluminum-hulled Sylvan. He seemed to prefer it to the sturdier Boston Whalers. Maybe because it was quieter, had a lower profile. All the better for sneaking up on evildoers.

Anna shouldered the net bag she used to carry her dive things.

"Oh," Bob said as she turned to go. "You got a big box from New York waiting for you. Teddy said if there's bagels in it, she'll trade you some of her homemade key lime pie for some."

Anna waved Bob off, then stood a moment, habit demanding she do a visual check of an area after an absence of hours. The campground, with space for only a handful of tents and, other than flush toilets on the public dock, no amenities, was quiet. Because there was so little dirt to be had on Garden Key, overnighters were by reservation only. Picnickers sat at tables nursing beers and sunburns, talking among themselves, families for the most part with lots of little kids scratching at mosquito bites, Kool-Aid smiles adding to the clownish colors of beach towels and bathing suits. Even Bob would have a hard time imagining an evil nemesis in the bunch.

Savoring the fact that she wasn't in a hurry, that, once again, her work for the National Park Service allowed her to rest her eyes and mind on a wonder most people would never take the time to see, she turned her attention to the fort.

Bob's motor's drone a pleasant burr in her ears, as comforting as the hum of bees in summer blooms, she looked across the moat at Fort Jefferson. More than the skyscrapers of Manhattan, the Golden Gate Bridge, or all of Bill Gates's cyber magic, it impressed her with man's determination to fight the world to a standstill and then reform it in his own design.

Seventy miles out in the sea, on the unprepossessing Bush Key, the magnitude of the effort awed her. Jefferson stood three stories high and was topped with earthworks and ammunition bunkers. A coal-black tower, built as a lighthouse but demoted to a harbor light when the taller lighthouse on Loggerhead Key was finished, thrust above the battlements. The black metal of its skin gave it an unearned sinister aspect. A wide moat, meeting the fortress walls on one side and contained by brick and mortar on the other, ran around the two bastions fronting the structure. Beyond was nothing but the Atlantic. At first the moat had amused Anna. Only in the front and along the eastern wall was it bordered by land. On the two other sides its outer wall separated it only from the sea.

When she'd first seen it, it had struck her as a conceit, the architect slavishly following the classic castle moat theme though this fort was set in a natural saltwater moat thousands of miles on one side and seventy on the other. Duncan, the island's historian and chief interpreter, had disabused her of that notion. Moats were not merely to keep land troops at bay but ships with malicious intent at their distance.

Trailing a young couple so in love they didn't notice it was too hot to be hanging all over each other, Anna crossed the bridge. As she stepped into the imagined cool and welcome dark of the entryway she heard the shivery sound of children giggling and saw a small head vanish into a stone slot. Anna laughed because heat and boredom had yet to diminish the childlike glee the fort engendered in her: "secret" rooms where ammunition had once been stored, dark and twisted caves where arches met and clashed and crossed at the bastions, designed by an architect who must have foreseen the genius of Escher. The formidable structure was now dissolving back into the sea with infinite slowness. Lime dripped out of solution as rain worked its way through ancient mortar. Stalactites formed, growing like teeth in the long, long passages through the casemates. Standing at a corner and looking down arch after arch after arch, perspective skewed. It was easy to feel as if one were falling through time itself.

Formerly an actress and a park ranger, **Nevada Barr** is now the award-winning, *New York Times*–bestselling author of the Anna Pigeon mysteries and numerous other books and short stories. She lives in New Orleans with her husband and various pets.